"GOOD NIGHT, SAM."

She turned to the door, but Sam got to the doorknob first.

He shut the door with a sickening click.

Ally's heart sank. "You cad."

"Rogue."

"I can go down to the front desk and get another key."

"Not if I don't let you." He stepped in front of her, blocking her path.

"Now see here, Sam—"

He grabbed her and kissed her, stopping the flow of words. His lips were warm and insistent against hers. She tried to pull away. "Sam!"

Only when he was thoroughly done kissing her did he mumble into her neck, "Why do you keep calling me Sam? I am the duke." Her hands were trapped between their bodies and all she could manage was a feeble struggle, which felt so enormously sexy, she struggled again just to feel him deny her.

Then, all at once, he swept her off her feet and into his arms.

"You're coming with me, Princess, whether you like it or not." His voice was gruff and dominating and not at all like the playful Sam she knew . . .

ᔕ

Please turn this page for rave reviews for Diana Holquist . . .

Praise for Diana Holquist

HUNGRY FOR MORE

"Fascinating and very sexy. Holquist shows us food isn't just love, it's magic!"
  —**Susan Mallery,** *New York Times* **bestselling author**

"4 Stars! The main characters are appealing, and the secondary ones add depth to the tale with intriguing stories of their own. A bit of psychic phenomena adds a delightful thread to this entertaining read."
  —*Romantic Times BOOKreviews Magazine*

"*Hungry for More* will keep you grinning throughout the whole novel. [It] is a light read that'll lift your spirits and make you . . . well . . . hungry for more from author Diana Holquist. The unique characters are loads of fun."

  —**NightsandWeekends.com**

"An intense, sexy, funny, wonderful redemption story . . . Feed me, Baby."

  —**AllAboutRomance.com**

∾

SEXIEST MAN ALIVE

more . . .

more . . .

"A funny, lighthearted tale of a match made in the stars."
—**RomRevToday.com**

"A laugh-out-loud book that looks at the wild and wacky ways in which we screw up our lives . . . the fast-paced, emotion-grabbing *Make Me a Match* is one story I truly enjoyed."
—FallenAngelsReviews.com

"If you enjoy stories where character development is right on par with sizzling romance, *Make Me a Match* will be the perfect match for you!"
—ARomanceReview.com

Also by Diana Holquist

Make Me a Match
Sexiest Man Alive
Hungry for More

How to Tame a Modern Rogue

Diana Holquist

FOREVER

NEW YORK   BOSTON

Copyright © 2009 by Diana Holquist

All rights reserved. Except as permitted under the U.S. Copyright Act of 1976, no part of this publication may be reproduced, distributed, or transmitted in any form or by any means, or stored in a database or retrieval system, without the prior written permission of the publisher.

Cover design by Christine Foltzer
Cover photography by Herman Estevez

Forever
Hachette Book Group
237 Park Avenue
New York, NY 10017
Visit our Web site at www.HachetteBookGroup.com.

Forever is an imprint of Grand Central Publishing. The Forever name and logo is a trademark of Hachette Book Group, Inc.

Printed in the United States of America

First Printing: August 2009

10 9 8 7 6 5 4 3 2 1

How to Tame a
Modern Rogue

Step One:

Every rogue has a weakness. Find it.

*The duke made his way out of Hyde Park with his usual
loose-limbed, easy gait. The evening was excellent for walking
despite the heat of early-summer London. Ahead waited his
luxuriously appointed town house, a snifter of brandy, and not
a woman in sight to scold him. In a word, perfection.*
—From *The Dulcet Duke*

Chapter 1

Manhattan; June 24, 2009

Sam Carson strolled out of Central Park, a long blade
of grass between his teeth. What a rush that meeting had
been, selling the client on his riskiest campaign, then dinner at Daniel with champagne corks flying and the ad
agency brass begging him to sign on for the long haul. As
if he would ever commit to an agency when his day rate
was so bloody—

Veronica.

He pulled the grass from his teeth and stuffed it into
his pocket. The spirited version of "For He's a Jolly Good
Fellow" he had been humming petered out into a single
flat note of dread.

Across the street, Veronica paced in front of his
building, looking pissed enough to vault the six lanes of
streaming traffic in a ferocious leap, plant one of her red

stiletto heels in his chest, and then fling him under the tires of the nearest SUV, after first, naturally, retrieving her Jimmy Choo.

Did he deserve punishment? He *had* told her from day one he wasn't the marrying kind. A pang of something that might have been pain sprang up, but he shook it off. *I told her not to expect more of me than good times and fun. Maybe a really nice birthday gift if the timing was right.*

He scowled. It had been up until now such a successful, lovely summer's evening.

He considered his options. Talking to her. Again. About how it was over. Again.

SUV tires crushing his skull sounded more appealing. Veronica was a lot of things. A subdued, rational conversationalist wasn't one of them.

On to plan B: Retire to Boule's Pub to argue about Premier League soccer with Angelo, the Italian bartender, until the danger had passed. With a pint of warm Guinness. Or two. Because Veronica notwithstanding, he'd had a *very* top-notch, lucrative day.

He looked around. Every cab was taken. There wasn't a bus in sight. He had ten more seconds at most before Veronica spotted him.

Nine, eight, seven . . .

On six, a horse and carriage trotted smartly out of Central Park, turned onto Central Park West, and stopped in front of him for a red light. A wrinkled, gray-haired speck of a woman in an elaborate gown in the back of the open carriage cried down to him, "A marquis walking! How charmingly odd!"

Not as charmingly odd as a costumed grandma in a

carriage on a sweltering June evening at West Seventy-second and the park, but this was no time to quibble. Sam's life had always been a precarious balance of creativity, luck, and strange circumstance, and he recognized this hatter-mad and/or drunk doddering woman for what she was at once: plan C.

He bowed deeply to the dowager and said, "Marquis? You are mistaken, madam. I am a duke. Duke Whatthe-hell." Then he added for good measure, "The third."

The opposing light turned yellow. He couldn't see Veronica, but he was sure her heels were clicking his death march on the opposite sidewalk.

"Ah! A duke!" The old woman gazed down at him adoringly. "But a duke *walking*? Do climb in! I'm on my way to see my granddaughter." Her accent was British, but just muddled enough for Sam to guess it was part of the act.

The opposing light clicked red.

Sam vaulted into the rig just as his light turned green. The horse pulled forward, incongruous and regal in the stream of yellow taxis and commuters. It was messy business, leaving a woman who, somehow, despite his up-front declarations of perpetual bachelorhood, had gotten the wrong idea.

He ought to be better at it by now.

He glanced back. Veronica stared down the avenue in the wrong direction. His doorman, Clive, however, had seen the whole affair and shot Sam a crisp salute.

Sam leaned back against the leather seat, bathed in triumph, even though he knew his escape was temporary. He found the blade of grass in his pocket and planted it back between his teeth. "To whom do I owe the pleasure?"

he asked the costumed woman beside him. She was delicate, practically see-through, with soft, unfocused pale
blue eyes. Her pink lace gown was high-waisted with puff
sleeves, spot-on for the dresses in the endless Jane Austen
movies he'd been dragged to by excited, weeping dates
whose names he had long forgotten, if he'd even bothered
to learn their names in the first place. Gad, those movies.
Besides the torture of having to see his native England
on-screen (he shuddered just to think about it), the movies
were too close to his own life for comfort. He preferred
The Terminator.

"I am Lady Donatella," the old woman said, her voice
clear and steady. "But since you will marry my granddaughter, you can call me Granny Donny."

Marry? Bollocks. The word chilled his heart.

He had almost been looking forward to finding out
Lady Donatella's story. Now he'd have to jump out at the
first red light and bid the sweet, unhinged woman a hasty
farewell.

Except that the blue of the old woman's eyes was so
pure, her lips so well drawn. That she was a gentlewoman
and as such required the escort of a duke was obvious,
and he rose to the occasion with a sense of duty his up-
bringing demanded, despite the sense of foreboding that
was spreading from his frozen heart to ice his veins.

Ally Giordano was leaving New York City. She had
waited exactly as long as she had promised herself she'd
wait—ten years. Time was up. Her parents hadn't come
back, and now it was time to move on.

In the last two weeks, she had sold her parents' left-
behind possessions, from her father's dusty brown over-

coat still hanging in the front closet to her mother's three jewelry boxes that had been crammed under the bed. What she couldn't sell, she'd given away.

The bittersweet, empty feeling of all this discarding was offset by the stunning success she'd had in planning her move, as if it was meant to be. She had found a ridiculously sunny, cheap studio in the Noe Valley section of San Francisco. A miracle, she was told. Then, to her utter surprise, another miracle. She'd gotten her dream job as a tenth-grade English teacher at the Ludington Charter School. It was the chance of a lifetime to teach at one of the most progressive, successful high schools in the country.

There was nothing to tie her to New York now but her beloved grandmother, who luckily was still ferocious and tenacious at eighty-four, perfectly capable of fending for herself and perfectly rich enough to jump on a plane to the coast to visit Ally whenever she pleased. In fact, Granny Donny had urged Ally to get out while the getting was good. She knew better than anyone how badly Ally needed to leave the past behind. "Go. Have fun. Get laid," Granny Donny had said when the move to San Francisco was set. She had patted Ally's hand, not taking her eyes from the mah-jongg table in her stately living room at the Plaza Hotel where she kept an elaborate apartment. The gray- and blue-haired mah-jongg ladies had nodded their agreement, Mrs. Ludith using the opportunity to slip a tile into the sleeve of her green cashmere cardigan.

That was two weeks ago. Ally had been so busy getting ready to go, she hadn't seen her grandmother since. She knew she was avoiding saying good-bye. She hated good-byes. She'd do it tomorrow. And she *wouldn't* cry.

As Ally sealed the last box with packing tape, her apartment mate, June, glided into Ally's bedroom. June had just come home from her three-hour afternoon workout with her dance company and was eating a mouse-size dinner of rice and greens, if pecking at a bowl with chopsticks could be considered eating.

June was gorgeous, smart, *and* happy. Her fiancé, William Cho, was moving in as soon as Ally moved out in three days.

Ally wasn't wild about Will. She thought he was a little on the cold side. It was June's enormous, extended family just over the bridge in Nutley, New Jersey, that made Ally jealous with longing. Just seeing the leftover dumplings from their family feasts in the fridge sometimes brought tears to Ally's eyes.

June flopped down onto a ratty red armchair Ally was leaving behind. Her muscular legs swung rhythmically over the armrest. She sniffed suspiciously at the grains of rice. Maybe she could smell which ones contained an extra fraction of a calorie.

June was edgier than usual this month because her dance troupe, the *Mephistopheles Project*, was deciding which ten dancers would go on tour to Europe this summer and which ten would be left behind. June was never the stay-at-home one, so Ally couldn't take her roomie's nerves seriously. Everything always worked out for June. She was that kind of person. But Ally liked her anyway.

"See you didn't manage to get dressed today," June said, motioning to Ally's pajamas. "How's the head?"

"Is it still there? It feels like I packed it by mistake." Being a Person Who Didn't Drink, Ally was still suffering from drinking three beers at her good-bye/birthday party the night before. She had never been a partier.

Or a smoker.

Or a drug user. Or a gambler. Or a sex kitten . . .

Hell, she wasn't even a jaywalker, which in New York City meant her ethical standards were just a smidge higher than, say, cloistered nuns circa 1602. Ally had never met a rule she didn't follow.

"Cutting loose before you move from an apartment you've lived in your whole life is allowed, you know." June chewed each grain of rice like it was a mouthful. Ally was going to miss the way her roommate ate, or rather, didn't eat. She was going to miss a lot about her. But Will's clothes were already in the drawers; his Mets poster was newly hung on the kitchen wall where Ally's Monet print had been. They were all ready to move on.

A rap at the front door startled both women out of their individual reveries. They lived in what their landlord Tony called a "garden" apartment, despite the lack of anything even remotely resembling a garden. What it really meant was that their door, shadowed under the grand stairs that led to the three aboveground apartments in their converted brownstone, opened directly onto 113th Street, and any nut who wanted to knock on it could.

But it wasn't the nuts that frightened Ally.

She braced herself for the dreaded hope that rose within her whenever there was an unexpected knock: *They came back for me.*

June's face got serious. "Hey, it's Ma and Pa," June said, just like she always said when someone knocked un-expectedly or the phone rang in the middle of the night or

Ally just got *that* look on her face for no reason beyond a sense that her parents were near.

"Think they bought me a lousy T-shirt?" Ally asked. *My parents got wicked into debt from their gambling problem, then went on the run, and all I got was this lousy T-shirt.*

June had been through this a million times with Ally. The two of them said the exact same thing every single time, and every single time, those few dumb words grounded Ally. *My fantasy about my parents returning is ridiculous. I am twenty-four years old. Twenty-five at 8:42 p.m. tomorrow. I don't need them and I don't care.* Especially now. *I am leaving.*

Ally could hug her friend for understanding how much it helped to state her ridiculous fantasies out loud so that she could hear how idiotic they were. "Why am I leaving you again?" Ally asked.

"So Will and I can have loud, wild sex without worrying about the schoolteacher in the next room." June softened her voice. "You okay?"

"Not a twinge of hope for the impossible," Ally lied. There was a twinge of hope. But just that. Totally manageable. "Let the wild sex begin." Another knock at the door, this time harder. "If that's Will, I'll go out and see a movie."

"Please. I'm much too tired to let the wild sex begin tonight. Plus, you and me only have three more nights together, so if it's Will, I'm kicking him out. He can cope for a few nights without me. That's what Internet porn is for." June floated to the living room.

Last chance, Mom and Dad. After I turn twenty-five tomorrow, I'm gone for you forever. It had been an arbitrary date—ten years since their running off and leaving Ally with her grandmother—but Ally was determined to stand by it. It was a childish test, she knew, but still, they had failed. Of course, Ally had been a ball of ridiculous, irrational emotion these last few days, wondering if they'd come through and show up at the last minute, as if they could sense her made-up time limit from wherever they were—a cosmic pull, an invisible thread that connected parents to daughter. She'd read about things like that. Like most things she read about families, though, it seemed to be bull.

June rose onto her toes to peer through the peephole. "Granny Donny!" she cried. She threw open the door, and in bustled Ally's granny Donatella. "What a lovely surprise."

Granny Donny launched herself into June's arms. For an instant, Ally thought she had seen a horse out on the street, but it was hard to tell, as the space over her grandmother's shoulder became filled with a tall man who entered the apartment behind her.

Tall beautiful man. He had a long piece of grass gone to seed sticking out of his mouth. He was beautifully and expensively dressed, yet somehow, remarkably *askew*.

Ally tried not to stare.

Which, despite the man's stunning beauty, wasn't hard, as Ally had just fully registered that Granny Donny was wearing a ball gown.

Of another century.

And it was pink.

"Granny Donny, how are you?" Ally asked her eccentric grandmother, not at all sure that she wanted to know.

*Rakes, rogues, ne'er-do-wells—Princess Alexandra despised
them all. Unfortunately, the only thing more insufferable than
a man of low morals was a man of high morals. This was why
she spent inordinate amounts of time with her horse, a mare.*
—From *The Dulcet Duke*

Chapter 2

"Ally, dear, may I present to you the Duke of—" Granny
Donny paused, confusion clouding her usually radiant
face.

The man bowed. "I am the Duke of Midfield. Duke
Whatthehell," he said. "At your service."

Ally's stomach lurched. The man, her grandmother's ball
gown, and the confused look on her grandmother's face all
signified the same thing: trouble. Ally tried to still the panic
building inside her. What was going on here? Eccentric as her
grandmother usually was, this felt different. It felt serious.

It felt sickening.

The man rose from his bow and Ally exhaled the
breath that had caught in her throat. His black hair was a
disheveled mess, sticking up in points here and there, as if
a personal wind had been blowing it around unmercifully
all afternoon. His black suit was ridiculously well cut, but
cockeyed and open. His yellow silk tie was loose and half

undone. The wind again. The guy was a walking tornado of invisible forces.

Hormones. Ally knew the type well from teaching high school. Only usually the type wasn't a grown-up.

But this was no time to be mesmerized by a beautiful man. She focused on her grandmother.

Oh, hell.

Granny Donny leaned in to kiss Ally's cheek. She smelled old-fashioned, like lavender water. Ally had been hoping she would smell of rum, and that this was just a drunken escapade. No such luck. "I've brought you a husband," she whispered.

Ally looked at the stunning man. His eyes were riveted on June's chest. "Not such a good one," she whispered back.

"It's your job to fix *that*, dear." Granny Donny gave her a shove toward the man.

Ally stumbled into him. He caught and righted her with an ease that said, *No worries. I'm used to women careening into me, willy-nilly, all day long.* She didn't make a dent in his concentration on June, who was leading a shaky Granny Donny to the couch.

Whatever was going on, the timing was lousy. *Not now, Grandma. I'm leaving. I can't stay. Remember my deadline?* But no matter how hard she thought it, she knew her plans were about to get thrown out the window. There was no one else to take care of her grandmother if something went wrong. And from the looks of things, something was clearly going very, very wrong.

She gathered her energy, determined to address the man with a sternness she usually reserved for her worst students. Mr. Wonderful had the smoothness, coldness, and assurance of the con men she'd watched prey on her parents while she was growing up. She had to be sure he knew something stood between Granny Donny's money and him. "I'm Ally Giordano. Mrs. Giordano's granddaughter."

"I am Duke—"

"How do you know my grandmother?" She cut him off before he could begin. No one survived teaching at PS 142 without becoming an expert in dealing with wiseasses.

"Oh. We go back bloody far. Generations of nasty inbreeding. You know how noble families are. I believe your great-uncle, the Earl of Flatulence, was the bastard twin of my father, the Marquis of Nosehair, who was also your grandmother's brother. And father." He paused. "Once removed."

The grass was gone from his mouth. Ally wondered if he had eaten it.

He cocked his head. "Oh, don't look at me like I just spiked the punch at the grand ball. Me and your granny, we go back"—he paused—"forty-one blocks." An upward twitch of one corner of his finely drawn mouth almost stirred Ally to swoon, but she sternly reminded herself that she was not the swooning type. He smelled like champagne. And money. And grass gone to seed. "Your grandmother rescued me, actually. I owe her my life."

"Careful, we might just hold you to that," June said.

"A duke never goes back on his word."

Was he faking the upper-class British accent? No, he was too well dressed to be an American male unless he was gay. Judging by the intensity he was now focusing on June's ass as she bent over the couch to tend to her grandmother, he wasn't gay.

Ally smiled, but she didn't mean it. Her grandmother's

money attracted the worst kinds of hangers-on, and this one seemed shameless. Usually, her grandmother could handle them: can't con a con woman. Her grandmother hadn't made her fantastic wealth selling Girl Scout cookies, after all. She and Ally's grandfather had gotten in early on the Cuban tobacco and rum trade before Castro cut it off in 1959, then taken the profits and invested heavily in Hollywood. Granny Donny had even starred in two fairly successful movies, back in her day.

Now her grandmother spared no expense in living her life. She wore only her signature Dior black silk suits. In winter, she topped them with a fox stole and in the summer sometimes accessorized with a floral silk scarf. But pink? Taffeta? A duke? Who was this woman, and what had she done with Donatella Regina Arabella Giordano? Whatever was going on in her grandmother's head now, it seemed to involve satin slippers and matchmaking and this phony duke, who had to be dispensed with immediately so she could figure out the whys and what-the-hells of the new wardrobe.

Ally followed his eyes to the slit of June's bare stomach peeking out above her yoga pants. "She's engaged," she informed him.

His eyes swept from June to Ally with rakish charm. His right shoulder quirked up, then down. A sinful smile spread across his lips. "To a duke?" he asked.

Ally was tempted to sucker punch the duke. "Duke Whatajerk, was it?"

"Whatthehell."

"My thoughts exactly."

They locked eyes. Ally had never seen a grown-up with such dancing eyes. No, wait, she had. They were the eyes of a gambler on a winning streak, a man who thought his luck would never run out.

Your luck stops here, buddy.

Granny Donny had finally settled her dainty dress on the couch to her satisfaction. "Tea. With biscuits. And cakes. Thank you, dear," Granny Donny said to June. She smiled sweetly up at the duke, patting the pillow next to her.

"And you, er, duke?" June asked.

"Whiskey. Straight." Duke Whatshisname sank beside Granny Donny, loose-limbed and easy. He watched June's ass openly and with deep admiration as she retreated to the kitchen for the tea and whiskey. Ally wouldn't have been the least surprised if he'd let loose a long, soft whistle.

"Excuse me." Ally maneuvered herself between the man and her grandmother, hip-checking him aside. Images of her grandmother in her pink dress on the streets of Manhattan picking up strangers made Ally rigid with apprehension and boldness.

They sat in steely silence until June returned with a bag of rice cakes and a glass that stank of cheap whiskey. "Tea'll be ready in a minute. This is the best I could do for cakes," June said to Granny Donny, covering the old woman's hand with her own. Her brown, smooth hand on Granny's blue-tinged, gnarled one gave the effect of a real hand resting on a crumbling marble statue.

Granny Donny didn't seem to hear June. She picked up the duke's glass and sipped, her pinky extended. Her face lit up with pleasure, a spot of color rising to her cheeks, and for an instant, Ally thought, *There's the Granny I know. Let's go sit in the Rose Club, and you can have your signature vodka martini and flirt with the twenty-something bartenders.*

Then Granny Donny took a bite of the rice cake and grimaced. She bent toward Ally and whispered loudly, "You really should look into procuring quality help. Orientals make lovely tea, but very dry cakes."

June's eyes met Ally's. Ally let out a soft whistle.

"Do you know where you are?" Ally asked her grandmother. This was the first question she always heard those TV doctors ask to see if people were nuts or not.

"Why, we're in London, of course, dear. Please, don't tell me you're going dotty on me, child." She had inhaled the entire double shot of whiskey. Hiccuping softly, she put the glass down carefully, as if unsure why the table was moving so erratically.

"What year is it?" Ally asked.

"Eighteen twelve, dear. What's the matter with you?"

"Who am I?"

"Why, you're my granddaughter, Princess Alexandra." *Oh, dear.*

"And now that you've turned sixteen," Granny Donny continued, "it's high time we found you a husband!"

Ally's stomach hit bottom. "Grandma Donny, I'm twenty-four. Twenty-five tomorrow."

"Oh, don't be ridiculous, darling. You're not *that* old! Out to pasture! On the shelf! Certainly not!" Granny Donny put her hands to her heart and rolled her eyes, then hiccuped again.

Ally turned to the duke, trying to pack her words with as much menace as possible, as if to say, *Mess with my granny, and I'll slit your throat.* What she actually said was, "I think you should go. Thank you for bringing her here safely."

The duke didn't move. Or rather, he stayed in one place

while he practically vibrated with energy. He studied her intently, and Ally had to hold on to the couch cushions to avoid spiraling into his orbit. Dark stubble shaded his face to sinister perfection, and between that and his steel eyes and his bow-shaped lips, she feared for the safety of all women within a ten-mile radius.

"Oh, I didn't bring her," he said finally. "Her coachman did. I was just along for the ride."

"Coachman?" Ally felt her world unhinge. There *was* a horse outside.

Granny Donny rose, slow and unsteady, the whiskey having taken hold. "I must be getting home for supper. I only wanted you to meet the duke so that you would see how lovely it will be when all of us retreat to my country estate, Carleton House, for the rest of the summer. London is no place for a girl of the ton after the season. Especially one in need of a husband. We'll have a house party and a ball and we'll see to your future, Alexandra! Before it's too late." She hiccuped and then smiled shyly from behind her hand. "After all, you must bear a male heir if you're to inherit my fortune!"

"Oh my God," June said under her breath. "Carleton House. Princess Alexandra. A dissolute duke. I read this book."

Ally looked at her friend but couldn't find the words to reply.

The duke raised his eyes to June's face, the first time he'd gotten his gaze that high.

"It's *The Dulcet Duke*, by Genevieve Lancet," June explained. "I must have read it fifty times. It's been on my keeper shelf for years!"

"Grandma," Ally said, her voice cracking. She cleared

her throat. "Have you been reading a book called *The Dulcet Duke*?" Granny Donny loved historical romance novels almost as much as June. They both inhaled them like air, trading them back and forth like blissed-out junkies. *You got the new Puffington in hard cover? Oh, baby, I've got to have it. Now.*

"I have no idea what you're gabbering about, dear."

"Gabbering. That's pure Lancet," June said. She covered her mouth with one hand and pointed at the duke with the other. "Which means he's Duke Blackmoore. Yeah, he looks just like him. Tall and dark and dissolute." June caught herself. "Not that you're dissolute, I mean. I'm sorry, I don't even know you."

"Of course I am," the duke assured her. "Horridly dissolute."

"Even the messy hair fits. And those burgundy lips . . ." She trailed off, lost for a moment in her memories of Duke Blackmoore and his lips. She shook herself, her dancer's control making the action startlingly erotic. "He's *trouble*. The ones with burgundy lips are always trouble."

The duke straightened proudly. "Am I? Sounds devilish and fun. What do I get to do?"

"Wenching. Gambling. Drinking. Dueling. The usual."

"I don't duel. But I could start."

Did Granny Donny think she was living in a Regency-era romance novel? Where a normal person might lapse into confusion, self-doubt, and depression, had something terrible happened to Granny Donny, and she gripped her lack of clarity with gusto, forming it into a world that pleased her? Had she, by the sheer force of her ferocious personality, taken even sickness—or whatever this was—and made it into something original, exciting, and fun?

Well, fun for her, at least.

Ally felt herself tumbling into an abyss of doctors and caretakers and possibly even an old-age home for her grandmother. No, she couldn't. Not that. Never. She'd take Granny Donny with her to San Francisco. How do you get a woman in a ball gown, plus her horse and coachman, on a plane? There had to be a way. But at the moment, Ally couldn't imagine it. It wasn't that they'd never discussed what they would do as Granny Donny aged, but the time had seemed so far off. Ally assumed she'd settle in San Francisco, marry, buy a big rambling house, fill it with kids, and only then would her grandmother move in after endless cajoling. She'd set up her mah-jongg game in the parlor, cheating the local blue hairs discreetly while she showed off her perfect great-grandkids.

June was still talking. "Which makes you, Ally—I mean, Princess *Alexandra*—the good woman who has to reform the duke. Oh, it's such a romantic, lovely story!" June hugged her body close.

"But why would a good woman want anything to do with a man as irresponsible and childish as Duke Blackmoore? He sounds like a jerk," Ally said, looking straight at the duke. If this *duke* thought he was getting anything out of her grandmother just because she temporarily (it just had to be temporary . . .) believed she was a bit player in a historical romance novel, he was sorely mistaken.

"Because he's very, very hot," June said.

The duke smiled. "Merci, mademoiselle."

June blushed. "Er. Not you. I mean, Duke Blackmoore."

"If the princess wants the duke because he's very, very hot, she must be very, very dumb," Ally said, her eyes meeting the duke's with what she hoped was steely menace. She tried not to notice that his dark hair against his white skin was crushingly beautiful.

"No. She's smart as a whip. See, she has to marry him to inherit the cash to support her oodles of siblings, and he has to marry her to get the wannabe Mrs. Dukes off his back."

"I don't have any siblings," Ally pointed out, inexplicably relieved.

"I don't have any wannabe . . . Wait . . . Oh. Bloody hell, I am the duke. But reformed? That's not a romance; that's a tragedy."

Ally hadn't read a romance in ages; there were too many high school classics to be reread with her students. But the romance novels she remembered involved very badly behaved men whom she had loved anyway, because of their rippling thighs and masterful ways that made her want to put the book down and just lie back and close her eyes and—

Ally realized with a start that she was staring at the duke's thighs.

So much for steely menace.

She yanked her gaze away, only to meet his dancing gray eyes. She felt herself blush. This was the dilemma, wasn't it? No matter how wickedly bad they were, the bad boys made the good girls swoon. But the truth was, you couldn't reform a person. People were what they were. Ally's life had confirmed that a million times over. She would never fall for a rogue the way her mother had fallen for her gambling-poisoned father, the world's number one toxic charmer. Never.

But the duke was hardly the point. Ally had bigger problems. She needed a plan. *One:* Lose the duke. *Two:* Get Granny Donny to the doctor and find out what was going on. *Three:* Postpone her move until she figured out what to do next. Self-pity caught in her throat, but she forced it down. She was her grandmother's only relative, unless her parents magically showed up. And that didn't seem to be happening anytime soon.

"Granny Donny, I'll take you home and stay with you tonight. I'll send your, er, your coachman home, and we'll catch a cab back to your place and put you to bed." Peering out the peephole, Ally got a fish-eye view of a thin man in a black top hat leaning against a carriage, reading a newspaper. The trouble with having too much money was the abundance of people who were willing to make any fantasy come true for a price. She wondered what she'd find at her grandmother's apartment. A matching set of eight liveried footmen? A pig roasting over an open fire?

Peasants?

She had to sit down.

"I'll escort your grandmother home," the duke assured Ally. "Isn't that the sort of thing I'd do? Being rich and idle, yet on my way to reform under your good-hearted, stern guidance? I won't even stop to duel on the way."

Ally considered telling the duke to beat it, but something about his accent and Granny Donny's dress and the coachmen waiting outside made her say, polite as could be, "You've done enough. Thank you." Sheesh, she sounded like she was reading for the role of Elizabeth Bennet.

Disgusted with herself, Ally stuck her bare feet into her slippers, pulled on her pink robe, and went to the sidewalk to settle matters with Granny Donny's coachman.

*It was scandalous to go out with only her coachman; but it
was possible, so Princess Alexandra did, daring the world to
contradict her. Luckily, being considered good occasionally had
its advantages. Just yesterday she overheard Lady Southerland
assert, rather too loudly, "When one looks as plain and serious
as Princess Alexandra, sadly there is little chance of her
attracting trouble of the masculine kind for which
she'd need a more suitable escort."*

—From *The Dulcet Duke*

Chapter 3

It was not love at first sight. Not even lust.

Not even close.

His duty done, Sam saw his chance to beat a hasty retreat. He bid the dear old lady and the nubile, engaged
roommate a fond farewell and followed the rather plain
and irritated woman named Ally out the door to the
coachman.

The granddaughter had been thoroughly disappointing after the delightful grandmother. That Ally was in
pajamas at eight in the evening, obviously still suffering a
hangover from the previous night, had been initially prom-
ising, true. But this woman's pajamas were just that: pajamas. Men's pajamas. Vintage, green striped, silk lounging
wear circa 1957. Clearly, she wore them for *sleeping*.

Time to move on.

The coachman looked up from his *New York Post*. The
headline screamed, "YANKEES WHANKEES." Sam didn't

get baseball any more than he got American football. English football, that is, soccer, was his game. He was an amateur midfielder; speedy, dirty, and agile. Baseball was one of those curious American afflictions that made no sense at all to him. Slow, plodding, and thick, without any of the grace of cricket.

He turned to Ally. "Well then. Pleasure to have met you. Good luck with your upcoming nuptials. I do hope you find, reform, and marry your naughty duke." He bowed low, then turned away.

She didn't acknowledge his departure. "I hope my grandmother hasn't caused you any trouble," Ally said to the coachman, as if she had just been shaken from the pages of a Jane Austen novel. "If she owes you money, I'll settle."

Sam was three steps toward home, but the idea of Ally paying seemed unchivalrous. He spun on his heel, cursing under his breath. The old woman had given him a hand, after all. "You'll do no such thing, Princess," Sam interrupted. Despite her grandmother's obvious wealth, it was clear from Ally's almost empty, dark, too-far-uptown home that Ally didn't have enough money for a decent life in Manhattan, much less a few spare twenties for a horse and carriage. He wondered at the disparity between the two generations of Giordanos. "I'll settle anything that needs settling."

He studied her as she refused his money with a lecture about god-knew-what. Her eyes were pretty enough, but it was hard to appreciate them, as they were separated from the world by black granny glasses. The light brown of her eyes was a slight improvement over the dark brown of her dull hair, which was pulled back in a messy bun. A few straight strands escaping around the edges made the effect of dowdy school marm so complete, he realized with considerable alarm, that her old-lady, man's jams, vintage look was by design.

She is a schoolteacher. He shuddered. He'd been thrown out of enough boarding schools to recognize a schoolteacher when he saw one. No wonder she was into lectures and obscure facts. He had a theory about spinster schoolteachers: They were surrounded by so many nubile adolescents, they had to shut down their own libidos just to make it to lunch. She had moved on to a soliloquy about her grandmother to the coachman that somehow segued into horse husbandry. He listened in silent horror.

When Ally finally paused for breath, the coachman held up his hand to stop her. "I'm Mateo," he said in heavily accented English. "And you must be Princess Alexandra. There's nothing to settle. Lady Donatella hired Paula and me for the week." He gestured to the horse, who must have been Paula. "I'm paid up till Saturday."

Sam snapped his roaming mind to attention. He recognized that accent. Almost Spanish, but more lilting. Portuguese. *Brazil?* Paula was decked out with a yellow, green, and blue plume. Brazil.

Had they ever met on the turf? He didn't recognize Mateo, but the coachman had the physical ease of a player about him. Sam could sniff out a soccer player the way he suspected a true Regency duke could peg another nobleman, down to rank and title with only a glance at his watch fob. Whatever a watch fob was. The point was, he just *knew* a player when he saw one.

Ally cringed. *"By the week?"*

Sam tore his attention from the far more interesting

coachman to Ally. The distress on her face touched him, and he reminded himself that he had no sympathy for hard-nosed schoolteachers. He'd been tortured by enough sadist teachers to last him a lifetime. "Really, you ought to pay better attention to your delightful grandmother," he scolded. "I'm not so sure you're cut out for the role of the good woman if you treat her so shabbily."

"I am not the good woman," Ally protested.

"Your glasses say otherwise. And your pajamas and your hair and your—"

Mateo interrupted their bickering. "Escorting your grandmother is an honor for Paula and me. Beats hoofing tourists around Central Park." He patted the horse.

Paula did not look honored.

Ally stroked the horse's side. "She's sweating."

"Went to eighty-four today at noon. It's not easy for old ladies in the city in this weather. Horse or human."

"Then you should take her somewhere cooler," Ally said.

"To the country house! She can pull your wedding carriage," Sam cried. Clients loved what they called his reckless enthusiasm, but Paula flicked her ears in annoyance. She turned her head to shoot him an evil stare around her blinders. She was speckled gray and white and looked small in her tack, dwarfed by the gleaming white, red, and chrome carriage looming behind her.

Bloody old ladies got him every time.

He offered her his blade of grass in apology.

She ignored him with a shake of her muzzle.

He turned his attention back to Mateo. He looked eerily familiar. "Striker?" he asked.

"Center mid," Mateo replied without missing a beat.

Sam's competitive juices stirred. "I don't remember ever seeing you around Central Park. But I've seen you somewhere."

Mateo folded up his *Post* after casting Sam the most cursory of dismissive glances. "If you saw me around, you'd remember." He turned to Ally, who was looking at them as if they were speaking Dutch. "Paula's got Arabian blood," he told her. "The heat doesn't bother her as much as the Belgians or Percherons you usually see around Manhattan. It's the cold Paula and I don't like much. I take good care of her." Mateo swung himself onto the carriage seat gracefully. Paula kicked at the curb with her hoof, as if she couldn't wait to get away from the lot of them. "Tell your grandmother I'll be at the Plaza in the morning as usual. Ten a.m. for our daily constitutional in the park."

"She won't be there," Ally insisted. "We'll be at the doctor all day."

Mateo shrugged. "Like I said, I'm paid for the week, so I'll be there anyway, in case you need me." Then he jostled the reins and Paula pulled back into the empty traffic lane and down 113th Street.

Nostalgia for London overcame Sam as he watched them clip-clop away. If you squinted away the parked cars, shut out the annoying, practical woman at your side, and focused on the setting sun and the echoing clip-clop of Paula's hooves, the scene could be, well, London, circa 1812.

He shook himself from his reverie. He hadn't been home in ten years for good reason. Bloody fool being nostalgic for a place that he'd spent his life getting away from. A place he was never going back to. A place he'd do anything to forget.

Ally watched the carriage pull away, struck by how wrong it looked on the filthy, New York street. It was like her dear granny in Manhattan—once natural, now hopelessly out of place. The clip-clops echoed in her head like a warning.

She gathered herself to go back inside and face her grandmother, sick with the understanding that her planned move was coming undone at the seams and then sicker with the understanding that she was thinking of herself when she ought to be thinking of Granny Donny then sickest, almost gagging, with the understanding that if something happened to Granny Donny then Ally was alone in this world, completely, utterly alone.

How had she ever even considered leaving New York? What had she been thinking? Ally had been blindsided. She knew it had been stupid to think her eighty-four-year-old grandmother could go on forever, but she had been doing so well—until tonight.

Her spiraling thoughts were interrupted by the duke's voice. He was talking into his cell. "Clive? It's Sam. Mr. Carson, yeah. Listen, there was a woman out front, red dress. Still? Bloody hell. Do you think Misha could meet me in the alley and sneak me in the back? Brilliant. Ten minutes." He clicked his phone shut and caught Ally staring, openmouthed. "Bon voyage!" He waved to her, then turned toward the park.

Mr. Sam Carson—*Duke* Sam Carson—was walking away from her. But of course, he didn't just walk. He trotted, invisible reins held high in the one hand, as if he were on a mighty steed.

As if he didn't have a care in the world.

Sneak me in past the woman in the red dress, Misha.

A pang of regret that Sam hadn't been a real hero, come on his white horse to save her, shot through Ally. Really, what did she want? To reform a self-centered, irresponsible, pleasure-seeking rogue? No, thanks. In real life, people never changed their true natures. A spoiled man with too much privilege, too much testosterone, and too much money was more trouble than he was worth.

Ally opened the door to her apartment, swallowed her foreboding, and went inside.

*Good help is impossible to find, and yet, a lady certainly
cannot be expected to boil her own water for tea.*
—From *The Dulcet Duke*

Chapter 4

After trips to the internist, the neurologist, and the hospital for endless tests and scans, all the doctors agreed: sudden onset of temporary *(please, God, let it be temporary)* dementia characteristic of that brought on by a mild but undetectable stroke. Pills and therapy and the advice to wait it out. *Granny Donny might return to normal. The brain is an amazing organ, capable of remarkable repair. Only time will tell.*

"Ally," Dr. Trawlbridge, the neurologist, said in a voice Ally was coming to recognize as the *You're-in-Deep* voice. "You must understand that her dementia might get better, but it might get worse. The most common forms of primary degenerative dementia are untreatable. But ten to twenty percent can be overcome with pharmacotherapy."

"Pharma what?"

"Pills. If we're very lucky and there was no stroke. But we don't know, so we'll try both approaches, physical therapy and pharmacotherapy, in case there are other indicators. But there's a chance there will still be no movement. You have to be sure that you live your life and don't get sucked into being a martyr. You're young. Your grandmother is quite wealthy. I advise you to hire as much help as you can and go on with your life as planned. No one suffers more in these situations than the caregivers if they don't put themselves first."

Ally had gotten stuck at *will probably get worse.* "Worse how?" she managed to choke out. Her grandmother had always put Ally first. Now Ally was supposed to put herself first?

"For example, she knows you're her granddaughter. She recognizes you. That's very reassuring."

Sixteen-year-old virgin princess granddaughter on the verge of spinsterhood, but Ally got his point.

"That might fade. She might not know who you are if there's another episode or if things deteriorate further. When there's one stroke, another becomes much more likely. So get help. Get ready. Then, take advantage of this time you have with her while she's somewhat lucid. But be ready to disengage and go on with your life."

"So here I am thinking this is a disaster, and you're saying that maybe it's a high point?" Ally's skin had gone cold and clammy.

"I'm saying that if there's anything you want to learn from your grandmother or say to her or do with her, now's the time. Yes, dear, it could get better, but it could also get worse."

Find my parents.
Ally couldn't get the thought out of her head as she

jogged her three miles through Central Park later that evening. She had only an hour before Brenda, Granny Donny's housekeeper, left for the day. She wanted to run out of the park and keep going, not stopping till she was over the George Washington Bridge and deep into Jersey where no one could find her. For the first time in her life, she understood her parents' urge to flee. *I can't handle this.*

But she could. She would. *I am not like them.* That was the guiding principle of Ally's life, her mantra.

Ally passed the Central Park Zoo with its hordes of happy, sane families. Ally had tried to look for her parents before, and she'd gotten nowhere. It was as if they had disappeared off the face of the earth. It was a fool's mission. And what would happen if she did find them? A trip to the zoo, complete with cotton candy and balloons? It was too late for all that.

But what did her grandmother want?

Ally reached the end of the park and slowed to a walk, crossing Central Park South. Elmore, the evening doorman, let her into the Plaza with a barely disguised I-Might-Be-Opening-Doors-for-a-Living-but-I'm-Still-Glad-I'm-Not-You smile. News of Granny Donny's abrupt decline had spread quickly through the staff.

Ally rode up to the fourth floor in the gilded elevator, the air-conditioning making her feel like she was riding the world's most beautiful refrigerator. She carefully opened the door to her grandmother's apartment and slipped off her sneakers in the foyer.

In the living room, her grandmother was sitting on the couch in a blue gown, hair done beautifully, thanks to Brenda. A full meal for two was laid before her. Ally recognized Delmonico's takeout, and her clenching stomach reminded her that she hadn't eaten all day in the flurry of doctors and hospitals.

"Oh, thank heavens you're finally here," Granny Donny said. "But what's happened to you? Did you fall in the creek?"

"I was jogging." Ally toweled off her face.

"Jogging? How ridiculous! Whatever are you talking about?"

"Never mind. This is lovely, Gran." Ally sat down on the gold couch with her grandmother. The room had always been formal and grand, and Ally couldn't help but notice that her grandmother fit the decor as if she'd aged along with it. They could film a period movie here if they hid the telephones and got rid of Ally in her running gear.

"Let's eat dessert first!" Granny Donny held up a small chocolate cake with a lit single red candle in the center. She mistook Ally's surprise for offense. She put the cake down. "Oh, me! I forgot you never eat dessert first, poor dear. Wet, practically naked, and yet still proper to the end." She mumbled something under her breath that sounded like *Poor virgin child.*

Before Ally could respond, Brenda, the housekeeper, peeked into the room. Her purse was on her arm and she winked, waved, mouthed "Enjoy," then slipped out the door.

"So, we'll save dessert and open the presents! Happy birthday, dear." Her grandmother held out a small box elaborately wrapped in gold with gold ribbons. "Go on. You're only sixteen once."

Well, in Ally's case, twice, apparently. But still, why

quibble? Granny Donny had forgotten it was the twenty-first century, but she had remembered Ally's birthday. Tears formed in Ally's eyes and she blinked them back. *This might be as good as it gets.* "Thank you, Grandma." She held the box carefully. "Do you remember when I really turned sixteen?"

Granny Donny looked confused. "Open it, dear. Then you can make a wish and blow out the candle and we can eat!"

But Ally couldn't stop herself from fishing for a sign that the old Granny Donny was somewhere in there, behind the confusion. "On my real sixteenth birthday, I had begged you for a sleepover with Alice Criddly, and you said yes and then you invited *boys*." Ally remembered Tim Whittle and Bobby Hemly showing up like it was yesterday. The two cutest boys in the tenth grade in their low-rise jeans and Yankees T-shirts, grinning stupidly. Alice had shrieked with terror and badly hidden glee, but Ally had been too mortified to make a sound. She knew Tim and Bobby would never look at a girl like her—mousy and quiet and studious. They had probably shown up on a dare. Or worse, maybe Granny Donny had paid them.

When Ally had confronted her grandmother in the kitchen, she had said, "Well, you have to learn sometime, so why not now, when I can make sure everyone's safe? And they are such lovely boys! Yummy!" The crowning highlight of the evening was Ally opening her gifts from her grandmother in front of everyone, including a box of birthday condoms. "Happy birthday!" Granny Donny had cried.

To Granny Donny's dismay, they had ended up playing Scrabble and watching old movies, until chastely sleeping

side by side in their respective sleeping bags. The next
Monday at school was torture, until she realized that mercifully she had become invisible; Tim and Bobby never
spoke to her again.

Maybe Granny Donny shouldn't have bought the extra-
small condoms.

Alice Criddly was forbidden from ever sleeping over
again.

"So, open it, dear."

Well, it couldn't be worse than condoms. "I really wish
you hadn't," Ally said. She opened the box.

It was worse. Ally's heart sank.

On a green velvet cushion sat her mother's pearl drop
earrings. Ally's heart broke in two at the sight of them.

"They're for your wedding day. To the duke. You'll
make such a lovely bride, dear," Granny Donny said.

"Grandma, I'm not sixteen, and I won't be a duke's
bride. But thank you." She closed the box and set it aside.
This was it, wasn't it? She had tried to sell, trade, and flee
her past, but it was no use. Her grandmother was handing
her the reins, giving her the family jewels. But Ally didn't
want even a pearl-sized piece of it. She wanted everything
to go back to exactly the way it had been yesterday so she
could leave for San Francisco. A clean break.

"We're going to get you all set up, dear, with such a
lovely husband. A duke! Everything is turning out so
splendidly!"

Ally looked at her grandmother, really looked at her for
the first time since last night. Ally had to turn away and
bite her lip in self-loathing. *Poor Granny.* She was fading.
All of her—the pale skin, the white hair, even her voice.
Soon, the old woman would disappear. And all Ally could

do was feel sorry for herself? She wasn't at all the good woman—she was selfish and tired and frustrated, and she didn't want to take care of her grandmother. Not now, when she had finally decided to look after herself.

And yet, she owed this woman everything. Without her grandmother, what would have become of Ally? She had even taken her grandmother's last name.

A drop of wax from the weeping candle fell onto the chocolate ganache.

"Grandma, for my birthday, will you make a wish? What do you want?" Ally braced herself for the answer. *I'll find your daughter, Granny Donny. My mother. Whatever it takes.*

Granny Donny closed her eyes like a child. She held her hands in a steeple of prayer. "I've already told you, dear. All I want is to go to my house in the country with you and the duke so you can fall in love and marry." She opened her eyes and blew out the candle like a child.

Relief washed over Ally. Just a trip to God knew where, a love affair with an arrogant jerk who wouldn't give her the time of day, marriage, and a couple of snotty kids. No problem. Way easier than having to find her parents. But the idea of finding them had taken hold, and Ally had to at least put it on the table. "I was thinking that maybe you might want to see Lisa again." The words hurt to say, but Ally kept on. "Your son-in-law, too? Lisa and Ross? Remember? Do you want me to try to find them before . . . before . . ." Ally couldn't get the words out. Her throat went tight.

"Before the marriage, dear?"

"Exactly." Ally swallowed.

"Oh, it's not necessary. I've taken care of everything.

We'll see them at the wedding!" Granny Donny said, as if she had thought the whole affair through and worked it out to her satisfaction. "I can't wait to get to Lewiston! Ah, the fresh air!"

Lewiston. Shock waves coursed through Ally and she inhaled to hold her emotions steady. Now she understood what Granny Donny meant by "the country." Her grandmother used to own a beach house in Lewiston, halfway out on Long Island. Could she still own the place? Ally hadn't thought about that house in ten years. "Didn't you sell that house?" They hadn't been there or even spoken of it since her parents left.

"Now why would I do that, dear? I love that house. There's nowhere better to escape the filth and heat of London. And we can embroider and play tiddlywinks and tend to our stables and inspect our tenants' farming."

Tiddlywinks? Tenants? Okay, fifty-fifty chance she still owned the house. But if Granny Donny did, a trip to "the country" would be easy and maybe even fun. If not, they could surely rent a house for a week or two nearby. It wasn't like Granny Donny was asking for a trip to a foreign country. Lewiston was just a few hours' drive from Manhattan in good traffic.

Ally felt a tug of guilt about giving up the plan of finding her parents so quickly, but if Granny Donny only wanted a trip to Lewiston, it surely was a waste of time, effort, and emotion to do more. After all, Dr. Trawlbridge had said that soon she might not even recognize Ally, so how would she ever recognize her daughter, whom she hadn't seen in ten years?

So, a trip to Long Island, to the beach. It was doable. Why not? Maybe it would be fun.

"I got you something else, too, dear." Her grandmother handed her another box, just as beautifully wrapped.

Ally tore off the wrapping without attention, her mind already in overdrive planning the trip ahead of them. She detested uncertainty, but planning was her comfort.

Ally's teaching job in San Francisco started in late August. She could spend the rest of the summer, if need be, with Granny Donny (and lots of hired help) on the beach. Maybe, in that time, the damage from the stroke would repair itself or the pills would kick in, and everything would return to normal. Or maybe, Ally would discover it was possible to live with Granny Donny in this state, and they could go to San Francisco together. In either case, she could focus on her grandmother's health with all her heart and soul.

She opened the box. Inside was a six-pack of Trojans, extra large.

"Oh, to be sixteen again!" Granny Donny giggled.

Ally hugged her grandmother, startled by her delicate bones. *She's still in there*, Ally thought. Maybe the trip to the beach would be like a trip back in time, to better days. Maybe it would be the ticket to getting her grandmother back. She'd recover from her stroke, get her bearings again, pull herself back into reality, and life would once again be normal.

*Everything was falling into place, which meant, of course,
that it was all about to fall to pieces. The princess
had seen enough of life to know that.*
—From *The Dulcet Duke*

Chapter 5

June came the next day, armed with take-out sushi and a six-pack of Diet Pepsi. They were in Granny Donny's living room, arguing as quietly as they could while Granny Donny had her post-tea nap. "You had a whole new life planned," June said. She was in her workout clothes, a loose sweatshirt thrown over her leotard to protect her muscles from Granny Donny's ferocious air-conditioning. "Please tell me that you're still going to San Francisco."

"Maybe. I don't know. I think I will. But later. Now, it's not about me. It's about Granny Donny. She wants to take this trip to Long Island, so we're going to do it." Ally sank back on the couch.

"To a house that you don't even know still exists?"

"I went through Granny Donny's papers last night, and I'm pretty sure she still owns the place. A real-estate management company had been renting it out and taking care of it. But the records end two years ago, so I'm thinking the

house must be empty. I didn't find any papers that indicated
a sale. I called and called the rental place, but no one answers. Anyway, no worries. If someone's there, we can get
another place nearby. It's not about the house. It's about me
and Granny Donny. Four days of adventure on the road."

"Four days? To Long Island? Um, more like two hours,
hon," June protested.

"Not if we go by horse and carriage." Ally didn't look
at her friend. She hadn't said that part of her plan out
loud yet, and she didn't like how crazy it sounded. Why
did things that seemed to make sense in her head always
sound wrong when she spoke them?

"No. You can't." June was so shocked, she popped an
entire piece of tuna roll into her mouth without even sniffing at it first.

"Why not?"

June chewed like a normal person, a sight Ally realized she'd never witnessed. "Why?"

"Because it's her wish to live in 1812 London, so I've
decided that I'm going to grant her this one last sort-of-
sane wish. She did lots of crazy stuff for me."

"This crazy?" June asked.

"Crazier," Ally insisted.

June looked doubtful.

"She moved out of this beautiful apartment and moved
into our crappy underground lair on 113th Street because
I refused to leave," Ally pointed out.

"You were young. Fourteen. You were abandoned.
Your parents had left you."

"She lived with me in that moldy, dark cave for four
years until I turned eighteen. That was an amazing thing
to do, and she didn't have to. She could have told me that I

was nuts and that I had to come and live with her. She had this beautiful suite in the Plaza, and she left it to live with me on the upper, Upper West Side in a dump."

"You were a child."

"So is she, sort of." Ally could just hear Granny Donny snoring soundly in the next room. "She lived in that apartment for four years, and I never let her change a single picture on the wall or carpet on the floor. And she never, ever complained. She let me keep it as a shrine to my parents, no matter how screwed up that was." Ally's voice lowered. "She let me wait, let me keep my fantasy that they'd come back. It might have been a stupid dream, but it kept me going."

"Okay. So she was awesome. But still. You're going to take a horse and carriage across Brooklyn, halfway across Long Island, to a beach house that might or might not exist, to have a house party, a ball, and end up marrying a duke?"

"Well, I'm kind of counting on her forgetting the duke part."

"Ally, I don't understand how you can do this. This isn't like you. It's totally nuts."

Ally shrugged. "I know. I sort of like it. I think, in a way, that was really her wish. That I do something crazy with her. She always wanted that, you know? And I always denied her. I was always the good girl. The responsible one. The one who wanted to stay home and wait, to do the right thing. So this time, I'm going to forget what makes sense and do something crazy."

June nodded, but she didn't look happy. "Well, then, it's official: You've both completely lost your minds."

"Mateo, how would you and Paula feel about taking Granny Donny and me to Long Island?" Ally asked the coachman three days later. "A town called Lewiston. It's about halfway out, on Fire Island. It's a beautiful old town, founded in 1652 when Richard Lewis bought it from the Matinecock tribe . . ." Ally rambled, unable to stop the history lesson for fear that if she did, Mateo would get a chance to say no. She hadn't expected to be so nervous asking him. Her throat was tight and dry. Talking to Granny Donny and June about the trip the last few days had made the plan almost seem normal. Now, with the traffic on Fifth Avenue snarled behind them and the rush of important-looking businesspeople streaming in and out of the Plaza, she felt absurd.

She willed herself to stop the lecture that was still tumbling out of her. "So, that's where the Dutch influence of the town originated and how it got its name. Um, what do you think?"

"It would be complicated," he said simply.

"Oh." Disappointment washed through her. "So. That's logical. I agree, actually. It was nuts. Crazy—"

"Complicated, but we could do it," Mateo said.

Ally perked up. She felt like hugging the coachman, but she didn't think he'd approve. There was something reserved, serious, and deeply sad about Mateo that she hadn't been able to put her finger on. "How many miles a day could we go?"

"Depends on the heat. The hills. How Paula reacts to the new surroundings. Conservative, twenty miles a day. More if conditions are right. The better question might be, how much can Lady Giordano handle?"

"I don't know." Twenty miles for Paula was the distance Ally had concluded, too. She'd done the research on horses, but her grandmother's endurance was harder to predict. She had cleared the trip with her grandmother's doctors, though. They thought she shouldn't have any problems, and if they did, they'd just be a quick cab-ride away from Manhattan. "We might have to play it day-by-day." Ally cringed. She hated not having a written-in-stone plan. But Dr. Trawlbridge had thought the trip was a lovely idea. He'd even given Ally leads on home care agencies he recommended on the Island so she'd have help.

Ally's plan was simple. She had arranged for June to meet them after the first day with a rental car packed with their things. Ally would take a cab back to the car every evening and drive to their new hotel. Then, once they got to the beach house and were sure they could stay, she'd have everything else sent. The only hitch was that she still hadn't gotten in touch with the rental agency that handled the house. But that seemed a minor detail when everything else was going so well. She had even found a set of keys for the place in a drawer, 237 Beachside Drive. She was feeling confident the house would be empty. "How would Paula cope?" Ally asked Mateo. "Stables, hay, what else does a horse need?"

"You leave that all to me. I've got friends," Mateo said. A sparkle began to glow behind his eyes, as if he was beginning to see the magic of the trip, too. Like maybe, if he'd let himself, he might smile. "There is one little issue."

"What's that?" Ally held her breath.

"Nada. Forget it. We'll be fine. Give me a week to get everything together," Mateo said. "Then, we're ready whenever you are." He patted Paula's flank. "We'll get you and Lady Donatella wherever you want to go. In style."

His world was just that, his. The princess, stumbling
in and out, didn't change that one bit. At least,
he was determined to think so.
—From The Dulcet Duke

Chapter 6

Such a lovely night for a ball! The air was warm and
balmy, the stars practically buzzing with excitement! Lady
Donatella couldn't hear the music, but surely it would
start soon. She picked up her pace as she approached the
ballroom. Ah! There was one of the musicians. "Dear sir,
a waltz!" she cried. She could still turn heads, even at her
age.

    She adored a waltz. How odd that no one was danc-
ing. Well, that wouldn't stop her. A woman of a certain
age could be forward with a gentleman about wanting to
dance, not like those young ones, wallflowers growing
dusty, waiting for a man. She picked out the most likely
prospect from the gentlemen strolling about the room.
Lord Vernon, if she wasn't mistaken, judging from his
swoon-worthy height and broad shoulders. It really was
awfully dark for a ballroom. So hard to see. "Dear sir,
would you abide an old woman the first dance?"

Lord Vernon smiled, obviously recognizing her. "Why, I'd be delighted! An honor!" And he took her by the hand and led her onto the dance floor.

Ally awoke with a start. Something was wrong; she felt it in her bones. She was in her grandmother's spare bedroom; the clock glowed 11:04 p.m.

She threw back the covers and raced to her grandmother's bedroom.

Her heart skittered to a stop. "Granny Donny?"

She ran into the living room. "Grandma?"

She searched the apartment. Her grandmother was gone.

She called downstairs to the lobby. No one had seen her. Ally's skin went clammy and her stomach churned. All night at dinner, Granny Donny had gone on and on about visiting the duke. Was Granny Donny walking the streets, searching for him?

Ally threw on a pair of jeans and a sweatshirt and bolted to the lobby. The Fifth Avenue doormen were adamant that Granny Donny hadn't passed that way. "We'd have stopped her for sure, Ms. Giordano," Ernest said. But then his face dropped. "But who's on the north side?"

They raced together to the door, Ernest a step ahead. Ally didn't recognize the man there. "Temporary," Ernest mumbled. "Damn staffing cuts." He took Ally by the elbow. "Evening, Tom. Did you see a little old lady leave this way?"

"In a ball gown," Ally added, fearing the worst.

"Sure thing. About an hour ago. Lovely woman," Tom said.

An hour. Ally was glad Ernest had her arm, as she felt faint.

"Did she get into a cab?" Ernest asked.

Tom was starting to detect Ally's panic. He looked uneasily from Ernest to Ally. "She, um, went, ah, I'm not sure I saw. I think, that way? I think she walked—I dunno."

Ally was trying to breathe. In. Out. In. In. In . . .

"I'll call the police. Don't you worry. Someone will have seen her," Ernest said. "She couldn't have gotten far."

Ally nodded, appreciative of his lie. Granny Donny could be on the subway, deep into the South Bronx by now. "Thank you. Thank you. Yes. Okay. I'm going out."

"Wait, it's not safe. Let me get—"

But Ally didn't hear the rest. She was already out the door and into the warm, dark night. The street was bustling with cabs and cars. Groups of post-dinner businessmen emerged from restaurants; tourists strolled arm in arm.

Surely Granny Donny wouldn't have gone into the park? Ally looked into the vast island of darkness that was Central Park at night.

Ally dodged the cars and raced across the street to where a line of cabs waited for fares. "Did you see an old lady? Alone? In a long dress?"

They shook their heads.

Ally didn't know what to do next. She looked both ways and didn't see her grandmother. She could be anywhere. Should she go east or west? South or—God forbid—north into the dark shadows of the park?

Okay. She had to think. To calm down. To cover all the bases. Granny Donny had been talking for days about her need to visit the duke. Surely she didn't know where he lived. Or did she? Ally dialed information. "Manhattan. Sam Carson. Residence. Thank you." The operator came up with three Sam Carsons before she found one at an address that seemed right for a man like Sam, on Central Park West. Ally waited while the operator put her through.

The phone rang and rang. Finally, a machine picked up with Sam's voice asking her to please leave a message.

"Sam. It's Ally Giordano. It's, uh, 11:13, and my grandmother is missing. I'm sure you remember her, remember us? The lady in the carriage? She's been talking about you nonstop, and, well, I'm afraid. I think she might be looking for *you*. Call my cell if you've seen her. I'm at the Plaza, looking for her. 212-022-5555." She hung up. Of course the man wasn't home. It was, after all, before midnight.

One of the cabdrivers approached her. "Ma'am? I just radioed one of my boys who was here earlier. Barky said he saw an old lady in a long pink dress go into the park. He said she looked like she knew where she was heading, so he didn't think much of it—"

He was still talking, but Ally was already on her way into the darkness.

Sam was almost through one of the most boring dinners he'd endured since childhood. He couldn't eat his crème brûlée fast enough. The woman across from him, Missy, was on her second martini, and she hadn't been shy about the wine either. She was waxing philosophical about Manhattan health clubs, going on and on about which clubs had the sexiest men. How his friend Jerry had thought he'd be able to connect with this woman was beyond him. Yes, she was built, but she was a vast, empty wasteland. Not that he usually cared. But lately, he cared.

Bollocks, was he ever off his game since meeting Ally

and her grandmother. He kept seeing himself through the grandmother's eyes, as a duke, and felt remarkably unworthy. It was ridiculous, really. A farce.

Sam checked his messages as discreetly as he could on his cell phone while he pretended to listen to his dinner companion. Two calls. Veronica. Again. Gad, would he ever be past her? And—

He sat forward. Ally? His interest sparked. Now that was a surprise. Her message was panicked, making only the slightest bit of sense. He listened to Ally's voice while looking at his dining partner.

"My grandmother is missing . . ."

"And I hate a man who sweats too much in public," Missy was saying.

"She's been talking about you nonstop, and I'm afraid . . ."

"The gay men don't sweat as much. Which maybe is a physical thing, you know? Like, hormonal? But then, what good are the gay ones? So it's a problem."

". . . I think she might be looking for you."

Sam stood up, waving the waiter over as he pushed in his chair. He was just a few blocks from the Plaza. "I have to go. Emergency," he told Missy. He wasn't entirely sure he meant his life was an emergency or helping Ally was. Or were they somehow one and the same? The waiter appeared and he handed him three hundreds. "Anything she needs, yes? Keep the change." He leaned over Missy and kissed the top of her head. "I'm sorry," he said.

"Call me?" she called after him.

"You bet," he lied.

He was both glad and confused to be out in the night. He ran the two blocks to the Plaza, wondering the whole way why he was running, why he felt nervous and worried. He didn't know Ally or her grandmother. Didn't owe them a thing. Didn't even particularly like Ally. And yet here he was, dashing across Fifth Avenue. A speeding Lexus cut him off and he pounded the hood. His heart was in his gut and he didn't know why. All he knew was that he wanted to see Ally again.

Two police cars were pulled up in front of the Plaza, their lights spinning. But he didn't see Ally. He dialed the number she had left.

Ally answered at once. "Hello?"

"It's Sam—"

"Sam? Is she with you?" She sounded so glad to hear from him, his chest puffed. It was an odd, pleasing feeling.

"No. Where are you?" He looked up and down Fifth Avenue.

"I'm in the park."

"In the park?" Pleasure drained away, replaced by dread.

"By the pond. A cabbie saw her come this way."

Sam spotted Ally at the top of the curved path, talking to a jogger who was pointing her deeper into the park. She took off running. Sam followed, catching up at the top of the next rise. He had walked on every continent, swam in every ocean, but he'd never been in Central Park at night. It was ethereal, otherworldly—romantic.

"He said he saw her go this way," Ally said, racing headlong, deeper into the darkness, hardly noting his presence.

Sam matched her pace. "What happened?"

"She snuck out. I don't know." Around them, the park

was deserted except for another hard-core runner, his head down, his feet pounding the trail. Sam wondered what kind of demons made a person come willingly into the park at night alone. But it wasn't the people he could see that worried Sam. The hairs on his neck rose in fear for Ally's grandmother because of what was hidden: drug dealers, psychotics, rats . . .

Ally stopped, and Sam had to catch himself from bumping into her. "Do you hear a violin?" Ally asked.

"A waltz," Sam said. "Mozart. G major." A small bridge crossed the path ahead where the trail dipped low. Under the bridge were two shadowed figures. Dancing.

"Oh my God, it's her." Ally started to run. "She's—"

"Waltzing," Sam said. "Pretty well, too." He took in the scene as he went. A violinist stood under the arch of the bridge, while the two dancers swept in and out of the shadows. Granny Donny was in a long pink gown that sparkled in the moonlight.

"Granny!" Ally called.

"Ally! Join us!" Granny Donny called back, not missing a step. "It's the loveliest ball of the season! I'm so pleased you've come!"

Ally stopped dead in her tracks, her mouth agape at the "ballroom" under the bridge.

Sam instinctively put his hand on Ally's back and they walked forward together, slower now, as one. Their unity felt natural and exhilarating. Sam wondered if Ally felt the rush of connection, too, as they stepped down the slope to the arch that formed the underside of the bridge. The violinist looked up but didn't stop playing. He was a grayed, wrinkled, unshaved man in ratty clothes. Homeless, Sam guessed, probably a busker during the day, with nowhere but the park to sleep at night. But he played beautifully, the music echoing and expanding under the bridge.

Granny Donny waltzed with a strapping, twenty-something man in a dark tie and white shirt that shimmered slightly in the lamplight. A woman Sam hadn't noticed at first stood to the side, holding the man's suit jacket and smiling at the scene. Two briefcases sat at her feet. As Sam's eyes adjusted to the light, other forms emerged from the darkness. Three teenage boys sat on a rock off to the right with an enormous boom box, mercifully silent. A bike messenger, his empty bag slung over his shoulder and his bike balanced between his legs, nodded in time to the music. Two runners stood under a birch tree, their arms around each other, mesmerized by the scene. They must have been dancing awhile for such a crowd to have formed in the otherwise deserted park. Sam felt an affinity for them all, kindred spirits in the dark, drawn together.

Except for Ally.

She stiffened under his hand. "Now see here," she began.

But Sam cut her off, taken with the moment she was determined to ruin. "A ball! Magnificent!"

"Granny Donny. Please stop dancing," Ally said, her voice rigid. "It's late and we need to go home."

"No time for talking, dear! Time for dancing! Oh, it's been too long," Granny Donny cried. The man spun her gracefully to the right. She was grinning up at him as if he were Rhett Butler. He was a surprisingly good waltzer, graceful and smooth. His eyes closed, his touch light, he looked as if he'd been preparing for this dance his whole life.

Sam took Ally's hand. "Well?"

"Well what?"

"Shall we dance?"

Disbelief vibrated over her features. "No. We shall not."

"But why not?"

"Because it's crazy."

Sam thought about his dull, totally sane dinner date. He thought about his proper-to-a-fault family. "So?" He took her hand and pulled her onto the path. He guided her in a stiff, unwilling waltz. "Ally," he whispered in her ear. "She's okay. It's okay. She's smiling. It's a beautiful night. Have you ever been in the park at night? Waltzing? It's unreal. I love this town."

"Of course I haven't. Because it's insane." Ally's body was rigid. She whipped her head from side to side to keep track of her grandmother, who was finishing a twirl, one foot peeping from under her gown, pointed delicately in its satin slipper. Could she even feel his touch with such stress gripping her body? Her situation was difficult; he understood that. And yet, the night was so lovely, her grandmother so radiantly happy, he felt, well, he felt like dancing. "If you don't concentrate, I'm going to step on your toes. Relax. Count. One, two, three. One, two, three. Don't you know how to waltz?"

"How can you ask that at a time like this?" Ally said.

"You don't know how to waltz. You'll make a lousy princess. It's a three-count." He started the waltz again. "One, two, three. One—"

"I don't care how to waltz, Sam."

"But this is lovely," Sam said, giving up mid-spin.

"This is dangerous—"

"Oh, no. Waltzing is quite safe. Now a tango can be dangerous. Especially my tango." He assumed the chin-up, chest-out posture of a bullfighter.

"Not the dancing! The park at night is unsafe. Crime statistics—"

He dropped his toreador pose. "Are you always this uptight?"

"I'm not uptight. I have responsibilities. You wouldn't understand."

"Oh, believe me, I would."

She stared him down, but he stared right back, anger blazing in his eyes.

When she finally spoke, her voice was hard. "You don't have to dance with me, Sam."

Her words took him by surprise. "Of course I don't have to. I want to."

"Why?"

No woman had ever asked him why. "Because you remind me of someone I used to know," he said. Did she remind him of Hana? How was that possible? They looked nothing alike. Were nothing alike. Except that they were both alone and fearless and determined.

She shook her head, puzzled. "Whatever. I need to get my grandmother home. And I should call Ernest. He's probably worried sick."

"Is Ernest your boyfriend?" Sam felt oddly territorial toward her. He wanted to kill the schmuck for not coming with Ally into the park.

"No. He's my doorman."

Jealousy was replaced with something softer: *recognition.* "Forget Ernest and dance. Look at the skyline, how the buildings light up against the black treetops. It's magical. They're glittering."

"Yeah, that's what I'll tell the cops after we've been mugged and they ask me why I brought my eighty-four-year-old grandmother in her diamonds into the park at midnight. *Didn't you see the lovely skyline, officers?*"

Sam started to smile, but the woman who had been standing with the briefcases came over to them, one briefcase in either hand. "I'd love to dance with you," she said to Sam. Then to Ally, "Do you mind watching these?"

Sam looked at Ally.

"Go. Dance," she said.

Ally was left with the cases, while Sam bowed, then waltzed into the lamplight with the woman.

He was determined not to glance back, no matter how much he wondered how she felt about him waltzing with another woman.

Ally tried to inhale the warm night air. She tried to look at the twinkling skyline. She tried to not care that Sam was dancing with Briefcase Lady. But after what seemed like an eternity, she couldn't take another moment. She picked up the cases, which were surprisingly heavy, and strode to her grandmother. She handed the man his case, somewhat roughly, then handed the woman dancing with Sam the other. "Grandma, we're going home."

"Oh, darling, are you tired? Me, too. It has been a long night!" Granny Donny had stopped dancing, but she still swayed to the music. Then she curtsied to her partner, to the violinist, and to the applauding crowd around them.

Sam and Ally walked her back to the Plaza.

"You need help getting upstairs?" Sam asked as they

stood on the sidewalk, looking at the lit-up facade, its flags still in the night air.

"No. We're fine," Ally said.

"Of course she needs help. Come!" Granny Donny said, taking Sam's arm.

"Really, no." Ally stood her ground. "Thank you, Sam, for coming. I really appreciate your showing up like that. But we're fine now."

"Speak for yourself," Granny Donny said, but she allowed herself to be disengaged from Sam.

"Well, good night, then," Sam said.

"Good night," Ally said. She pointed Granny Donny toward Ernest, who was holding the door open.

But Ally couldn't help herself. Just before she went inside, she glanced back to see Sam still standing on the sidewalk, looking at her.

Her heart beat a wild flutter, and she thought, *I should have danced with him*. Regret filtered through her, but she kept moving. Soon the door closed behind her, and she was alone, again, with her grandmother.

But not *quite* as alone as before.

After all, Sam did have her cell number.

Which might have mattered, if only she hadn't behaved like an insufferable stick-in-the-mud.

She reminded herself that she had been right, and he had been irresponsible and childish.

She reminded herself that he was everything she despised in a man.

She reminded herself that she never had to see him ever again.

And somehow, none of it helped a bit.

*To live the life of a princess was to live the life
of a woman in service to society.*
—From *The Dulcet Duke*

Chapter 7

Over the next few days, the details of how Granny
Donny had mentally arranged her new life in 1812 London revealed themselves one by one. The more Ally saw
of her grandmother's machinations, the more she could
see the peculiar genius of Granny Donny's sickness.

On Thursday afternoon, Ally came home from buying
new traveling bags to find Granny Donny's apartment a
hive of activity.

"Darling! Meet Salvatore," Granny Donny cooed.
"The famous tailor. All the way from Italy."

"Well, Little Italy," Salvatore said. "Mott Street, actually." Sal busied himself around the apartment as if
he'd been there often, which, judging by the perfection of
Granny Donny's dresses, he must have been.

"Oh, don't be silly. Compared to England, Italy is huge,
not little." Granny Donny waved him away dismissively.
"And these are his two assistants, Marco and Lily!"

Salvatore and his crew had taken over the living room with a rack of period dresses, bolts of silks and satins, and a terrifying array of pins and needles. A tape measure was draped around Sal's neck. He clapped at his assistants as they scurried about.

So this was how her grandmother got the clothes so right. Ally excused the home aide she had hired to watch over Granny Donny while she had been gone. She settled onto the couch and into the middle of the chaos of nineteenth-century aristocratic life.

"How many dresses do you need?" Ally asked her grandmother.

"At least five new country dresses. And then gowns for evening! Salvatore will take care of it all."

"Final alterations will be ready by first thing Monday," Salvatore said.

"Then we're almost ready to go," Ally said. She had just secured the last piece in the puzzle for going to Long Island, a full-time, live-in home aide for as many weeks as necessary. Mrs. McGill, a delightful Irish nurse, would meet them in Lewiston as soon as she was done with her current assignment.

It was a huge relief to find help. After the episode in the park, their trip had taken on a new urgency. In fact, she was beginning to wonder if Long Island might be a permanent move for her grandmother. Ally wanted her grandmother as far away from Manhattan and midnight violinists as possible.

And as far as possible from Sam. Not that Ally had seen or spoken to him again. Which was good. He had been so cavalier about the situation in the park. It had been just another evening of fun for him. No responsibilities. No worries. Just dance! It was infuriating. She wished she could be so daft and outrageous, treat life as a game.

And yet she had called Sam, he had come running, and she had acted like a nun and hadn't heard from him since. Not that she cared—certainly not. Why would she care? She had too many other things to deal with.

The obsessive checking of her cell phone was utter childish silliness.

"Oh, Ally!" Granny Donny cried, breaking into her thoughts. "Look! Salvatore brought along a wedding gown for you!"

"How did you arrange all this?" Ally asked her grandmother, ignoring the wedding gown the way she was learning to ignore talk of corsets and earls and roasted pigs. Amazing how quickly the impossible became routine.

"What kind of silly question is that, dear? Salvatore and I correspond by post, like normal people," Granny Donny exclaimed.

"She messengers me letters," Salvatore explained.

"You act as if I'm too dumb to know how to write," Granny Donny went on. "I might be old, but I'm not doddering, you know."

Sal nodded at Ally, four pins sticking out of his mouth. "We write with fountain pens," he said with some difficulty. He used the pins, then said more clearly, "On very heavy paper. It's delightful! Did you know Lady Donatella also has extensive correspondence with Jane Bonds, New York's best antique milliner, and a man from Sotheby's who specializes in antique jewels and accessories?"

Ally didn't doubt it. No one wanted to remind Granny

Donny it was the twenty-first century if they could make a fortune keeping her thinking it was the nineteenth.

Ally made a mental note to call Granny Donny's accountant.

"I usually do costumes for Broadway," Sal admitted when Granny Donny was out of hearing and Ally had questioned him further. "But I'm between shows, and this is a lovely distraction. I adore your grandmother. Would do anything for her. Now, let's get you fitted, darling." Salvatore held up the wedding dress for her to admire.

The gown was gorgeous. It had a tiered bottom and a fitted bodice with long, capped sleeves.

Her grandmother and all three assistants descended on her. "Oh, yes. Try it on."

"You must, go on."

Before Ally knew what was happening, she was stripped of her sundress, positioned on a small riser, and draped in white.

The vintage satin was unspeakably delicate on her skin.

"It's a 1907 gown," Sal explained as he turned Ally this way and that, measuring and pinning. "We could adjust it to suit the Regency age so you'd match Mrs. Giordano better, but I hate to ruin its integrity."

Ally fingered the ancient lace, awed by the intricate workmanship. She didn't want to think about how much the dress must have cost her grandmother. "You don't have to make it fit the age or fit me," she told Sal. "I'm trying it on this once. For fun."

But Sal shook his head in disgust. "What good is a wedding gown that doesn't fit?" He and Granny Donny shared a look. "Such an odd girl."

Realizing resistance was futile, she allowed them all to fuss. But the more they fussed, the more Ally couldn't stop thinking about Sam. How had that man gotten under her skin like this? It was humiliating to take a man seriously who didn't take anything in life seriously. As soon as she could, she shed the gown. Granny Donny reclaimed the spotlight, and Ally sank onto the couch to watch the proceedings, mercifully forgotten.

It was an elaborate process to fit the gowns. Even with two assistants, it took what seemed like forever to get just one dress right on her grandmother's tiny frame. Three more dresses still waited on the chrome rack, but no one seemed in any sort of hurry to get to them. After all, they had to break for tea and cakes and gossip about made-up earls and viscounts.

In the old days, Ally realized as she sipped her third cup of tea, with the absurd conversation swirling around her, an elderly woman living alone was still surrounded by her servants and still had important things to do, like having necklines adjusted and waists taken in. There were letters to write and send by urgent messenger. And, of course, everything had to stop for tea. Then, if you happened to forget you'd stopped for tea just moments ago, you could stop again!

"I can't wait to tell the duke we're almost ready to go," Granny Donny said as Sal turned her this way and that in her gray silk gown.

"He'll catch up with us later," Ally lied.

"Oh, no!" Granny Donny cried. "I won't leave London without him. Absolutely not. We need an escort, after all, if we're to go into the wild countryside."

*   *   *

Sam.

He was the only piece of the trip to Lewiston that Ally didn't know how to handle. She looked at the lists spread before her on her grandmother's coffee table: medicines, phone numbers, supplies. Which list did Sam fit in? Imaginary Nobles? Beautiful but Dangerous Dukes? She had hoped that Granny Donny would be satisfied with her virgin teenage granddaughter and vague excuses that "the duke was on his way." But as the days of planning passed, that was looking less and less likely, and now it was midnight, four days before she and Mateo had decided they'd leave, and Ally had no answers. She wanted to give her grandmother the trip of her dreams. She wanted even more to get her grandmother out of Manhattan until she was well again. But if Granny Donny kept insisting on the duke's presence, would it all fall apart?

Of course it would. Granny Donny was as stubborn as a mule. It was impossible to explain to her that Sam Carson would never come on a trip that was obviously nuts with Ally, a woman without enormous boobs or a yen to rip off her clothes at the sight of his angled cheekbones.

She tried not to think of his angled cheekbones.

She picked up her yellow pad and started her own list: *What I Want.*

For a long moment, the paper remained blank. Did she still want San Francisco? Her new job? Did she want to go back to June and sleep in her childhood bed?

Sam Carson.

She wrote the name before she could think it through.

She resisted the urge to crumple the paper and toss it away.

So, she would take a deep breath and admit to herself

that a part of her wanted him to come, too. The dumb-ass, moronic part. She stared down at his name. Okay, it wasn't so bad to admit it. After all, Sam *was* dashing and handsome and rich, and he *had* come to the park and behaved like a perfect gentleman.

But he hated her. That much was clear. His scorn in the park when she broke up the "ball" was palpable. He had come out of duty, or maybe a sense of adventure, and she had disappointed him somehow. Of course she had disappointed him. She had called like a damsel in distress, *like a princess*, and then refused to swoon.

And now she needed his help again.

How did the princess in *The Dulcet Duke* handle Duke Blackmoore?

I have to read the book.

Why hadn't she thought of that before?

Ally crept into her grandmother's bedroom. Granny Donny slept, snoring quietly, a pitifully small bundle of sharp-angled bones in her enormous king-size bed.

Don't worry; I'll take care of us, Ally thought. She hoped she could back up her intentions, but images of her grandmother lost in the park shook her.

The room was filled with romance novels. They overflowed the bookcases and were stacked on the floor. *The Wilted Flower, The Rose and the Vulture, To Tame a Maiden* . . .

Then she saw it. On the bed stand, the cover worn and creased. *The Dulcet Duke*. Ally snatched the book and replaced it with a copy of *Dog Fancy*, which one of the home aides had left behind.

I'll just read a few pages. Skim it for pertinent information.

But when she looked up hours later, she was on the couch, thirsty and needing to pee, but unable to put the book down. She was breathless, alarmed, confused, and only up to page 172.

The dulcet duke of the title, Duke Blackmoore, was tall, manly, rich, and impossibly sexy. Ally got the resemblance to Sam Carson after the first paragraph. Not that Sam Carson had "rippling" thigh muscles that "gripped his horse's heaving, sweating sides." Well, Sam certainly might have grippy thighs; Ally couldn't be sure. What was more disturbing was the spiritual affinity—the rakish charm, the devil-may-care attitude, and the lack of anything resembling responsibility for himself or his fellow creatures, especially his fellow *female* creatures.

And the hair. Both dukes had alarmingly unruly hair. Except that Sam wasn't a duke. Why was that so hard to remember?

Still, the facts stood undisputed. Duke Blackmoore was a womanizing, irresponsible rake who didn't deserve the incredible privilege he took as his due. He didn't deserve the good woman, who at this point in the novel was avoiding him at all costs with a disgust Ally found deliciously exciting. *Good sir,* spoke the princess, *I do not find your childish antics delightful as the other females who seem to fawn over you.*

Right on, Princess! Don't fall for adolescent swagger. For classic beauty. For that longing in your soul—

Oh, hell. Ally wanted more of that swagger. At least, she wanted it on the page. Why fight it? It was only a book, after all. She got herself a bowl of chocolate ice cream, a few more pillows, and settled down on the couch for a night with the dashing duke.

*   *   *

The princess wore a translucent nightgown. Her hair was loose and flowed behind her as if there were a constant wind. She walked, barefoot, through the dark night. Her body trembled with fright, but she kept going forward. She held a candle, its flame also trembling, the flickering light making the night seem alive with evil. The path under her naked feet was cold and scattered with fallen leaves that crunched ominously.

Suddenly, a hand gripped her. Before she could scream, she was pulled into the briar hedge.

Duke Blackmoore!

"Don't scream, Princess. It won't do you any good."

The princess was furious, but she was also relieved to be in the duke's arms and no longer alone in the dark.

The weight of him crushed into her and then, somehow, they were in his bed, still outside, the leaves of the massive oaks rustling against the black, starless sky above. "This is what you want," Duke Blackmoore growled.

"No. I want to find my grandmother." She was Ally, and she tried to pull away but was no match for the more powerful man.

"She's fine. She's with your mother." He grasped her closer.

"No. That's not possible. My mother is dead."

"Shhh . . . it's okay. You don't need her anymore. All you need is me." Duke Blackmoore had transformed into Sam.

He pulled her against him, catching her mouth with his own. And then, they were making love. A violin played a waltz in the distance as he ravaged her, his ferocious, savage rhythm out of sync with the playful waltz. She *gripped the posts of the mahogany bed, trying not to cry out in ecstasy. He was too much for her. Too powerful. But there was nothing she could do. Her body responded to him, rising up to meet his. It was too good. She spiraled deeper into the sensation of him—*

The violin music stopped, replaced with the heavy bass of a boom box—

Ally awoke with a jolt.

Around her, the night was silent.

The book had slipped to the floor along with her covers. Had she been *thrashing* in her sleep?

She let her head fall back on the pillows. Oh, hell. She was hot and sweaty—and thank God, alone on her grandmother's couch. But lovely sensations of the dream still tingled in her nerve endings. Ally felt a rush of hope. She could use a hero these next few weeks.

Wait. No. Reality check. Dream over. She wasn't some wimpy nineteenth-century woman who needed a man to save her from the dark. She was no virgin Princess Alexandra, swooning and fawning. In her dream, what had happened to her grandmother? She couldn't remember exactly, but the haze of unease she still felt meant it had been nothing good. Ally had abandoned her grandmother, left her in the park while she fulfilled her own desires.

The dream felt like a warning: *I must not abandon Granny Donny the way my parents abandoned me.* She shoved the book under the seat cushions, determined not to read another word.

Ally didn't need a hero. She would get Granny Donny to the beach house and they'd have a good time doing it. She would figure out a way to make sure her grandmother was safe and cared for. She would get by, with help from no one. After all, she'd lived most of her life without help from anyone but Granny Donny. She didn't need a man's help now.

Except the increasingly irritating fact was that she did. Her grandmother wouldn't leave Manhattan without the duke.

Ally got up and paced the dark apartment. The grand windows opened onto the shadow that was Central Park at night: dangerous, unknown, unsafe, beautiful, magical, unpredictable.

Just like Sam.

And then it struck her: Ally wasn't capable of lying to her grandmother about Sam coming.

But she knew someone who probably wouldn't mind lying one bit.

A man's house said everything about him. The rooms of
Blackmoore Manor said, "Enter at your own risk, for herein,
the rules of polite society do not signify."
—From *The Dulcet Duke*

Chapter 8

The next day, Ally stood outside Sam Carson's ornate prewar building, pacing. The unbearable heat wave hadn't let up, and even in her vintage cotton sundress, she was sweltering.

She had called Sam, and he had agreed to see her with surprisingly little hesitation. In fact, he had seemed almost *glad* to hear from her.

Maybe he had forgotten who she was, thought she was one of his floozies.

She practiced her speech as she paced outside his building: *Sam, my grandmother has the delusion that you will escort us to the country and then marry me. So if you could spare a few moments, pretend to be the duke again, come and visit her, and tell her you'll go, I'd be very appreciative.*

Ally reconsidered. She ought to cut out the bit about marriage.

She practiced again. Then, with a final huff, she strode past the doorman and presented herself to the Russian-looking man behind the marble desk. "Mr. Carson," she said. She had meant to say "Sam," but in the face of the gilded marble lobby and the exceedingly handsome Slav in the blue uniform with gold buttons and braided trim behind the grand desk, "Mr." had slipped out, then "Sam" had retreated, leaving only "Carson." At least she hadn't asked for the duke. "He's expecting me. Ally Giordano."

The man, whose name tag read Misha, looked her over and shook his blond bangs. He had blue eyes, slanted and heavy. "Mr. Carson isn't in." He put out both hands palms up in an old-world gesture of apology.

Great. Sam had said he would be here, she had walked all the way across the park and up to Seventy-second Street in the awful heat, and now he was gone? "I can't believe he's not here. I just spoke to him."

Misha shook his head. "Gone. Just left."

Ally felt the weight of dealing with her stubborn grandmother crash down on her. She sank onto a too-small, upright chair across from Misha's desk. Caring for her grandmother kept putting her in these straight-backed chairs—at the doctor's, the therapist's, the Rite-Aid pharmacy with its endless take-a-number line. She saw her life as a series of hard, straight-backed chairs stretching to infinity. *The good woman . . .* She could hear echoes of June's voice in her head: *Taking this trip is crazy . . .*

"I'll wait."

She was annoyed but not surprised that Sam could be so rude as to tell her to come, and then not be here. She looked at her watch. She had hired a new woman from the agency to watch Granny Donny, but she was anxious to get back.

Misha darted a sly glance around the deserted lobby and then came around his desk to her side. He leaned in close, his hands on his knees. He sighed and stared into her eyes with the peculiar intensity only foreigners would dare in New York City. Ally wondered if he was about to tell her that she was supposed to slip him a twenty.

"You should go," Misha whispered. *Youshooghoh*.

He said it with such gentleness, it took Ally a moment to understand him. "Go? Oh, I really have to see Sam, er, Mr. Carson."

Misha clasped his hands together, interlacing his fingers. He shook them with urgency, as if in prayer. "You find a better man." *Youfindabeddermin*. "Mr. Carson is no good."

"Oh. No. It's not that." Ally was amazed that the man had taken so much risk to warn her off Sam. The things Misha must see. She didn't want to think about it. "I know Mr. Carson is—" Dangerously gorgeous? Childishly irresponsible? All of the above? "It's just business."

"I don't want that such a good woman to be hurt." Coming from Misha's mouth, "hurt" was drawn out and softened, so that it ended up sounding like a thing that one became forever, for others to stare at in pity. "He's with someone. Yes? You know?"

I'm not the good woman, and no, I didn't know, and tell me, what does he do that's so awful? Ally composed herself. "Of course I know he's with someone," she lied. The news struck her harder than made sense. She had to stop reading *The Dulcet Duke* so those upsetting, lovely, very wrong dreams about Sam Carson and his four-poster bed in the park would stop. The book was in her purse now, and she touched it like a talisman. She had not intended to finish it, but this morning she couldn't resist taking it with her, so she'd dug it out from under the seat cushions. One had to finish what one started, after all. "Really, it's business."

Misha looked at her like he was a priest and she was a sinner condemned to a particularly nasty level of hell.

They stared at each other a few moments. Ally tapped her foot impatiently. She looked around the same way Misha had earlier, then lowered her voice to a whisper. "Besides the women, what's so bad about him?"

"The drinking," Misha said, shaking his head sadly.

"Anything else I should know?" *Buggering? Swordplay? Snuff?*

"Elbows."

Ally blinked. "Really?" Why did the thought of Sam's elbows suddenly seem obscene? She nodded, as if she understood what Misha was talking about.

"Like a Brazilian," Misha added meaningfully.

"Oh. I didn't know." Ally still didn't have a clue, but she didn't want Misha to think she was too innocent and good to know about the implications of elbows and Brazilians. Something about extreme waxing? What a sicko. "But I still need to see him. I'll watch his elbows."

Misha cocked his head to the right.

"Or, rather, I won't look at them," Ally tried.

Misha stared at her, confused, then shrugged and threw up his hands, as if washing himself of responsibility for what would happen next. He mumbled something in his Slavic lilt, went back behind the desk, picked up the phone, dialed, spoke her name (*Ms. Giordano, sir*), nodded, hung up, and pointed to a single elevator Ally hadn't noticed before, off to the side and apart from the main elevator bank. "Penthouse."

"Thank you." A disturbing sense of helplessness descended over her. She had known that Sam Carson, *Mr. Carson,* was rich from his tailored clothes and his eccentric manner, but in Manhattan, rich had so many not-so-subtle levels, and a private elevator to the penthouse at Seventy-second and the park was more than she had bargained for. Ally shook away her naïveté. Who knew where his money came from? Maybe he swindled his fortune from unsuspecting grannies with his waxed Brazilian elbows.

The elevator was as ornate as the lobby and had only two buttons, P and L. Guess people who lived in penthouses didn't borrow cups of sugar from their neighbors. She practiced her speech on the way up, tripping over the words. This just sucked. The gilded elevator made her feel underdressed. Maybe Sam Carson would answer the door in a velvet dressing gown, smoking a pipe and holding a crystal snifter of brandy.

Maybe his butler would answer the door. Or his manservant, whatever that was. Maybe he *was* a duke.

She pushed the lobby button frantically. This was a terrible idea. There had to be another way to get Granny to Lewiston besides begging from a man who was so despicable, his doorman tried to protect strangers from him.

The elevator kept rising. It came to a stop and the P light glowed red accompanied by a soft chime.

This was a fool's errand. There was no way a rich, self-centered stranger like Sam Carson was going to agree to—

The doors slid open.

Hello.

The duke was insufferable. He was insolent. He was charming.
And then, all at once, he was kissing her.
—From *The Dulcet Duke*

Chapter 9

Sam stood alone in the center of his private foyer. He wore only a pair of very nicely broken-in jeans, which he hadn't bothered to button. After all, when you weren't wearing underwear, which she could see the man wasn't as his jeans rode so low, buttons were so potentially nippy. She caught her breath. No shirt. No shoes. Just the jeans. And the chest. And those toes. Even the man's toes looked strong and powerful, well-tanned and cared for.

She looked Sam in the eye, pointedly holding her face neutral as if she were speaking to a misbehaving teenager caught in the hall between periods. She nodded curtly, not quite admitting to herself that she was, as the heroine in *The Dulcet Duke* too often said, stilling her heart.

Look away from the hot, mostly naked duke.

Er, not duke. Man. Oh, dear . . .

She pretended to admire the architecture. The small entry was white marble from floor to ceiling. A black, modern wooden table, the only furniture in the foyer, stood by an open door through which she could see the corner of a similar white marble living room filled with white leather furniture. The table held a vase packed with at least a hundred dollars' worth of artfully arranged white tulips. What was this supposed to be, heaven? The man should live in the basement, with an entirely red apartment . . .

"Ally!" he said too loudly. "I told you not to come here."

"Yes, you most certainly did tell me to—" She stopped. He was shushing her. What was he doing and why was she intrigued and why was he coming so close to her and why was it so lovely the way that swirl of black hair whorled around his belly button then tapered down into the waistband of his jeans? She had known on first sight where his personal storm came from and now it was confirmed. A whirlpool, a vortex, drawing in unsuspecting travelers. *Must remove eyes from vortex . . .*

He was glancing back into his apartment with expectation as he closed the space between them. She stepped back, so stiff that her shoulder blades were the first part of her to hit against the now-closed elevator doors. He grabbed her elbow and leaned in. *Elbows! Not that!* She tried not to panic, but she could smell the warm, lovely scent of him, forest mixed with sleep and skin—and *sex*. "Shh. Play along," he whispered.

"I am not here to play." Ally inhaled, her prepared speech wiped out by the scent of Sam. "Mr.—er, Sam." Why was she letting his lovely almost-nakedness rattle her? "I need to ask you to tell my grandmother that you'll come to her house on Long Island. Of course, you don't have to actually come. That would be crazy. Just tell her you'll come so she'll leave New York with me. I'm very sorry for the inconvenience. She's taken an inexplicable liking to you, and, well, she won't consent to go without you. Not that you'd have to go. Did I say that already?" She felt so flushed and awkward. "Just tell her you'll come. That's all. A little lie. Not that I think it's okay to lie, but she's very confused. I know that this is a lot to ask of a stranger." She trailed off, unsure of what to say to his belly button.

To him. She forced her eyes to his face.

"I'll do it." He glanced back into his apartment.

"You'll do it? Wait. Why?" *Who cares?* She studied the curve of his left shoulder, scolding herself for studying the curve of his left shoulder. She glanced down at his elbows. They didn't look Brazilian.

"*If* you play along," he hissed just as a stunning redhead appeared at the door.

"Sammy?" The redhead looked from Ally to Sam. She looked confused. And gorgeous. She must have been six-foot-two at least and maybe a hundred thirty pounds with her clothes on. Not that she had her clothes on. She was wearing a man's button-down white linen shirt and nothing else as far as Ally could tell. Between the two of them, they almost had an outfit—if anyone was wearing underwear, which she doubted.

Sam dropped Ally's arm and took a step back, shuffling his feet as if caught in an illicit embrace. He cleared his throat. "Um, Veronica, this is Ally. Ally, Veronica."

"Sammy?" Veronica's cheeks were just a shade shy of her hair color.

"Ally, I think you should go," Sam said, moving to

stand beside Veronica. "I told you it was over between us."

"I really need to talk to you. I just need a yes or a no," Ally said, before she realized that she sounded like a woman scorned.

"Is she—?" Veronica couldn't form the sentence. "No way. She's why you wouldn't make love to me last night?"

Sam shot Ally a warning look. "Veronica." He stopped as if he didn't know what else to say. "I told you you could stay because the pipes were broken at your place, but that was all."

Veronica squinted at Ally and cocked her head. "I don't believe it. You wouldn't sleep with me because of *her*?"

Ally's jaw dropped. She straightened to her full five-foot-four, feeling the inadequacy of every inch. Her sundress suddenly seemed childish and inadequate. Her B-cup breasts ridiculously small.

Sam shrugged. "It does seem unlikely, doesn't it? But she is"—he paused, searching—"kind. To horses. And old people. Well, not so much old people." He paused again. "Or horses, actually." Ally could see in his eyes that he was enjoying this immensely. She wanted to stomp on his bare foot.

"But she's . . ." Veronica was at a loss. She threw up her hands. "Short," she declared finally, the word a challenge tossed down like a gauntlet at Ally's size-six feet.

Ally understood Sam's game and she didn't like it, but she needed his help. She raised her voice. "Samuel, I've decided to give you one more chance." She struggled not to roll her eyes.

"Alexandra!" To Ally's intense alarm, he crossed the

room in two quick strides and took her into his arms. She felt her eyes widen in terror as he bent to her. And. Then. He. Kissed. Her.

This was so not okay.

She couldn't move. Because, actually, it was pretty okay. His lips were warm and soft. His bare chest, pressed against her thin cotton dress, was warm and hard.

And she really couldn't help but dislike Veronica, who was pouty and overdyed and insulting to the vertically challenged. That woman deserved to be one-upped by a short schoolteacher in a vintage polyester dress gotten for a steal from a hole-in-the-wall shop on Seventh Street and Avenue D.

The kiss was still going. In fact, it was growing, deepening.

Unsure of where to put her hands, Ally let them flutter about idiotically, before resolutely reaching down, as if to push Sam away. The fingertips of her right hand touched the whorl of hair at his belly button, and a rush of adrenaline swirled through her. For a split second before she regained her sanity, she swooned, blown over by a gust of lust.

Sam pulled away and met her eyes with a curious, amused stare, as if to say, *Really, Ally? I had no idea.*

Ally yanked her hand away, but it was too late. She would never, ever, forget the feeling of his taut stomach against her fingertips. When would she ever get the chance to touch such an insanely beautiful thing as his narrow, sculpted abs ever again in her life? To be on the receiving end of one of his wicked looks? To be kissed by his burgundy lips?

Let's waltz, baby.

Before she could pursue the thought, Veronica had had enough. She spun around, yanked her shirt off like a man, gripping it from behind the neck and pulling it over her head. She tossed it at Sam's feet and strode out of the room, stark naked and raving. "You are such an asshole."

"I told you at the beginning," he called to her. "From day one!"

Ally was still lost in the memory of Sam's skin against her fingertips. Which came first, being a womanizing jerk or an incredible kisser with rock-hard abs? She swallowed, her throat parched as if with longing. Gah. She shook herself free from the spell of him. Not possible. She would not fall for a rake. "That was despicable," she hissed at Sam. *That was incredible.*

"Really? I thought it was actually one of the nicest kisses I've had in a while." He was looking at her curiously, the white shirt in a puddle at his feet, his hair a tousled mess. "I didn't expect you to, you know—" He smiled mischievously, touching his fingers to belly button as if the touch had been mutually pleasing. "Kiss back."

"I did *not* kiss back." She sounded like one of her students. She cleared her throat again. Then again, stalling. Man, she needed water. She needed air. She needed sanity. She needed to stop thinking about dropping to her knees and putting her lips against that taut stomach and following the trail with her tongue, down, down—

"Ally?"

"Oh. Right. Sorry. So Dr. Trawlbridge said that my grandmother needs—"

"Wait." He held up a finger, then pushed the elevator call button. "One, two, three." The elevator doors opened with a soft ding and a softer whoosh.

Veronica, now fully dressed in a sophisticated white shift and white sandals with an enormous white purse slung over her shoulder, flew out of the apartment. Her oversized white sunglasses with giant Chanel "C's" reduced her upturned nose to a tiny button, making her look like a child playing dress-up in her mother's clothes. She didn't pause to look at either of them as she strode into the waiting elevator. Before the doors shut, she was on her cell phone, saying, "Sarah, you won't believe this asshole. Yeah, the one with the Porsche. No, the *red* Porsche not the yellow; that's the other Sam, Samson McGrath, the lawyer, in Princeton . . ."

Then they were alone.

"Well, now that that's taken care of," Sam said, "come in and tell me what I can do for you."

The duke did not suffer females gladly. Especially females of the well-bred variety. But the agitated woman in his sitting room didn't want to be there any more than he wanted her there, and this was so unusual, he couldn't help but be intrigued.
—From *The Dulcet Duke*

Chapter 10

By the time he had poured them both a glass of Perrier and settled on the couch, Sam had pulled himself together. More or less together, considering that very unexpected kiss and Ally's very unexpected fingertips catching fire on his stomach.

He hadn't meant to kiss her so deeply, in fact, he hadn't meant to kiss her at all, but he had known Veronica wasn't buying a word he said about Ally being his lover. Veronica was predatory, but she knew his type when she saw it, and Ally was decidedly not his type.

Why did he have to keep reminding himself of that?

As he buttoned his shirt—he felt somehow *obliged* to be fully dressed and buttoned around this woman—Ally crossed the expansive room and sat herself primly on the couch, allowing a full three-foot pillow length between them. She didn't seem to notice his place, which he liked and didn't like simultaneously. Most women gaped at his view of Central Park and went on and on about his imported Italian tile and his Sub-Zero refrigerator and who was his decorator (Josh Allen Lord, LLC). Ally had marched right across his living room with barely a look around, her arms crossed over her chest, her considerable wrath completely focused on him.

She behaved as she had that mysterious night in the park: impervious to her physical surroundings. Something stood between her and the rest of the world. He wanted to know what it was. Her dissociation from life fascinated him. And angered him. He couldn't help thinking of his wife, Hana. She had died so young, no chance to live.

A trace of the taste of Ally lingered on his lips. She had shaken him in a way a whole night next to Veronica had failed to. And Lord knows, she had tried just about everything.

He secured the last button and leaned back on the arm of the couch to face her, resting one arm over the back pillow and crossing his ankle over his knee. "Before you say anything," he said, anticipating one of her lectures, "I want you to know that I tell any woman who is willing to have anything to do with me that I'm a confirmed bachelor." Widower, really, but that was none of anyone's business but his own. "One month and it's over. That's my limit. Not that it matters a whit to me, but if I let them stay longer, they tend to grow acquisitive. I never lie. But they never believe me. Ever. At least, not once they see my place and my possessions and my—"

"I don't want to hear what else they see." Ally jumped up. She glanced out the window and huffed, as if the view offended her.

Now that she was in a dress, albeit an alarming,

orange-green-pink floral print, he could see that her legs were well formed and her neck was long and regal, unusual in such a short person. In fact, she was graceful and solid and powerful, like a runner. If only she'd quit with the prim, ugly vintage clothes and those black granny glasses.

"We think my grandmother suffered a stroke, leaving her very confused. It's a common side effect of mild strokes. All she wants is to go to 'the country,' by which she means her beach house on Long Island, and plan a ball for . . ." She trailed off, shaking her head as if to negate the very thought of something as distasteful as a ball. "Anyway . . ." She kept talking and pacing, and he took the opportunity to study her ass. Eight, maybe even a nine. Hard to tell until she got into some decent clothes.

How had he missed all this on their first meeting?

Her words began to slow, and, mercifully, after a brief explanation of the history and significance of house parties in Regency times, she stopped and sat back down.

He felt as if he had to climb out from under a huge pile of facts she had dumped on his head. He hadn't taken in more than the general gist of her story, but it was obviously time to respond. "So? Take the dear old lady to the country. I think that's a great plan. Much safer there."

That set her off on a new avalanche of words and obscure facts. The floral print on her dress was irritating him like a personal affront. In a way, it *was* a personal affront because it said, *I am not here to turn you on.* A very odd thing for a woman's clothes to say.

And yet, he liked it. It felt like a challenge. As if the clothes were taunting him: *You impress me, and then maybe we can take things further.*

The dress, like her, wouldn't shut up.

And then she did. She looked as if she intended to rip off his head. "You didn't listen to a word I just said, did you?"

"No. Not really," he admitted. He couldn't get his mind around the combination of her awful dress and her not-so-awful legs. Her hot kiss and her not-so-hot shoes.

"You're checking me out."

"Well, yes. Of course. I am a man and you're a woman and you are in my apartment."

"To ask you for help, not to sleep with you, for heaven's sake."

"But why be so rigid?"

She looked shocked down to her pink ballet flats, and he enjoyed it immensely. "It's fascinating," he went on, "how you and your grandmother both ignore reality."

"I do no such thing!"

"Of course you do. You push on as if you were made of stone, not flesh. As if the physical reality around you isn't there. Why? Why pretend I'm not here? That you're not drawn to me? That kiss in the foyer was—"

"A mistake!" she cried. She had turned bright red and was wringing her hands in dismay. She stood, then sat back down on the edge of the couch, barely touching the cushions almost as if levitating, her back bolt upright. "I don't have time for this. Now listen, Mr. Carson. *This* is reality: My grandmother has taken a perverse liking to you."

"Perverse?" Sam studied every inch of her as deliberately as possible. The buttons on her dress were tiny oranges. What a detail. Sam leaned forward and she leaned back, as if she were pulling him with a string. He tried it a few more times, just for fun.

"What are you smiling about?"

He sat back, perplexed. She wasn't a slob who didn't care about her appearance. She cared deeply about her clothes and probably went to great lengths to plan her wardrobe. But her choices had nothing whatsoever to do with the male of the species. Clothes to her were like a tulip garden, solely for her own pleasure, perhaps the pleasure of other females, but the gate was decidedly closed and locked to the male of the species.

And that riled him beyond measure.

He wanted to vault the fence, stride through her prissy bed of tulips, scoop her up, and take her to his jungle lair to show her what nature left to its own devices could come up with. He could almost hear the snapping tulip stems under his feet. Or, better yet, her orange buttons snapping as he yanked her dress free.

He felt himself stir and adjusted his posture to hide his arousal. That would surely make her mad and let loose the guard dogs.

She was waiting for another reply. What had she said? From somewhere deep in his jungle, he heard echoes of her civilized conversation: She had gone off on a dissertation of the psychological reasons her grandmother liked him. "I often affect women that way," he interrupted.

"Demented ones," Ally amended.

"Do you mean Veronica or your grandmother or yourself, Ally?" An image of Veronica lying about the broken pipes in her apartment hit him. There *was* something demented about Veronica, vibrating behind the facade of her beauty. The quest for perfection had sent her mad with botox and bleach and gravity-defying heels. That woman was a whole different kind of tulip garden, a Day-Glo one made of plastic, taking him for a fool, as if he wouldn't notice it was all a put-on.

But at least Veronica was trying to impress him. Not like this woman, who clearly didn't give a rat's ass if he liked her or not. A garden full of poison ivy if he wasn't careful.

Ally sighed. "Granny Donny won't go without you because . . ." She took a careful, tiny sip of water, then set the glass gently on the glass table. "She wants us to marry. It's a delusion. She's very difficult and confused. But very stubborn. I need her to make this trip."

"Why?" The word *marry* brought him to full attention. But unlike the terror that word usually instilled in him, he felt intrigued. A woman like Ally would have to be fought for, broken down, uncovered layer by reluctant layer. And he had the feeling that every layer would reveal something fascinating, unusual, worth the fight. Deep roots, as it were, instead of plastic artifice.

"Long story."

He braced for another onslaught of words. But she didn't seem inclined to speak. Behind her eyes, he saw a flash of distress that fairly shouted, *Rescue me*.

They stared at each other across the expanse of couch. He wanted to close the gap between them, but he didn't know how with a woman like Ally. His body vibrated with indecision. "Let me ask you a hypothetical question. Do you think your grandmother is completely mad, or do you think she's on to something?"

"Excuse me?"

"Don't you want to marry me even the tiniest little bit?

Just for the sex and money?" He was testing her, probing for her weakness. *Show it. Show me.*

"Maybe for the Porsche," she said dryly. "*If* it was yellow."

What did she think would happen if she let him in? "You despise me. Why?"

"You're reckless," she said.

"So?"

"So. Reckless people leave disasters in their wake for other people to clean up. They only see the fun, and they don't look back to see the problems they cause for everyone else. Like Veronica. Or Misha."

"Misha?" Was she talking about his doorman? "You know, sometimes, reckless is good. Sometimes, things need a little stirring up." He could read in the narrowing of her eyes that she thought he meant she needed stirring. But face-to-face with her, he saw it was *his* life that needed a good whisk. Because she was definitely agitating him, and although he didn't know why, he was enjoying it.

She stared him down as she would a bad dog. "If you hate Veronica, she shouldn't have been here."

"I don't hate her. I just don't want to marry her. There's a difference. I actually enjoy her company a great deal. She's a very funny, sexy person. We both enjoyed sex with each other. A lot. Is that a crime?"

"How you just treated her is a crime."

Bollocks. His arousal for Ally faded enough so that he could stand. He looked out the floor-to-ceiling windows over the park, which from the twelfth floor opened onto a view of green treetops and the blues of shimmering ponds. "You have no idea how she treated *me*. I'm like a bank to her. Arm candy, too, of course. You think she'd stay with me a half-second if I were poor and ugly?" He spun to face Ally, his agitation growing. "How dare you accuse *me* of being awful? That woman has no one to blame but herself. At least I'm honest."

"Oh, for God's sake." Ally took a deep breath and looked him in the eyes. "I really don't care about your and Veronica's sad, shallow relationship. But you promised you'd talk to my grandmother, Sam. So there's nothing more for us to talk about. Come to the Plaza before Monday. That gives you the whole weekend to find a moment between floozies to put some clothes on. Ask for Donatella Giordano. We're leaving first thing Monday morning. Tell her you'll come with us." She stood up.

She was leaving. Just like that. She had come on a mission, and nothing about him or his place had fazed her. She was a bulldog. Relentless.

He liked that in a woman.

Then she pushed a strand of escaped hair behind her ear and for a split second, there it was again, the flash of exposure into her soul. He saw that she was exhausted, alone.

That was her weakness.

She needed him and she despised him for it. And wasn't that the very definition of a rogue—a lone wolf, a person outside society, unwilling to conform to society's demands? She was the rogue as much as he was. And he had her trapped.

"Where are your parents?" he asked.

She stared at him a long moment before she said, "Gone." Did she mean they were dead?

"Brothers? Sisters?"

"None."

"So it's you and Granny Dotty?"

"Donny. Donatella Giordano. This weekend at the Plaza. I'll leave your name with the doormen."

She was completely alone in the world. Her grandmother was all Ally had, and she was slipping away. He wanted to protect Ally, to pull her back in. "How are you going to get to the beach? Do you have a car? A driver?"

"Sort of."

"Sort of? Sort of what?"

She was looking out the window, gloriously immune to the multimillion-dollar view. "A driver. No car."

He came next to her, close enough to touch her. The scent of lilacs mixed with lily of the valley swirled around her. *A driver. No car.* He grasped her shoulder and turned her to him. "No. You can't." She didn't shake off his touch, but she didn't respond to it either. "Not Paula," he said, aghast.

She met his gaze with defiance. "Paula."

"It'll take days. It's got to be, what, a hundred miles to Fire Island?"

"Eighty-four and a half."

"Eighty-four and a half miles through some pretty shady neighborhoods. Have you ever been through Brooklyn?" He wanted to shake her, but the delicate skin under his hand and the smallness of her shoulder bones held him back. As did the look of pure determination on her face.

"It's really not your concern. We'll be fine." She looked at her watch, a clunky antique man's silver contraption with a thick metal band. Awful on her delicate wrist. "Thank you, Sam. I appreciate your going to talk to her." She dislodged his hand from her shoulder like it was a pesky wasp, crossed his apartment, and soon was into his private foyer, pushing the elevator call button.

The elevator doors whooshed open and she stepped inside.

He raced after her and caught the doors with his hand before they could close. "Ally, I'm sorry about your grandmother. I hope she gets better. Of course I'll talk to her. And I'm sorry about your parents. And—"He was going to say he liked the way she smelled, but it seemed a both inappropriate and insufficient way to express the tenderness he felt for her at that moment. *You don't have to be alone. I will help you.*

Why? Why would he want to do that? What had she just done to him? And how? And how the devil would he extricate himself?

She jabbed at the lobby button. "The Plaza. This weekend. We leave first thing Monday. Thank you. Now excuse me, I really have to go."

At first, Sam didn't see it since it blended with the couch. But after a few moments of agitated pacing— damn, that woman agitated him—it caught his eye: Ally had left her purse. It was a small white bag with a tiny orange-shaped button for a clasp.

He was about to call down to Misha to stop her, then reconsidered. If she thought he was a despicable rake, unworthy of anything but her scorn, he'd be a rake all the way.

He popped the clasp.

He had been with enough women to know that a woman's purse was the key to her soul. But Ally's purse was nothing like he suspected it would be: a purple rabbit's foot keychain; a small wallet that held a picture of a couple with a child (Ally?); a bright pink cell phone; and a small white card that read, "Carpe diem."

Carpe diem? Her?

Also, there was a tattered copy of *The Dulcet Duke*.

He felt a rush of hope; she had a *fun* side.

He lifted the book from the purse. The cover sported a painting of a stunning redhead in a long, pink gown who stared out the window over rolling green hills. The cover was slightly narrower than the rest of the book, and from underneath peeked out what looked to be a second cover. He turned the page and was startled at what he saw. Another full-color painting, but this one of a shirtless man smashing the heavily bosomed redhead onto a red couch. Her clothes were torn and their torsos met violently. The man's face was savage; the woman's head thrown back in surrender.

Sam flicked back and forth between the image of the prim, composed woman on the front cover and her ribald, passionate abandon on the inside cover.

He glanced out the window to see Ally emerge onto the street below, her head held high and her gait tight and focused as she marched away, prim and composed.

He flipped to the inside cover.

Hot damn.

Getting to know Ally might be more fun than he imagined. She was hiding her true self—her fun, waltz-in-the-park, make-out-in-the-foyer self.

He poured himself another Perrier, sank onto the couch, and started to read.

The duke had taken her glove, and in her haste to flee,
Alexandra had neglected to retrieve it. She imagined him pressing
it to his face, smelling it perhaps. The image made her flush with
shame. And with other emotions she dared not address.
—From *The Dulcet Duke*

Chapter 11

Ally had walked ten blocks before she realized she didn't
have her purse. She stopped in her tracks, the humid air
thickening around her. She considered calling Sam, but
of course she didn't have her cell. She considered turning
back, but she didn't feel steady enough to face Sam again,
and no way was she dealing with that nosy Misha a second
time. She needed space and air. Well, what air there was
in the mid-morning heat of a July day. Sam would bring
her purse to her this weekend when he came to talk to her
grandmother. Until then, her grandmother had everything
she needed. Ally was late meeting June for coffee, but her
friend wouldn't mind spotting her the tab this once.

Ally strode into Edgar's Coffeehouse, still feeling unsettled. June was waiting at a corner table with two small
coffees in steaming white mugs. Ally tried to hold off her
words until she sat down, but she couldn't. "Sam Carson
is the worst kind of man: a man who hasn't grown up.

After all, why would he? He has it all—money, looks, success. He's a child who lives for his own pleasure with no responsibility to anyone!"

June's eyes lit up with delight as Ally took her seat. "Hello, dear. Nice to see you, too." A small, knowing smile played around her lips. "So, why are we talking about Sam Carson?"

Ally was too worked up to address June's question. "I see teenagers like Sam in my classes every single day, and it's my job—my life's mission!—to teach them that good looks and charming personalities are not enough to get them through life."

"Too bad it's a lie," June pointed out. "You love Sam Carson already just the way those teenage girls love the bad boys, Professor."

"I do not love him."

"Ally, why fight it? I saw that man. Love him. Want to sleep with him. Want to reform him. He's not ordinary in any way. He's beautiful and funny as hell and smart and, well, exciting." She paused. "But, um, Ally, why are we now *arguing* about Sam Carson?"

Ally blew on the coffee June had bought her and emptied in a sugar packet. "Because he is exactly like my father, and I will not be exactly like my mother." She stirred her coffee angrily, the metal spoon clanking against the mug. "I will never forgive my mother for leaving with that, that, scoundrel," Ally said, upset that she couldn't find a more modern word for the reckless man her father was. "My father might have been an irresponsible gambler, a drinker, a charming rake—a rogue. But my mother was worse because she was the good woman who threw her life—and me—away to be with him." Ally poured in another packet of sugar. "I will not be a too-stupid-to-live fawning groupie, going after an irresponsible, idiotic man just because he has hot abs."

"Your dad had hot abs?"

Ally was too frustrated to respond to June's teasing. "My point is, I will not fall for a rogue like my mother did. Ever. It ruined her life."

"Such a protest," June said. "It's not like anyone's disagreeing with you. Hey. Wait." She pointed a coffee stirrer at Ally. "Did something happen?"

Ally's fingers went to her still-heated lips before she could stop them.

"You kissed him!" June cried.

"No! Certainly not!" Ally stirred her coffee, watching the whorl of coffee like the whorl of . . . *Oh, stop.* There were more important things to be thinking about than that man's belly-hair trail. Or the way he seemed to see right through her, into her soul. *Why pretend that you're not drawn to me . . . ?*

"You did." June looked dreamily at her. "I want every single disgusting detail."

"I didn't." Ally ripped open another sugar. "Well, not exactly."

June took the sugar gently from her before she could pour it into her coffee. "Not exactly?"

"He kissed *me*," Ally said quietly. She winced as she sipped her oversweetened coffee.

June clapped her hands and smiled like a child. "And?"

"And, it was the most unbelievable, sexiest kiss of my life."

June started to squeal, but Ally held up a hand to stop

her. "That doesn't make Sam any more acceptable. In fact, it makes him worse. *Dangerous.* He's still a man led by hormones, and I'm still a woman with a brain."

"So then why did you go to see him?"

Ally told June the story of her grandmother's growing insistence that Sam come with them.

After June took it all in, she asked, "So, is Sam going to talk to your grandmother?"

"Yes."

"Then how bad could he be? I think that's very nice of him. He could have said no."

Sheesh, June sounded ready to go after the man herself. "Trust me, it wasn't nice of him. He had other motives. He was trying to blow off a naked floozy who was in his apartment, trying to get him to marry her. I pretended to be his"—Ally blushed at the memory—"his girlfriend. So he owed me." Ally replayed in her mind everything that had happened in his apartment, ending with her missing purse. "Listen, speaking of owing, can I pay you back for the coffee later? I forgot my purse."

"You went out without your purse?" June shook her head in a worried way. "You never go out without your purse. You must be exhausted, honey. You really need a break."

"That's why I'm going to the beach. Anyway, I'm fine. And I didn't go out without it."

"Then where is it?"

"At Sam's."

June's eyes went wide. "Oh. Now that's a whole 'nother kind of upset." June tried to suppress her grin. "You so want that man."

"That is ridiculous."

"Oh, Ally, it's turning out just like the book. Remember? The princess forgets her gloves. Now, he'll come to your house to return the purse. And you'll have a *moment*. Another kiss that becomes more than a kiss!" June put her hands to her heart. "Lovely! Oh, Ally. If it turns out like the book, I want to be your maid of honor."

"I am not controlled by that stupid book."

June pointed her finger at Ally and said sternly, "You're also not controlled by your mother's genes. Just because she followed your father to God-knows-where doesn't mean this situation is the same. You need to see Sam on his own terms, Ally. He's a beautiful man." She took a sip of coffee. "A beautiful, rich man."

Ally couldn't help herself. "A beautiful, rich, smart man. With an apartment you would not believe." She paused. "And a Porsche."

"Yellow?"

"Red."

June grinned. "You're all lit up. You so have a torch for that man; admit it."

"I do not!" Ally insisted. "He's the most irresponsible person I've ever met."

June wagged her finger at Ally. "You think any woman who has a torch for Sam Carson is going to get burned. But maybe, hon, just maybe, it's about time you faced a little fire. Maybe, because of your past, you're the one woman who can reel him in."

Sam read the last page of *The Dulcet Duke* and angrily snapped the book shut. His bedroom felt eerie, like he had just awakened from a disturbing dream. It was dark outside. He'd been reading for hours, missing his dinner date. He paced his apartment, then gave up and set off for Boule's Pub.

The place was packed. All of the women and most of the men greeted him by name. He shook hands and kissed cheeks European-style and patted backs. Then, as soon as he could extricate himself, he took a stool in the back.

"The usual?" Angelo, the bartender, asked when he had managed to work his way down the crowded bar.

Sam nodded.

Angelo put a pint of warm Guinness in front of him. "You look like shit. You must have watched the Chelsea game, eh? Nil-nil. Bloody hell." The man shook his head in disgust.

"I just read the story of my life," Sam said.

"Yeah? I'd like to read that," a blonde said, sidling up to him. It was Veronica's best friend, Sarah. Or Sylvie. Or something. She cooed, "Or better yet, we can start writing the sequel. Together."

"Another night, kid." The bartender gave her an icy stare and she backed off with a little wave and a, "Bye, Sammy. Call me." She mimed holding a phone to her ear.

When she was gone, Sam started up again. "I'm a character in a romance novel, Angelo. A two-bit duke."

"Congratulations!"

"Congratulations?"

"My girlfriend reads those. I think those guys get lucky every ten pages or so."

"Lucky!" Sam said it too loud, and heads turned. He inhaled a long, warm chug of the dark, bitter beer until everyone went back to his or her own business. Sam leaned in and lowered his voice. "I'm telling you, Angelo, it's spooky. The guy even looks like me. Well, except he's got this hair that sticks up all over the place."

Angelo looked at Sam's head and sucked in his cheeks but didn't comment. "Since when did you start reading romance novels, tough guy?"

Sam considered joking, but he wasn't in the mood. His head was swirling. He told Angelo about Granny Donny and Paula and Ally leaving her book behind. "It's like we're the same guy. For instance—"

"The hair."

"What? No. My hair's fine. Listen, every eligible female this duke meets wants to marry him for his money."

"I see the resemblance." Angelo put his elbows on the bar and watched Sam. "But let's face it, English, that describes half the SOBs in here."

Sam drained the rest of the beer while he looked around the bar filled with strutting men in Hugo Boss suits and Bagatto loafers. He knew he could count on Angelo to put things in perspective. He was, as usual, getting carried away. Exuberance and creativity were what made his advertising work shine, pushing ideas to their limits and making connections where ordinary people didn't see them, but in the real world, those attributes made life dicier than it needed to be. Got him into all kinds of trouble. Like this. Because, frankly, despite his body's traitorous reactions, Ally wasn't his type. "You know what makes me want to eat my own head?"

"The Italy-Germany game last Wednesday?" Angelo asked hopefully.

"The duke doesn't go near a respectable woman with a ten-foot pole—"

"Are we still talking about that book?"

"He won't consider a woman who's respectable."

Angelo sighed. "Because of the marriage problem."

"Right. But the writer of the book, Somethingor-other Lancet, implies that this is a weakness. A character flaw!"

Angelo nodded. "Well, Lancet is most likely female."

"Exactly! Just because a man doesn't commit to marrying every woman he beds doesn't mean he's miserable."

"Right."

"Or childish."

"Certainly not."

"Nothing wrong with fun, mate. Right? Places to go, people to meet."

"Party on, buddy." Angelo pulled a light beer from the tap then passed it over Sam to a blonde in a black dress behind him.

"I have my work, which is important," Sam asserted.

"Yeah? I thought you sold your ad agency last year for a coupla mill." The blonde sidled closer. "That you just take advertising freelance gigs now when it doesn't interfere with your other, er, pursuits." Angelo watched the blonde with the light beer rub up against Sam.

Sam shook off the woman and Angelo's observation, but the truth of it stung. Only working when he felt like it was more a gentleman's hobby than work, wasn't it? Panic was starting to rise in his gut. *I am the duke.*

When Angelo came back from mixing a martini, Sam said, "Last week, Angie, I flew to L.A. for a Nike shoot with Anthony DeGenisis, the tennis phenom. We made an ad with him that's gonna sweep the award shows in Cannes and New York. It's bloody brilliant. Then when I got back, another grateful client gave me behind-the-plate

Yankees–Red Sox tickets. Yanks and Sox! I work hard for my pleasure."

"It's a book, Sam. Don't you think you're getting a little worked up?"

"A damn bad one." Sam gazed into his half-empty beer. He *was* getting worked up, and he had drunk enough by now to face the worst part of *The Dulcet Duke,* the part that even his beloved Guinness couldn't touch. "This Duke Blackmoore meets Princess Alexandra, and he's reduced to a trembling vat of jelly." He drained the rest of his beer, willing it to take hold. "A grown, successful, happy man, reduced to jelly! By a sixteen-year-old virgin."

"You're in love with a sixteen-year-old virgin?"

Conversation around them stopped as everyone looked at Sam.

"No! That's the book. Me, I'm . . ." *Trying to waltz in Central Park with a twenty-something schoolteacher in horrid, vintage clothes. Wanting to understand a woman who despises me. Curious about the whys and hows of reaching her.* Damn, that was even worse. At least the teenage virgin made some kind of sense. "Me, I'm in need of another beer."

Angelo pulled the tap slowly, waiting for the hum of the bar to go back to normal. He set the glass down in front of Sam and leaned in close. "So you met your princess," Angelo said. "This is good, Sammy."

Bloody hell, even Angelo was going soft on him. Sarah—or was it Sandy? Sally?—was watching their exchange. She was a knockout, and yet, Sam didn't care. The woman looked like every other woman in the place: carbon copies. Beautiful carbon copies, but they all wore the same pointy heels, had the same highlights, and even the same vine tattoos peeking out from under the spaghetti straps of the same baby-doll dresses. *If Ally was here, which she never would be, she'd look—* He hesitated. *Different. Real.* Sam lowered his voice, looked both ways, and said, "What am I gonna do, Angelo?"

Angelo nodded. "Get on your wild steed, grab your sword, and get your princess. Or something like that. I dunno. I only read the juicy bits. Turn the corners down to mark the pages when I need a little reading material in the loo."

Sam ran his hand through his hair. "The duke has to beg the princess to *consider* him. She despises him. She treats him like a—"

All at once it hit Sam like a freight train. He looked toward Sarah/Sally/Sandy; she winked at him, and he felt sick.

I'm her.

I am Ally's Veronica.

Less than her Veronica, because Ally wouldn't even condescend to sleep with me.

A rage beyond any he'd felt in years took hold of him.

He tried to drink down the anger in a swig of Guinness, but it was stuck to him, part of him. Who did she think she was? He wasn't a man to be used and disposed of with scorn because he wasn't serious enough to rate better treatment.

"You okay, Sam?" Angelo asked. "You went a little pale and quiet there, mate."

"I don't beg," Sam growled. "Not for a woman in flats!"

"Met your challenge, eh, English?" Angelo delivered

the barb, then darted down the bar to pour drinks for another couple.

He should have been frightened, because Sam was mad enough to lunge over the bar and grab the man. A challenge. Hell, he was no floozy. He was Sam Carson. Ally might hate his guts, but she wanted something from him, too. Not just help with her grandmother, but something else, something she kept trying to hide behind those brown eyes and granny glasses.

She wants me.

He looked around the bar. For a minute, he lost his bearings. *Who am I? What am I doing here?* In this strange, adopted country, thousands of miles from his home, from his nearest blood relative, he was no one. He might as well not exist. If he left this bar tonight and got stabbed in a back alley, who would care? Misha? Angelo? The clients who called only when they needed help? He watched Angelo mix a whiskey sour for another man in expensive clothes. That man would slip onto Sam's empty barstool, and Angelo might wonder a few weeks later, *What ever happened to English?* Or he might not.

Sam drained his beer in two long swigs. What number was he up to? He didn't care. He was getting blotto tonight to get his mind off that woman.

But two beers later, his rage had turned to a kind of despair he hadn't felt in years. "Angelo, what in bloody hell are rippling thighs?"

"Don't know, friend, but if I were you, I'd find out. Because there's a princess out there who needs her duke in shining armor. And he'd better be rippling, or else all the begging in the world isn't going to get him anywhere. At least, that's how I think it works. Plus, you have to grow a mullet. Those guys on the covers always have the mullets. Oh, and lose the shirt, buddy. They never have those either. Plus, I have two words for you that you're not gonna want to hear."

"Hit me."

"My girlfriend must have a stack of these books waist-high by the bed, Sammy. I've studied these things for clues about what women want. It is my business, after all, to know. So I can give advice."

"You read the books, Angie. Just admit it and spit it out, mate." Sam was exhausted, wrung out, grasping for anything that he could use to understand that blasted woman.

"Chest-waxing, Sam. Those romance-novel dudes always have smooth, shiny chests. Not a hair in sight."

Sam left the bar alone, which was disturbing enough. He had drunk all night and was still stone-cold sober. Which didn't help explain his tripping over that bloody curb. Or the spinning ground. Or the way he couldn't stop thinking about Ally Giordano.

She made him laugh and made him hard and made him think about things he hadn't thought about in ages. What was happening with his family in England? Was the ancient, crumbling mansion waiting for his stewardship in Leicestershire still standing? Who was sitting at his father's side, learning to lead the Carson Financial Group in his absence? Did his parents ever think of him, or was he truly dead to them forever as they had declared with their cold, clipped words when he left England with his new wife, Hana, at the age of twenty-one? Of course he was still dead to them. Not a single word in response to Hana's funeral. Not a visit. Not a flower. Total silence. Until the plane ticket came with a terse note: *We will forget this ever happened.* Naturally, he had ripped it to shreds.

He tripped over another curb. He hoped it was a curb. It definitely was as hard as a curb. Two women walking the other way gave him wide berth.

He sat down on the next slab of dangerous concrete before it could attack. He held his head in his hands, but his world didn't stop spinning. Ally, like the princess, like *everyone,* wasn't *all* good. He had felt her fingertips press against his skin, her warm lips grow hot under his. It didn't matter a whit what she *thought* of him because lust was irrational, physical.

And love? He stared into the gutter. A crushed Starbucks cup. Cigarette butts. Wasn't love also irrational? He wouldn't know. He'd experienced it only once, in the whirlwind with Hana. And then she died. And before Hana? Nothing. Hell, at one point he must have loved his parents, his brothers and sisters. Was love that shooting pain in his side he'd felt when he was loaded alone at noon on Christmas Day into the chauffeured car to go back to boarding school after just twelve hours home? Was it the burst of agony left radiating through his head after the blind, mad anger of being told that if he married that commoner, he wouldn't receive his position at Carson Financial Group, and he might as well go to America and never come back? *You'll be dead to us.* And then Hana was dead and here he was alone, on the hard sidewalk, feeling sick as a dog.

Oh, he knew love. Love was the empty, blank rage of having his letters returned and his calls not answered by his mother. To be treated as if he were dead, with hardly a backward glance, because he had dared to want something other than finance and the uptight aristocrat they had picked out for him to marry.

He stood warily as he reminded himself, *I don't love Ally. I don't even like her.* She surely had no idea how to please a man. No woman who wore glasses like hers could possibly care about pleasing a man.

But if I took the glasses off . . .

He walked slower now, carefully, toward home. Cabs slowed behind him, hoping for the well-dressed drunk's extravagant tip, but he waved them off. This was Manhattan of the twenty-first century, not Regency England. If he was going to be a hero in a romance novel—which he was not—it sure as hell wasn't going to be one about him changing into a good wee lad, like clay in a moralizing author's hands. No, his book would be about the "good" woman realizing that comfortable shoes and vintage prints do not make a woman good any more than loving fun and women (and fun women) make a bloke bad. In this day and age, it was no terrible thing for a woman to give in to a rake now and again, just for the fun of it. Because life was short. Shorter than Ally knew.

He stumbled into his lobby. Bollocks. Misha stared him down like he was coming home from a mass-murder spree. *Got a towel for my bloody knife, mate?* Misha just stared. Why did that man despise him? Sam ignored him and rode up in his private elevator, remembering Ally stepping out of it, taking him in hungrily with her eyes, stumbling over her endless words. Rubbish that a woman with decent legs like Ally's would go willingly at twenty-five onto a shelf, when what she really wanted was to bed a naughty, wealthy duke.

The doors opened and he stumbled out. He knew she wanted him. Not just by the hungry look in her eyes, but also because *The Dulcet Duke* was a guidebook to "good" women like Ally Giordano. It explained in endless adverbs how Princess Alexandra *really* felt around the man she fought to despise. Sexually, Ally had been his from the first time their eyes met.

He threw himself onto his bed fully dressed.

What did he care what she wanted? What did he want?

Why would he want to bed Ally when there were so many other women out there willing and able, better dressed and experienced, and way more fun?

He sat up and kicked off his shoes.

I don't beg.

He took off his shirt and threw it across the room.

I don't want her.

He'd see her grandmother this weekend as promised, return Ally's purse and that cursed book, and he'd never have to see or even think about either one of them ever again. Never have to feel the pain and hurt of his past that she and her grandmother dredged up in him.

But as he drifted off to sleep, one blasted thought circled through his mind, trumping all others: No duke worth his title would let two women venture into the depths of Brooklyn in an open carriage without being at their side to protect them, no matter how much one of the women despised him.

The princess had a way of always being in the midst of doing good whenever he saw her, making whatever he was doing feel downright silly and selfish the moment he laid eyes on her.
—From *The Dulcet Duke*

Chapter 12

Sam left his apartment the next day at eight. He dropped off Ally's purse at the Plaza with the doorman, but he didn't go up to see Lady Giordano. It felt too early to call on a lady. Plus, he was in his soccer gear. Jockstrap and shin guards hardly became a duke.

He took a slow jog around the lower park to warm up for the game. He had barely slept last night, dreaming of Ally, which was disturbing enough. Now, his mind was racing faster than his feet seemed able to manage, as if his past were about to catch him. He had to get rid of his obligation to her and get back to his old life.

After his lap, he walked to the soccer field. This Saturday morning game in Central Park was a rough, fast, take-no-prisoners pickup game. (Game, ha! As if soccer was ever a mere game.) The European Union expats joined forces against the Brazilians and other assorted South American ringers. Once in a while, a brave, foolhardy American tried to join the carnage, but he almost always was handed his head on a platter. This was the real deal.

Two Brazilians were lacing up. Sam sat next to them. "Hey, Paulo," Sam asked as casually as he could, "you ever hear of a player named Mateo? Drives a horse and carriage around the park. Brazilian. Midfielder."

Paulo shook his head. "Sorry, English. But if you're looking for some real skills, I could teach you a few things."

"In your dreams, Paulo."

"So who's this guy? Someone we should see? Not like we need more talent to kick your pussy European asses."

"Nah. Just met him, that's all. Let's get out there so I can make you eat your words, eh, *caras*?"

The game was brutal. That Misha showed up and joined the Latin team, determined to take Sam's head off, didn't help any. The players cursed in twenty different languages. By the second half, blood flowed freely down Sam's leg, most of it his own, and he was covered in mud. The park was starting to fill around them with couples pushing babies in strollers. Wide-eyed tourists took pictures of one another on benches.

A line of picnic blankets began to form around the field as people settled in for their vigil to receive free Shakespeare-in-the-Park tickets. The park service handed out the free tickets at one o'clock, first-come-first-serve, and the crowd was thicker than usual today because the theater group was doing *Hamlet* tonight. Sam hated playing on the days they handed out the tickets, as whole families came with elaborate picnics, small children, and old people, prepared to spend a peaceful day in the park, ignorant of the battle taking place on the soccer field just yards from their crosswords and potato salads. The makings of a Shakespearean tragedy, indeed.

Ally and her grandmother sat in the back of the carriage as it made its way slowly around the park. Ally had to admit that she thoroughly enjoyed her grandmother's daily constitutional with Paula and Mateo through the park. Ally had never allowed herself the luxury of a carriage ride, and it was lovely. Out of habit, she always refused her grandmother's offers of money and luxuries. She never wanted to have anything her parents might want. She wanted them to come back for her alone, not for help with their debts. She lived on her teacher's salary just fine. It suited her.

But what harm was a carriage ride? Not like her parents could snatch this away from her, even if they were near, which seemed beyond unlikely.

Ally put her head back to take in the flawless blue sky peeking between the green leaves. Paula trotted in front of the carriage effortlessly. Mateo had explained that the carriage was so light, even Ally could have pulled it loaded with four of the fattest people they could find. The flat, shaded park was child's play for such a powerful creature as Paula, he had said. And to look at her trotting proudly, it seemed true.

"Look, darling, the duke!" Her grandmother pointed toward a field of half-naked, bleeding, mud-covered men as if they were dandies strolling about in top hats and tails.

Talk about a powerful creature. Even in a field of beautiful men, Sam stood out. Of course, in a game of shirts vs. skins, he just had to be a skin. His bare chest glistened with sweat; his legs were strong and tanned; even from this distance, she could see the outlines of his abs. But Ally already knew the man was gorgeous. Nothing new there.

"He is a handsome man! Mateo, pull over, would you?"

"Mateo, no. Keep going," Ally said.

But Mateo ignored Ally and pulled Paula to a stop by the side of the road. He seemed as mesmerized by the game as her grandmother was by Sam.

"He does cut a fine, fine figure," Granny Donny observed.

Ally couldn't care less about soccer or Sam's fine figure, which was why it was so upsetting that it took a herculean effort to rip her gaze away from his effortless, physical grace. She looked everywhere but at Sam and gasped. A toddler meandered over the sideline, oblivious to the men on the field. Ally stood up in the carriage. "Who's watching that child?"

Apparently, no one. The players began to move up the field as the child toddled farther into the line of play, oblivious. Why didn't the goalie notice the girl and blow a whistle or call out? He was blind to her. No, not blind, preoccupied with the game. No. Worse. *He saw her, and he didn't care.*

Ally looked at her grandmother. Then at the girl. She didn't want to leave Granny Donny alone, but the goalie clearly had no intention of leaving his goal for the girl, who had crouched to examine something on the ground.

"Go. I'll watch Lady Giordano," Mateo said. He had spotted the toddler, too.

Ally jumped from the carriage. She dashed toward the little girl, but it was slow going through the picnic blankets and she was too far away. "Hey! Someone!"

"Tell the duke to come and say hello!" Granny Donny cried cheerfully after her. "Way to go after your man!"

Ally recognized Misha with the ball, his head down as he ran full-speed, leading a pack of men right toward the toddler.

Finally, the goalie moved out of the goal, toward the girl. *Oh, thank heavens . . .*

But Misha was picking up speed. He darted around the last defender.

The goalie crossed himself and then aligned himself against Misha, the girl obviously sacrificed.

What a jerk! Ally was too slow, tripping over sunbathing teenagers and novel-reading couples in beach chairs. "Sam!"

Sam didn't seem to hear. But he had looked up the field and stopped cold. Did he spot the toddler, too? And would he care?

He took off for Misha at full speed.

Ally watched, out of breath, her heart pounding.

Misha pushed the ball up the field. He must have seen the girl by now, but, like the goalie, he obviously didn't care. He was running full tilt, two players on his heels. Sam coming on strong.

At the last moment Sam dived, tackling the bigger man. Sam, Misha, and two other players fell in a pile, crumpling just yards from the little girl's feet.

The little girl looked down at them and clapped, as if they'd planned the spectacular crash for her amusement.

Then, distracted by a butterfly, she abruptly wandered off the field as if nothing had happened.

Ally's heart started up again.

But then it stopped.

As the pile cleared, Sam, who was at the bottom, wasn't getting up.

Ally didn't think. She ran to his side. "Sam?"

Sam was dead still. The other players gathered around.

"Foul in the box," Misha protested. "Penalty kick."

The other men cursed and argued whether it was in the box or not, whatever the heck that meant, as if Sam weren't in a heap on the ground, not moving.

"Sam?" Ally whispered. He looked peaceful lying there, like a fallen warrior. *Please don't be dead.* To her utter dismay, she felt a rush of emotion. She put her hand on his chest. His heart was beating. That was good. Did he need CPR? She had taken a course ages ago, but the class dummy had never made her feel like this. She bent close to him to feel if he was breathing.

His eyes fluttered, then opened. "Ally?"

Ally jumped upright and removed her uncomfortably hot hand from his chest. "Oh. Ah. Hi. Hello."

"Hello." He stared up at her with a curious sort of regard.

"Are you okay?" she asked.

"Did you tackle me?"

"Me?" Her face fell. Had Sam become as confused as her grandmother?

"Gad, woman. Just kidding," he said, trying a slight smile but then wincing. "Is the girl okay?" he asked.

She wished he'd get up, as he looked so helpless and sexy stretched out on the grass. Maybe just a little CPR? Just in case? Her throat was dry and her skin tingled and it was hard to form words. Of all the ass-hats on the field, only Sam had cared about the toddler. "She's fine." Her voice was rougher than she intended. It was hard to take her eyes from the fallen warrior.

He tried to sit up, winced, then lay back down.

"Sam, I don't think you're okay."

He blinked a few times, then, to Ally's relief, he painfully pulled himself to a sitting position. Unfortunately for her ability to speak, he looked as good sitting as he had lying down. He shook his head as if he had water in his ears. "You don't have to pretend to care, Ally. I'm fine." He looked around and spotted the carriage. He tried to wave to her grandmother but winced and lowered his hand.

"It's a goal kick," Misha insisted.

"Penalty was clearly outside the box," someone else cried.

"Shut up," Ally snapped at them all. She had been so entranced by Sam, she'd forgotten ignorant brutes surrounded her. "Can't you see this man is hurt?"

"Get the woman and the wounded off the field so we can play," a man called out in a heavy Italian accent.

"Nice friends," Ally commented as two players pulled Sam to his feet, none too gently. They were mumbling about Sam's foul. *Stupid bastard. Kick on goal. Merde. Mierda. Merdoso.*

Sam hobbled off the field, holding his side. She followed, ready to catch him if he stumbled, or collapsed, or wanted to turn and kiss her—

No. Not that. What was with her? It was her dream last night of Sam, confusing reality and fantasy just as badly as Granny Donny. She started to babble. "I think you lost consciousness. Concussions are very dire medical emergencies that are undertreated in ninety-four percent of cases. You need to go to the hospital."

He collapsed onto the grass at the sideline, obviously still in pain. But his attention had gone back to the game. Misha was setting up for his penalty kick.

"Sam? Hello? Concussion? Broken ribs? Internal organ damage? The sooner you get to the doctor, the less the permanent damage. They've done studies."

The sooner she got away from Sam, the less *her* permanent damage. It wasn't just his physical form, but his physical bravado at saving the girl. *It was just one more example of his recklessness.* But she had to admit, that kind of recklessness was impossible not to admire. Good thing it was tempered by his idiocy of refusing medical evaluation. "We can take you out of the park in the carriage."

"Nonsense. Just had the wind knocked out of me," he said, but he winced as he tried to stand to watch the action on the field, so he stayed put. Sam's team formed a wall in front of the goal, but Misha's powerful shot cleared it and scored easily. The Russian danced around the field until he was buried under a pile of his teammates.

"Bloody hell," Sam said. He stood up shakily. "I'm back in," he called.

"Sam, no!" Ally hated how she sounded, so she added, "Don't be a fool."

He stopped in his tracks and stared at her. "But why not? That's what you think I am, isn't it?"

"Excuse me?" Ally said. The edge in his tone alarmed her. Was he really that upset about a stupid goal?

"You think you're too good for me. That I'm nothing. I'm your Veronica, Ally, aren't I? Only worse, because you wouldn't dream of sleeping with me even just for fun."

Ally felt as if he had just flattened her the way he'd taken down Misha, knocking the air out of her. She and Sam *had* collided these past few weeks, but she had thought she was the only one feeling the impact. "Sam, I have no idea what you're talking about," she blundered. But she did. She knew exactly what he meant. He had nailed it. Her fantasies of him were just fantasies, to be put in a box and ignored as insane.

"Give it up, Princess. You wouldn't deign to give me the time of day if you didn't need me to help your grandmother. Well, don't worry, I'll live long enough to talk to her. To lie to her. Because that's what you think a man like me is good for, right? I see through you, Princess. Now, excuse me, I have to go. I just cost my team a goal, and as dumb as you think that is, it matters to me."

"Well, if all you're worried about is a goal, then you are an idiot," Ally called after him, flustered.

He stopped and turned, his eyes flaring with anger. "I'm not worried about a goal, Princess. I'm worried about my team. But you wouldn't know about that, because you do everything alone, don't you? You're too good to ask for help from anyone, especially someone like me. It kills you, doesn't it, that you need my help? Good thing I'm a gentleman and won't demand anything in return." He started walking again and this time didn't look back.

Ally was left alone on the sidelines, overcome with anger and confusion. Where had that attack come from?

On the field, Misha delivered a stiff elbow to Sam's injured ribs, and she winced as if the blow had hit her. Sam kept up with the play. He was hobbling but determined. His teammates patted his butt and mumbled monosyllabic grunts of approval at his idiocy. *Men.*

He didn't spare her another glance, so she turned on her heel and hurried back to the carriage as steadily as she could despite her pounding heart. He didn't know a thing about her. He didn't know anything about the pain of not having parents to rely on, about making it on her own, about being the only one left to care for her last link to family, to be the only responsible one—the one who couldn't give in to passion and idiocy. He had no idea how long and how hard she had waited for people who never came. Yes, you learned to be on your own. So what? Who was he to criticize her?

When she got back to the carriage, Mateo was feeding Paula. "Let's go," she said, climbing into the carriage.

But Mateo shook his head. "I've got to give Paula time to digest. Her colic. Fifteen minutes, *si*?"

Ally cursed her bad luck. She jumped back down out of the carriage. "Okay. Of course." Mateo had explained to her about the old horse's delicate stomach.

Now she just had to keep her eyes and mind off Sam for fifteen minutes.

No problem.

No problem at all.

When halftime finally came, Sam was surprised to see Ally and the carriage still under the trees by the side of the path. Mateo, the coachman, stood by Paula, whose nose was buried deep in a silver bucket. Mateo adjusted the tack here and there, but his attention was on the men on the sidelines, as if appraising them with expert eyes. Ally paced impatiently beside the carriage, her arms crossed.

God, he had been an ass, lashing out at her like that. Why was he so mad at her? What was it about her?

Sam tried to ignore the scene, but images of Ally bending over him, asking him if he was okay, clouded his head, and something deep inside him tightened as memories he usually blocked rushed him. *The only day Mum ever appeared on my sideline. Kingsbridge United vs. Waldron Prep. Me, number twelve, playing a brutal, punishing game for her. Bloody brilliant my cross at eighty-nine minutes. Assist on the winning goal, a header just under the crossbar by my winger, Manny Cypress. My head high, strutting to the sideline after the game. Mum saying, "Number twelve? Why, Samuel, I had thought the whole game you were number six, the boy who scored. Now he was very good."*

He knew his mother from a football field away at a glance, knew her every mannerism, her every nuance, had it all inscribed into his soul. He had been able to pick her out of the crowd of parents with an eagle's eye.

Sam never told her about another match. Only Hana, much later, had ever come to see him play.

He shook off the childish memory only to see Ally watching him with cold appraisal. Pleasing a certain kind of woman was impossible. A waste of time and effort. When a woman was cold inside, there was no touching her.

He ought to go and talk to Donatella Giordano now,

save himself the trip to her apartment later, get rid of these people once and for all who seemed to dredge up memories of his past. He limped to Ally's carriage as best he could, aware that the pain in his side was getting steadily worse.

He bowed to Lady Giordano, who nodded back, her face bathed in a radiant smile that pained him almost as badly as his side.

"Nice game," Mateo said.

"I cost us the tying goal."

"You saved that little girl from getting crushed," Ally said. Her eyes had softened, or maybe he had only imagined that they had been hard. Oh, hell, maybe he really did have a head injury, because he cared. *I don't care.*

"Tell that to my teammates," he said.

Mateo rearranged Paula's bucket. "You're too slow with the left foot. And you turn into traffic on the defense. But not bad. For a Brit."

Paula snuffed agreement, her nose still buried in the bucket.

"He's also not bad for a husband," Granny Donny called down from her seat in the carriage. "Right, Alexandra?"

"How are you feeling?" Ally asked, changing the subject.

"Fine. No problems," he lied. Every breath was like a stab wound.

"Then you'll still be able to come with us to the country?" she asked. Her voice trembled slightly.

A wave of roiling, conflicting emotion engulfed him: *her hand on her chest, the worried look in her eyes as she bent over him.* Was she only worried that he wouldn't help her, or was she alive inside? *Her touch had been*

*more. Her touch had been nothing. She despises me. She
wants me. I despise her.*

I want her.

He did?

No. He didn't. That would be emotional suicide. But
his pride was hurt. He wanted to prove to her that he was
no Veronica. Why? What was happening to him? He had
nothing, absolutely nothing to prove to this woman. His
breath quickened and the stabs got stronger and he hoped
maybe he'd just keel over now, and save himself the agony
of trying to understand his feelings for Ally Giordano.

"Sam?" Ally asked. "I *really* think you should get to a
doctor. You don't look so good."

He didn't feel so good, but it had nothing to do with his
ribs. It had to do with what he was considering doing despite his foreboding. "Lady Donatella," Sam began. Then
he stopped, frozen by the regal woman in the carriage
staring down at him like he was the most worthy man on
the planet.

Sweat dripped down his back. Mud and blood coated
his legs. It hurt to breathe. And yet, this one female, this
gentle, crazy old woman, didn't see him for what he was,
but for what he was raised to be. He was her knight in
shining armor, a nobleman, a gentleman. *Worthy.*

Of course, there was the little issue of her being
insane.

But he was feeling more than a little insane himself.
Must have been the head injury. *You want me, Ally. And
I want you. I want to know what makes you so alone. I
want to understand why you can't trust anyone. I want to
hear your discussion on the percentage of head injuries
treated vs. untreated and how you segue from that into*

the mating habits of the Central Park pigeon. I want to dance with you at midnight in the dark.

I want you to look at me the way your grandmother does—with respect.

He looked back at his teammates on the sidelines, then at Ally and her grandmother.

I want to stop playing games.

The verdict was in: He had bloody well lost his mind. But there it was: He wanted Ally, God knows why, and he was determined to make her admit that she wanted him, too.

He bowed to Lady Giordano. "May I pay you a visit later this evening? After supper?" he asked. He would go home, wash up, and come to Lady Giordano properly, in her sitting room, as a respectable duke, not as a half-naked bleeding slob caked in sweat, a boy on a field playing a boy's game.

"Of course, good man, of course!" cried Lady Donatella.

Ally's jaw dropped. "Sam?"

"A problem?" he asked.

"No. No problem," she said, but her eyes said otherwise.

"Tonight, then." Sam took Ally's hand and kissed it, meeting her eyes with his own. She was off-balance, confused, angry—and intrigued.

She was just where he wanted her.

There comes a time in every scoundrel's life when he catches a glimpse of what he might have been. Only if he catches it in the reflection of the right woman's eye, is there hope for reform.
—From *The Dulcet Duke*

Chapter 13

Granny Donny didn't like the new skinny housemaid any more than she liked the fat, flatulent housemaid before her. But she couldn't concentrate on the help when her granddaughter was on the edge of ruin. *Unmarried. With no prospects in sight.*

The plan to marry off Ally to a worthy man had come to her a few weeks ago. Or was it months? Days? It was all so confusing! It was the day after waking with that disturbing pain in her right ear, which had gone as quickly as it had come. So strange, that pain. Anyway, it didn't signify. A phantom pain in the ear; who ever heard of such a ridiculous thing? She had thought maybe it was a tooth. But the pain had gone quickly, and the teeth were still there. Every single one! Eighty-four years old and perfect teeth! She had always been blessed.

But now she felt distracted, as if she'd missed something important. Something she couldn't put her finger on. Since the real pain was gone, though, she didn't take the pills. Oh, she pretended to. But they never noticed that she slipped them into her sleeve. Silly Alexandra and her endless pills. She wondered if they affected the ficus tree whose dirt she shoved them down into as soon as Ally or the nursemaid was gone. The healthiest tree in London!

Donatella Giordano took another sip of tea as she wondered why she hadn't seen the necessity of her intervention in the girl's affairs before. Why ever had she waited so long? The poor dear's parents were gone—her own daughter and son-in-law, gone! He a scoundrel and she a devoted wife to a man who couldn't be saved. No one to care for the girl and her future. Except for her, Lady Donatella Giordano!

She did so enjoy *action*.

If only she wasn't so confused all the time. Nothing fit the way it should. People came and went. Her daughter. Her son-in-law. She felt as if she saw them around her, but everyone said they weren't here. She felt as if they were near. It was like living in a dream that almost made sense. Only when she focused on Ally did her head clear.

Help the child.

The country house was empty when it should have been full of generations of Giordanos. Herself, in the parlor, embroidering. Hmm . . . did she know how to embroider? Of course she must know. A woman of her position. She was just tired, that was all. So hard to focus. What was she thinking about? Oh, yes, how she must take Ally and the duke to the country! How delightful! Her daughter, Lisa, by her side, chatting over tea. Oh, her dear, dear daughter. It seemed as if she had just left.

Where was Lisa again? Why wasn't she caring for the

child if she was here? Donatella squeezed her eyes shut. She had such a headache. It was so hard lately to keep on a happy face. To keep it all straight. But as the family matriarch, it was her job to keep the family intact.

Lisa is in the country, at the family estate. We are going to see her and her dear husband so they can meet Alexandra's betrothed and I can die in peace, the family united and carrying on into the future.

It was just after seven when Sam arrived at the Plaza. His afternoon in the emergency room after the game (he had played to the end and his team had won 3–2 on his assist off the left wing) had confirmed a bruised rib, a minor injury he'd endured before, but no concussion. A little ice, some ibuprofen, no big deal. Just as long as he didn't try to breathe too deeply.

Unfortunately, what he was about to do was making him breathe much deeper than he preferred.

A skinny, balding nurse in uniform let him into Granny Donny's apartment, where the elegant old woman was perched on the edge of a gold couch, taking tea in a gown and gloves. The toes of purple silk beaded slippers peeked out from under her long skirt.

She held out her hand. He obliged with a kiss, then sat next to her, refusing her offer of cakes and Earl Grey. He had put on his best black Armani suit and silk tie, but next to Lady Giordano's grandeur, he felt like a stablehand.

"I hope you've decided to join us in the country," Granny Donny said. "We have such enjoyment planned. Lawn tennis and quail hunting and whist!"

"How could I refuse whist?" He made a mental note to look up what the bloody hell whist was.

Ally came into the room, and he stood on instinct and bowed. Under her icy stare, he almost lost his resolve.

She nodded at him curtly. "Glad to see you're still with the living."

Was he mistaken, or was she a little breathless, too? "Delightful as always," he said.

They all sat. Ally didn't touch the tea.

"The duke just told me that he'll join us in the country, dear! Isn't that delightful!" Lady Giordano positively beamed.

Ally nodded. "Delightful."

"I really am joining you," Sam said to Ally. "To play whist."

"Good. It will be a pleasure," Ally said, playing her role.

"No, you don't understand. I mean, really. I'm coming."

Ally's eyes went wide. "Are you? Really?" The bottom had fallen out of her voice.

"Yes."

"Don't you have a flooz—?" She stopped herself. "A job?" she substituted.

"I do. In fact, I couldn't get Monday morning off. A small matter of a photo shoot I have to tend to. But I'll catch up with you by the afternoon."

"You will?" Ally was at a loss for words, which pleased him immensely. "Why?" She practically squeaked the word.

"I couldn't leave two women alone in a carriage to cross such dangerous territory."

Ally looked like she wanted to kill him, so of course he smiled his most wicked smile. This was going to be fun.

Granny Donny took his hand. "No brigand would dare

attack our carriage with you on board, Duke. Your skills with the sword are nothing short of legend."

Sam stood before Ally could protest his nonexistent sword skills. "I really have to be going. Next time we meet, we shall continue this delightful conversation in the back of Paula's carriage. Good evening, ladies. Until Monday afternoon, adieu."

He had her alone in the garden. Her moist lips.
The moonlight in her eyes. A lesser man would be merely
tempted. A greater man would surely resist. A man like
him would indulge, and without regret.
—From *The Dulcet Duke*

Chapter 14

*A*lly followed him into the hallway, closing the apartment door behind her. "What the hell do you think you're doing?" she asked. She smoothed her vintage yellow dress, as if it were as riled as she was.

"A man of honor doesn't lie to a gentlewoman," he said smoothly.

"But you're not a man of honor."

"That's what you think. I'm out to prove you wrong."

"Why are you doing this, Sam?" Ally asked.

"Because you're not up to the task of escorting your grandmother back to 1812, much less to Long Island."

"You think you're going to protect us from brigands with your invisible sword?"

"No. I'm going to protect your delightful grandmother from you. You wouldn't know how to show that grand, worthy woman a fun adventure if you tried. Just look how you bungled the dancing in the park."

"You're not a noble duke, Sam." Ally was bright red and flushed over with a mist of perspiration despite the over-air-conditioned hall. "And I'm no sixteen-year-old virgin. I will not allow you to rush in and play hero to my damsel in distress."

"You can't stop me," he said. He liked that she was so upset. It meant that she cared.

The blaze that erupted behind her eyes told him he had her on that point. She said, "You want to come? Fine, come. Actually, it does me the favor of pleasing my grandmother. But that doesn't mean I'll play that stupid role. You'll always be my Veronica, Sam. I don't fall for men who treat life and other people like they're disposable."

"Ah. Is that a challenge? You and me. Four days in a carriage." He hit the elevator button. "You'll have no problem resisting my dangerous charms?"

"Four days in a carriage with my eighty-four-year-old grandmother," she pointed out.

"Four days for me to prove that I am a gentleman, and you, my dear, are the rogue." The elevator doors opened.

"Me?"

"Yes. The loner. The one who is lost, cut off from society. I will make you admit that you need me more than you could ever imagine and for reasons that you can't control. G'day, m'lady."

He caught the doors before they slid closed, caught her, pulled her to him, and kissed her. Hard. Solidly. Thoroughly. He let her go and she fell away from him, shock on her face. "For old times' sake," he said. "Next time, you kiss me."

The doors closed with a soft click.

He was alone. He sank against the back wall of the
elevator, the heat of her lips vibrating across his own.

I found her weakness, and it's me.

Monday, he'd go on a carriage ride through Brooklyn
and beyond with a woman who professed to hate him, her
crazy grandmother, a worn-out horse, and a coachman he
was starting to suspect might not be what he seemed.

And he couldn't wait.

Ally slammed the door behind her and leaned against it,
catching her breath as if she had escaped a wild animal.

In a way, she had.

There she went again, "stilling her heart." Ridiculous.

It was lust, and she knew firsthand from her mother
what happened when a woman forgot her responsibilities
and gave in to lust. Because Sam was dead wrong—Ally
was no rogue. He was the rogue that needed taming. And
she knew now what his weakness was. She had seen it in
his eyes when he addressed her grandmother in the park
and then seen it again tonight, as he sipped his tea: *He
wants to be respected. By me.*

I found his weakness, and it's me.

Ally returned to Granny Donny in the living room.
Her grandmother wore her emeralds and diamonds, looking beautiful, defenseless, and wealthy beyond belief. *If
their trip was anything like* The Dulcet Duke, *brigands
on the road to the country would attack and the duke
would save them.*

Ha! What would Sam do? Kick the bad guy in the head
with a soccer ball? He'd be useless. They were all going to
die in a gutter before she even got a chance to be ravaged
by him . . .

Oh, hell. That wasn't what she meant. But the sizzling memory of his kiss was hard to ignore. She had to be careful. He had challenged her to resist him. Which wouldn't be a problem.

She deserved a good man.

Whatever the heck a *good man* was.

And after Sam—with his raw passion, his heat, and the look in his eyes—did she really want a good man?

Or had she already lost herself to a hopeless, unrepentant rogue determined to drive her to ruin?

Or, at least, to Long Island?

Step Two:

Every rogue has something they hold dear.
Take it.

The roads from London to the estate in Derbyshire were filled with bandits, highwaymen, and countless other dangers. One needed a man, a gun, and a great deal of bravery. Princess Alexandra had the latter in great supply. The previous necessities, unfortunately, she had to hire and endure.
—From *The Dulcet Duke*

Chapter 15

Monday morning, Ally and Mateo helped Granny Donny into the carriage in front of the Plaza. Granny Donny wore her pale blue dress with yellow ribbons and her diamonds. Despite her apprehension, Ally had to admit that her grandmother looked beautiful against the red velvet of the carriage seat.

Granny Donny sat herself primly in the center of the seat and crossed her hands in her lap. "Where is the duke, dear?"

"He's going to meet us as soon as he's finished his photo shoot."

"His what, dear?"

"His, er, as soon as he's finished touring his estates."

Ally climbed in beside Granny Donny, nervous, no matter how she tried not to show it. She had been to Brooklyn plenty of times, but, as June had pointed out over the course of the last week, always in a closed, locked

car on a freeway. Frankly, she had no idea what to expect
on the back roads of Brooklyn, if there were such things
as back roads in New York's most populous borough. In
her wakeful hours, unable to sleep, she'd done as much
research as she could on their trip. The first few neighborhoods would be spotty but okay since they were so close
to Manhattan, full of artists, musicians, and Hasidim. But
as they traveled deeper into the borough and beyond, it
became harder to know what to expect. She had no idea
what they'd find. Or who would find them.

Oh, hell. She was acting as wussy as a nineteenth-
century princess. They'd be fine. This was supposed to
be a fun adventure. Could Sam be right, that she was too
rigid to give her grandmother her wish of fun and fantasy? She was determined to enjoy the ride.

If only the carriage didn't look so fragile and open. Its
chrome railings gleamed against white fiberglass sides.
The red velvet seats were plush and luxurious. They might
as well just put up a flashing neon sign that read "WE'RE
LOADED! ROB US!"

The original plan was to walk Paula at an easy pace of
five miles per hour for five hours. Then, after some discussion, she and Mateo had reduced today's ride to four
hours for Granny Donny's sake—the sitting and jostling
in the heat was easier for Paula than for Granny Donny,
who had not a drop of Arabian blood in her veins.

But today was truly, dreadfully hot, and they recalcu-
lated and decided to shoot for going just past JFK Airport,
where Mateo had a friend who could board Paula for the
night. The change in plans was fine; Ally had every hotel
and motel between them and Lewiston mapped out, as
well as the address of every police precinct, every public

park, and every public and private horse stable (amazingly, there were four stables in Brooklyn alone). She also had the names and numbers of every acquaintance she had ever had even the slightest contact with who lived along their route programmed into her BlackBerry. She rebooked her and her grandmother at the airport Hilton, pleased with herself for being open to new plans.

See, she wasn't rigid.

She wrung her hands.

Were they having fun yet?

"I mapped out three different routes," Ally said to Mateo, handing him sheaves of paper with routes highlighted in yellow. "Some ways are shorter, but some have less elevation—"

Mateo took her maps, but he didn't look at them. "You let me worry about getting you there. Climb in. Let's hit the streets."

Ally caught something new in the set of Mateo's jaw. Was he nervous?

Ally climbed into the back of the carriage and settled herself next to Granny Donny. "Have you ever taken Paula to Brooklyn before?" she asked Mateo. The rigidity of the coachman's face was starting to make her sweat.

"No." Mateo adjusted Paula's tack.

"Why not?"

He swung himself onto the box and gave the reins a shake while cooing words of encouragement to Paula as they started off in the "wrong" direction, away from her usual route through the park. She hesitated a moment but didn't protest. Mateo didn't lose his rigid stance. "Because it's illegal to take Paula onto the streets of Manhattan during the day," he said.

Ally's stomach clenched. "But we're always out during the day."

"Just to and from Central Park and her stables."

Of course. How had Ally not noticed that before? They never had a reason to take Paula anywhere else. She looked back to the line of horses waiting for tourists at the edge of the park.

"Also, it's illegal to take her over the bridges," he said as Paula pulled toward the busy Fifth Avenue traffic. "So hold your breath, Princess. We're going to break some laws."

"Why didn't you tell me this before?" Ally asked. Break a few laws. No big deal. Just laws. Breaking. Her skin felt chilled despite the repressive heat.

"Because I didn't think you'd go for it if you knew," Mateo said.

"I wouldn't have!" Ally felt ill remembering how her parents broke every law in the book, from "harmless" shoplifting after Granny Donny had cut them off from her money completely for losing too much at the track to sneaking onto the back of busy buses to avoid the fares. Breaking little laws was a slippery slope . . .

And yet, her grandmother looked so happy as they trotted down Fifth Avenue. *This is the trip I promised her. The adventure. I'm going to be the fun one, the one up for adventure.*

"Didn't want to worry you," Mateo said.

Ally's heart was beating wildly as she scanned the vicinity for policemen. "Who's worried?" she said as a new worry occurred to her. "Is the no-horse rule because it's dangerous for Paula? Is she going to be okay?"

"She'll be fine. The morning traffic moves so slowly,

it's not the danger of the cars; it's the police we have to keep an eye on. It's not a big deal."

Ally tried to rally her sense of adventure. She could be fun and wild. If only it didn't make her feel so ill. She wished Sam was there. She felt certain he could talk himself out of any trouble. "Well, at least this couldn't get any worse," she said as gamely as she could manage.

And then, it got worse.

"Where's the duke?" Granny Donny asked again, looking around at the early-morning crush of humanity that streamed through the streets, cutting through the canyons of midtown like water flowing along the path of least resistance. Paula clip-clopped down Fifth Avenue easily, the traffic so slow, she blended right in. Ally kept waiting for a policeman to stop them, but the cops they passed didn't seem to care about them. Maybe they were as ignorant of the no-horse law as Ally had been.

"Sam's meeting us later. Work held him up. He'll be here. He has my cell."

"Well of course he'll be here," Granny Donny said, sinking back onto the seat. "A duke always keeps his word. But he better meet us soon. I won't leave London without him, no matter how excited I am to see my daughter."

Ally tried not to panic. "Your daughter?" *My mother?*

"Of course, dear. Lisa and your father are at the country house, waiting for your arrival. Where do you think they've been all this time? They can't wait to meet your duke."

Ally tried to hold herself together. *Just illegally passing through the streets of Manhattan, about to see my mother and father, who disappeared ten years ago.*

"Granny Donny, are you sure they're there?" Ally had to remind herself that Granny Donny had said a lot of things in the past two weeks that were highly questionable: the imaginary visits from viscounts and earls, the imaginary scandals among the cooks and servants and footmen and tenants, even an imaginary case of measles from which the "parlor maid" perished. (Brenda, the maid, had quit to follow her boyfriend to Cal State on a football scholarship.) But the end of the Lewiston house's rental records loomed in Ally's mind: There had been a change at the house two years ago. No more rental records. Why hadn't she paid more attention?

"Of course I'm sure they're there. We speak often."

Ally had to hold on to the carriage sides to stop herself from jumping out and running away. She'd been ambushed, but not by brigands, by her past. *It's not true. She's crazy, confused.* They made their way past the chic stores and high-rises of midtown, past the prewar apartment buildings of the twenties, past the funky boutiques and restaurants of downtown, and finally into the chaos of Chinatown, with its mid-morning crowds moving in every direction like the Chinese character signs mounted on every spare inch of the buildings. Paula pulled the carriage like a pro and no one stopped them, every police officer unconcerned. Some even waved, and Granny Donny waved back, filled with childish delight.

As the neighborhood petered out into kosher delis and high-rise tenements, Ally started to relax. Her parents were not at that house. They'd have contacted her. Granny Donny was unsettled, confused. Identical redbrick former tenement buildings rose up around them. The final approach to the bridge loomed ahead.

But what if her parents were in Lewiston because they had somehow learned about Granny Donny's loss of her faculties and were there to take her money? *Turn back. Forget it. Never mind.* The only thing worse than seeing her parents would be seeing her parents try to lay down one last con on Granny Donny to get her money.

She had to get back to the apartment so she could make more calls, do more research.

The traffic was rowdier now that the orderly woven streets of midtown had tangled into the chaotic fringe of lower Manhattan. Paula seemed twitchier, although it was hard to tell if that was because she could sense that Mateo was tense or because of the new sights and sounds and smells that surrounded them.

Mateo's back stiffened as he directed Paula into the bridge-access lane. Ally's skin went clammy as the traffic crawled toward the bridge. If Mateo had planned on making a speedy crossing before anyone noticed them, that didn't look likely.

Ahead, tucked into the triangle beside the entrance columns, a police car was stopped, its lights spinning idly while the policeman inside did paperwork. Mateo cursed under his breath. Paula flicked her ears in annoyance. With each step closer to the stopped police car, Ally felt her heart thump faster.

Her parents. Had they been at the house for the last two years, since the rental records stopped? Been there and not called her? Not wanted to see her? Anger and pain made her bend over, pulling her stomach toward her thighs.

Let's forget this whole thing. I can go back to living my old life. No problem. I'll get back my old job at PS 142 and live with Granny Donny and be quite happy, thank you very much.

Even Granny Donny was looking uneasy. "Where is Duke Whatthehell? Where could he be?" Confusion clouded her eyes. Maybe Granny Donny was having second thoughts, too. Was the trip too much for her? Was this all a huge mistake?

Ally checked her watch. It was eleven-thirty. "Any minute," Ally reassured her, having no idea if her words were true or not. How long did it take for a "photo shoot" or whatever Sam had called it? "He'll be here."

Mateo stared straight ahead. The officer inside the car didn't seem to notice them.

They were directly alongside the police car, its lights strobing blue and red across Paula's flank.

The window of the cruiser slid down and the officer looked out at the horse, then up at Mateo. "You've got to be kidding," he said.

Oh, thank you, God. She loved the police, loved law and order. Good man, stopping them. They could forget this whole trip and go home.

The policeman pointed to the side of the road. "No horses on the bridge," he said to Mateo. He didn't add "asshole," but his tone implied it.

"Well, we tried," Ally said. "Mateo. Let's just go home. It's no big deal."

"Certainly not!" Granny Donny cried indignantly. "We have such plans! Lady Lisa and Lord Ross are waiting!"

Ally winced at the mention of her parents' names.

The policeman hauled himself from his car, stopping traffic so that they could get the rig to the side of the road.

Paula snuffed and shuffled testily, as if the delay was a personal affront, an outdated species segregation she had no time or patience for.

Ally, however, felt like a death-row convict suddenly freed.

This was a terrible idea. My parents? What if it's true? I can go home and think about what to do now, for about, say, ten years . . .

But where was home? She'd given up her childhood apartment to Will and June. She'd quit her job. She'd sold everything. Would she go back to living the rest of her life with her grandmother? And what of Granny Donny? Her birthday wish to go to the country? The need to get her out of the dangerous city? How could Ally be relieved at this monumental failure? *Her failure to have fun and cut loose.*

When they got to the curb, the police officer leisurely made his way to Mateo, who was so nervous his hands shook on the reins. The officer looked suspiciously at them, although suspicious of what, Ally was sure he couldn't say. *Just a dotty old lady in a Regency-era traveling gown, her panicked granddaughter, and a very oddly behaving coachman trying to trespass a bridge with a horse and carriage. Is there a problem, Officer?*

Ally felt weightless as Mateo spoke with the impassive officer. "Just one carriage across the bridge? It's for the old lady? Just once?"

The officer remained unmoved. He pulled his enormous ticket book from his belt and flicked it open. "License," the officer demanded.

Mateo turned sheet-white and Ally wondered not for the first time about the mysterious coachman.

But before Mateo could respond, Ally heard someone call her name. "Ally. Mateo. Lady Giordano. Paula. There you all are! Sorry we're late. Let's go. Time is money, folks. Time is money!"

Needless to say, it was Sam.

One could solve almost any problem with money and title. The princess, however, had only a title, and so depended upon wit and skill. When these failed, she turned, reluctantly, to friends.
—From *The Dulcet Duke*

Chapter 16

Sam was hanging out the driver's window of a black Jeep that had pulled up behind the police cruiser. Stuffed in the open-topped Jeep with him were a mob of twenty-somethings with various degrees of floppy hair and face piercings. Sam pulled to a stop behind the police car and everyone began unloading, first themselves, and then—what was all that stuff? The last one out of the vehicle, from the passenger-side front seat, was a stunningly gorgeous woman, who towered over everyone, even Sam. She was in full makeup, a slinky silver dress that barely covered her, and five-inch heels.

The gang descended on the carriage like ants, talking and squinting at it critically while the elegant woman, obviously a model, climbed into the carriage with a grace that seemed otherworldly in those shoes and that dress.

Ally was pushed into the far corner as the beautiful woman settled in between her and Granny Donny.

"This'll be fun," she whispered to Ally. "Isn't Sammy just a gas?"

Before Ally could say she surely wouldn't know, a man climbed into the carriage. He held a camera with an enormous lens, which he pointed at the model. He squatted this way and that at her feet, trying different angles, working the camera's dials and knobs and mumbling to himself. Two more cameras were slung around his neck on thick straps. Everyone, in fact, had complicated and expensive-looking filming equipment: lights and poles and boxes. A short pink-haired woman swept into the carriage behind the photographer, engaging Granny Donny in discussion as if she'd known her all her life while she settled herself on the seat opposite.

Sam strode up to the police officer. "We have a bridge permit for two hours," Sam told the policeman.

The policeman squinted at the group critically. "No one told me anything about a permit."

Sam was going to get them over the bridge. Ally had to stop him. "You haven't heard because he's lying."

"That's funny, Ally. Lenny, give the officer the permit," Sam said.

The tallest of the young men leaped from where he'd been hanging like a monkey on the sideboard of the carriage and loped back to the Jeep. He rummaged through the glove compartment. Ally was pretty sure there was no permit. There couldn't really be a permit, right? The makeup artist began dotting blush on Granny Donny's cheeks. Granny Donny was delighted at the attention.

Ally tapped Sam's shoulder. "Sam! Psst. Forget it. We don't want to go anymore," she hissed at him.

"Don't be silly. It's no problem," Sam responded happily. "You can owe me later."

Another police car pulled up alongside the first. The officer inside rolled down the passenger window, leaned over, and called out, "All right, Eddie?"

"Excellent!" Sam cried before Eddie could answer. "The escort cars are here, boys. We were expecting the crew from the film unit, but this is a quickie; two cars'll be fine. Let's shoot this thing." He shook the confused new officer's hand. "By the way, have you met Chloe?" Sam called the model's name, and she leaned down, offering her slender hand and a great view of her not-so-slender cleavage.

"Hello," she cooed as if she were saying, "Let's get it on, coppers."

They grinned. The one named Eddie blushed.

"Nice ta meet ya!"

"There's no permit!" Ally cried to the smitten men. "Let's all go home." But no one seemed to hear her.

"The light is getting too high," the pink-haired woman called, holding up an electronic contraption.

"I never heard anything about a permit," Eddie said to the new officer. "But I never do. Permits are a mess with that new guy in. And I think I saw something in the *Post* about a big shoot on the West Side with De Niro. Probably got lost in the shuffle."

Sam was looking at the sky with a worried face. "We need to catch the sun before it gets too high. No one over twenty looks good in the noontime sun. Not that Chloe is anywhere near twenty." Sam added the last bit quietly to the younger officer, but Ally overheard.

"I do not want to cross this bridge," Ally repeated.

Sam ignored her. "If you want Chloe's phone number, not a problem," Sam assured the officer in a whisper.

Ally wanted to break both their skulls.

The second officer came to life. "Yeah, ya know, I think I did get word about a permit from Central," he began. "Let me call it in and we'll escort you."

"Nice to see you," Sam said to Ally as the chaos he had put in gear swirled around them. He leaned against the carriage, his arms crossed as he watched the two officers discuss the situation, not a trace of anxiety on his face.

A small crowd was forming on the sidewalk to watch the commotion. A mother and child had stopped beside Paula. The mother put down her grocery bags and held out the toddler, who shyly petted Paula's side. At least someone wasn't entranced by the half-naked model. "Isn't it against the law to lie to a police officer?"

"Nah. The jails would be too full," Sam said. "Anyway, who says I'm lying? You're always trying to make me out as a bad guy, Ally. I may be a lot of things, but I always tell the whole truth. You should try it sometime."

They watched Eddie shake his head no. The other officer kept talking, gesturing with his hand to the model. Mateo chatted up the young mother, who pulled an apple from her bag for Paula.

"Who are these people?" Ally asked.

"Crew from the Maybelline shoot. Old buddies. We've been working together on and off for ages. They're happy to help." He looked at his watch. "At least for another hour. We got through shooting Chloe early, and the second model is still in makeup. We got lucky."

Lucky. The confusion around her was disorienting.

The horse ate the apple. The officers were on their radios. Granny Donny was discussing milliners with the makeup lady while the model smiled and posed for curious tourists with digital cameras. And then there was Sam, looking totally in charge and smug and sure of himself. "I don't want you to do this," Ally said to Sam.

"Why not?"

"Doesn't matter. Trip's off. It was a terrible idea."

He turned to her, astonished. "You lost your nerve. You're terrified of me."

"Oh, for heaven's sake! My world doesn't revolve around you, Sam."

"Not yet, anyway." He smiled his wicked grin. "After I get us over this bridge, you'll owe me twice, and then how will you defend yourself from my considerable charms?"

"How did you know we wouldn't get over the bridge?" Ally asked, trying to change the subject from his considerable charms.

"Oh, I was telling the Maybelline producer, Charlie Frank, about our strange journey, and he said there was no way you were getting over a bridge with a horse and carriage. In fact, he didn't think you'd even get this far. You were lucky as hell. Anyway, Charlie and me and the crew here worked out an idea to get you over the bridge if you did make it this far. And here you are!"

"And your idea was to lie to the police?"

"I have connections, Ally. As does Charlie. The magic of being of the noble classes in this city full of the great unwashed. We dukes have our own rules."

Ally had heard that one before. *Our own rules.* It helped her steel her will against his. "What does this noble Charlie know about horses?"

"Charlie Frank? He's a pro. Been shooting in New York City for decades. Even back when the NYPD would help out on the porno shoots, shutting down the streets for privacy. That man can tell stories like no one. I once did a shoot with Charlie from a helicopter. A model hanging off the top of the Chrysler Building. He knows everything about shooting in New York."

"We could all be arrested if you're lying."

"You know, Ally, you really are an awful coward. Say the word, and I'll split right now. You could go back to your old, dull life. That's what you want, isn't it?"

Was it? Ally's head was swimming with the heat of the day and the fumes of the passing traffic and the chaos of Sam, who, of course, looked stunning in his jeans and china blue, button-down silk shirt that brought out the steel blue in his gray eyes. He was such a beautiful man. But more, he was right and she knew it. She couldn't go back. Now that they had begun, she had to face whatever was waiting for her in Lewiston. Chances were it was nothing but an empty, broken-down house. She had promised her grandmother this trip, and she had promised herself she'd be wild and fun. "No. Stay. Let's do this."

"That's my girl," Sam said.

And for an insane moment, she actually wished it was true.

*The trouble with meddling in a lady's affairs was that most
ladies' affairs were such pits of mismanagement, that once one
got started, it was frighteningly difficult to find a way out.*
—From *The Dulcet Duke*

Chapter 17

One police cruiser, its lights flashing, led them over
the bridge. The second brought up the rear. Paula clopped
along elegantly between them, ignoring the police cars
and their flashy display. The black Jeep trailed them, almost empty now, as most of the crew was piled in the
carriage. The model and Granny Donny sat on one bench.
Ally, Sam, and the makeup artist were crunched together
on the facing bench. The pretend photographer knelt in
the space between the seats, crouched on the floor of the
carriage, clicking away.

Ally wondered if he was really taking pictures or mim-
ing for the police.

Sam had sped over this bridge hundreds of times, but
this was different, and it was hard to say why. He leaned
back on the seat, enjoying the sunshine. Something about
the open carriage and Lady Giordano, smiling so serenely,
sure that life was just one big elegant ball waiting to be

thrown. She hadn't been the least bit surprised to see him. She'd counted on him, believed in him.

And then there was Ally, who sat beside him, looking shell-shocked. She kept looking back toward Manhattan, as if she had forgotten something important. She didn't seem to notice the sparkling water below or the shining bridge above, or the clip-clop of Paula's hooves as the road-mad Manhattan drivers slowed to give them a wide berth and curious stares. Classic Ally. Just like waltzing—or rather, not waltzing—in the park.

"Ally, you okay?" he asked.

"You know, this bridge took fourteen years to build. John Roebling, who designed it, died from an accident before it was done. He never even saw it."

"Ally?"

"In fact, lots of men died. Two were hit by a giant snapped cable in 1872—"

"Ally?"

"And Washington Roebling, who took over the work after his father died, was hit by such a bad attack of the bends that—"

"Ally!"

She stopped. "What?"

"Shhhh . . ."

"But—"

He put a finger to her lips. "Shh. It's okay."

She seemed to stop.

He cautiously lowered his finger. "You look a little green around the gills."

"I'm great. Super. Never better."

He looked at her a long minute. She wasn't super by a

long shot. He put his arm around her shoulders and pulled her close, wondering why she was so spooked.

They sat like that all the way to the other side.

They were over the bridge.

Ally tried to still her mind. She was, possibly, on her way to see her parents. And Sam was by her side and he'd been—

Oh, hell . . .

He'd been . . .

Their hero.

It was exasperating. Infuriating.

Mateo had stopped Paula on the shoulder to unload the film crew, who climbed back into their black Jeep. All except Sam, who unloaded a small travel bag from the Jeep and waved his good-byes and thanks to his friends. When the Jeep and the two police officers (the younger one with Chloe's number, and, Ally couldn't help notice, a bit of a boner) were gone, Mateo swung back onto the carriage seat. "Ready?" he called back to them. Mateo looked delighted to be out of Manhattan. He called a gentle "haw" to Paula, and the carriage started forward.

Ally tried not to fret. Modern women didn't fret, after all. She patted Granny Donny's hand in what she hoped was a reassuring way. "Almost there."

"Oh, yes, you are," Granny Donny said somewhat mysteriously. "Yes, you are finally on your way."

A stroll in the park is one of the least civilized pursuits a true lady can undertake. What happens in London's parks—the flirting, the stolen kisses, the bold innuendos—is nothing short of scandal.
—From The Dulcet Duke

Chapter 18

Mateo pulled Paula off the road and into Prospect Park to give her oats, rest, and shade. They were quite the crowd-pleaser in the park, the old costumed woman sitting under her parasol next to her horse and carriage.

Mateo had to wait before he gave Paula water after her oats so as not to upset her colicky stomach. To bide the time, he pulled out a soccer ball and a pair of sneakers from his box. Sam sat up at the sight of them like a dog seeing his favorite stick. Mateo rolled up his black livery pants to the knee, and Sam kicked off his dress shoes and socks and removed his silk shirt (of course). And now they were going at it, the goal marked by Paula's feed and water buckets and Sam's discarded footwear, while Ally and Granny Donny watched.

"Oh, dear, perhaps your gaze is upsetting the duke's play, Princess," Granny Donny commented as Sam got snuffed for the third time in a row.

"No. I think he's just out of his league." Ally felt like a Roman queen watching gladiators perform. Of course, Sam couldn't possibly have left his shirt on. After a while, neither could Mateo. Ally took a moment to thank the sun god for his good work. Both men were beautiful, sleek and athletic. But it was Sam whom Ally couldn't stop staring at. His shoulders were so broad, his waist so tapered. Running, diving, wrestling Mateo off the ball—or trying to, at least. Muscle, strength, speed, and power—a magnificent show of what made a man a man.

"Good thing that wasn't a duel," Ally said to Sam as he collapsed onto the park bench beside her, the game mercifully over. "You'd be dead."

"He is dead," Mateo pointed out. "I killed him. Tennil."

"You got lucky today," Sam said. He sat up and rubbed mud off his jeans. "Ah, excellent, a bath. Shall we?"

Ally looked at the fountain across the square, shooting water twenty feet into the air. "You can't."

"Of course I can. You should come in, too, Ally. Give yourself a break."

Ally looked at the glorious fountain. She wanted to go in, and yet—yet what? She was frozen.

"Oh, go on, dear," Granny Donny said. "Remember when you and your dear mother waded in that fountain and the constable chased you out? Oh, the scandal."

Sam watched Ally closely. "I won't let anyone chase you."

"She must be remembering some book," Ally began. But then she stopped, because she and her mother *had* been in this fountain. How could her grandmother not remember what century she's in, but she could recall this? Was this trip bringing her grandmother back?

"Well, you guys can talk all day. I'm burnt." Mateo set off for the fountain. He walked like a natural athlete, and all four of them (including Paula) watched him go with admiration.

"That man is not who he seems to be," Sam said.

Ally was grateful for the distraction of Mateo. It gave her time to think. So, she'd gone into this fountain with her mother when she was little? She had moved on from caring. And yet, she felt hollow.

Mateo, in the distance, sat on the edge of the fountain. He kicked off his sneakers, stripped his socks, and stepped into the water like he was on the beach. He dunked his head over and over, whipping it back each time and sending a stream of water flying. He waved to them and called, "Come on, amigos! The water's fine." He had been like a new person after they crossed that bridge and Ally wondered at the transformation.

"You're afraid," Sam said to Ally. "Look, there's a three-year-old in there. You're more frightened than a three-year-old."

"I'm frightened *of* the three-year-old. Who knows what kind of diseases he has. There's no chlorine in there to kill the germs."

"That's not what you're afraid of, Ally."

She shook her head in denial. "Gastrointestinal illness is not fun, Sam. *Shigella sonnei* and *Cryptosporidium parvum* infections are proven side effects of improper bathing."

Sam touched her hand. "Come in. We'll do it together."

"No."

"Okay, that's it. You're going in just so the Shigella can kill you and save me the trouble." He took a step toward her and she took a step back.

She yelped as he gripped her wrist.

Mateo climbed out of the fountain. Two excited young boys approached him, but Mateo shrugged them off. Ally couldn't hear the conversation, but the boys looked suspicious of whatever Mateo told them as they whispered together, their heads touching and shaking a silent *no*. They tried to follow him, but he spun and faced them down and told them something not in English that made them stop. The boys went back to their game in the fountain, casting lingering looks after Mateo. Mateo picked up his shoes and started back toward them without putting them on.

Sam still had her arm, and he began to pull her toward the fountain. "Ally, you can do this. Don't you see what's happening here?"

"My coachman is about to contract polio, and I'm going to be abandoned in Brooklyn with my grandmother, a colicky horse, and you?"

"No. You're going to face your deepest fears, whether you want to or not. And don't ask me why, but I'm pretty sure they're in that fountain."

Mateo reached them, shaking water from his black hair and wringing out his shirt. He was soaked to the bone and didn't seem to care. *Men.* He sat on the bench next to Granny Donny, let his head fall back, and began to bake dry in the sun. What did that man do when he wasn't driving the carriage? Bench-press Paula? His body was like steel.

"C'mon, Princess. Risk almost certain death and come into that fountain with me," Sam said. "If you die of some

nasty disease, at least you'll die a happy criminal instead
of a sweaty wimp, smelling of horse and bus exhaust."

"I do not," she began. But then she stopped. Because
the truth was, it had been a long, hot, horsy morning.

The fountain's round base was filled with two feet of
sparkling, inviting water. In the middle stood a bronze
statue of a naked man and woman, back-to-back. Water
spurted into the air around them. A cherubic statue of a
child played around their legs and various mythical statues lounged around their feet. Sam rolled up his jeans
and, without a moment's hesitation, strode to the center
of the fountain to join the happy naked romping statues,
the spray raining down on his head. "This. Is. The. Life."

Sam wet looked even better than Sam dry, no mean
feat. Rivulets of water streamed down his lovely chest,
down his cut abs, and into his low-riding jeans. Ally followed the lucky drops with her eyes until they disappeared
into the soaked denim that clung to him.

Sam plopped down next to one of the mythical statues,
his sleek muscles a match for those of the godly companion, as if both men had been chiseled from stone. He
patted the statue on the head. "I'm still alive; it can't be
all bad."

Ally could almost feel the cool, delicious water on her
skin. It must have been ninety degrees out, and the dust
and grime of the road coated her. It was ridiculous not to
go into the fountain because she'd done it once with her
mother.

Well, maybe she'd dunk her feet. She sat down on the
edge of the fountain and kicked off her sandals.

With no warning, Sam scooped her up from behind. He cradled her like a child. A very angry child.

"Put me down this instant!"

"Never!"

She hit him about his shoulders with little effect. "Sam, I am not playing along with your stupid game." It felt deliciously good to be in his arms, the spray of water hitting her skin.

"It's not a game. It's a mission of mercy." He strode to the middle of the fountain, sheets of water raining down on them. He was stonily serious, as if he understood the root of her fear and had taken it upon himself to rip it out, by force if necessary.

"If you drop me—!" *I'll hit you with my ineffective girly-fists.* "Damn you, Sam. Put me down."

Sam held her as if he could have stood there all day. As if they were normal people, having a normal conversation, *in the middle of a fountain full of children and naked statues.*

He was watching her, his eyes intent and blazing. "Forget the past."

She didn't know what to say. Part of her wanted to throw herself at his mercy and cry, "Yes, I'm scared." But how could she trust him? The fact that he seemed to instinctively understand her innermost fears made him more dangerous, not less. She was determined to be the one who controlled her fear. "Oh, just drop me in, for heaven's sake. I'm already soaked."

"Certainly, my lady." He lowered her gently into the water until she could feel the hard stone of the fountain's base under her. Despite already being wet, the water was shockingly cold. It felt delicious. He said, "Whatever your heart desires. I exist to serve. Don't worry, I'll preserve your modesty and let you bathe in peace. I'll pretend I didn't see the outline of that very lacy demi-cut. Victoria's Secret, fall collection?"

"Spring." It felt wonderful in the water. She waited for more perilous emotions to overcome her, but they didn't. She was fine.

Sam sat down next to her. They both leaned back onto the base of the statue. She closed her eyes.

"Really? I don't usually misjudge these sorts of things. Let me get a closer look." He peered down her shirt. "Love the pink. Very good-girlish. Thirty-four B?"

"Sam!" What other memories had been holding her back? What other fear could she overcome so simply? Just by saying yes?

"Ally, sleep with me tonight."

She sat up. "You think I'm that easy?"

"I think you're that human."

She tried not to smile. *He thinks I'm human.* Why did that seem like a tremendously nice compliment coming from Sam? She felt her face flush. "I don't know. It's just that—"

"That you're scared. Like going into the fountain. But then you dive in, and it feels good. Problem solved."

Her insides shifted. She had to hold herself back from grabbing him then and there. Her mouth was too dry to speak.

He leaned in close. "I have a better idea. Don't sleep with me."

Disappointment filled her. Dismay, even. If it showed on her face, she would have to shoot herself.

"Send a message to the princess. Tell her Duke Blackmoore will await her. Tonight. Where are we staying? I mean, where are they staying, the princess and the duke?"

"The airport Hilton."

"Tell her to come to his room."

"I, er, the princess . . . her grandmother," she stammered. She was having trouble breathing.

"Leave her for an hour. When she's asleep. She'll be fine. Tell her to come to me, Ally. It won't mean you lose our challenge because it won't be you, and it certainly won't be me."

She gulped. "Sam, I—"

"You can." He leaned close. The water around him seemed to heat. And then he kissed her

His lips were soft, yet insistent.

After a while they broke apart, and she tried to breathe again and succeeded, but now her breath was too deep. He was watching her again with his piercing gray eyes and she felt panicked to fill the silence. "So if the princess slept with the duke, it wouldn't be me and you?"

"Certainly not. I would never sleep with you until you admit that I'm your emotional, mental, spiritual equal."

"And I would never sleep with you, because—"

But she stopped. Because the truth was, face-to-face with dripping-wet Sam, she had forgotten why she wouldn't sleep with him.

That the princess was indebted to the duke was inconvenient.
That she enjoyed it was insufferable.
—From *The Dulcet Duke*

Chapter 19

An hour later they were finally dry, Paula was rested and watered, and they were back on the road.

The streets were getting grittier and narrower as they went. Ally chided herself for imagining that their trip would mimic *The Dulcet Duke*. Brigands would not attack them. It was absurd. And yet, their surroundings were becoming grimmer by the block. *It's broad daylight,* she reminded herself.

And Granny Donny's diamonds are sparkling in the afternoon sun.

Luckily, her grandmother had fallen asleep almost as soon as they got back into the carriage. Now she slept softly next to Ally, leaning against the carriage side.

They passed a menacing man muttering obscenities on a street corner who shook a grizzled finger at them. Ally pulled herself as deeply into the carriage as she could. Check-cashing, phone-card, lottery-ticket, and liquor stores had taken over the storefronts that weren't boarded up or marred by shattered glass. Narrow Chinese food joints served takeout from behind what looked like bulletproof glass, the workers sliding the food out of tiny slits like bank tellers passing bills. "So, did you bring your sword?" she asked Sam as she watched a fight break out in front of a pizza parlor.

"How lewd to ask a man about his sword, Princess. You'll have to wait for tonight to find out."

Ally rolled her eyes. The fountain had been delicious. And that kiss. Even discussing her bra had been exciting in a way she didn't like to admit. Still, she had no intention of sleeping with him tonight. It was absurd. Impossible.

"Don't worry about us, Ally. I do a mean impression of John Wayne."

"We're going to die."

"Maybe. But let's enjoy ourselves until then. Let's play twenty questions."

"That'll scare 'em off."

"It's to get our minds off the, er, countryside."

A car backfired and Ally jumped.

"You first. Think of something," he said.

Two huge men threw a noisy drunk out of a liquor store. He swore and threw a bottle at the storefront. It exploded against the door, and red wine dripped to the sidewalk like blood. Ally glanced at Granny Donny, who was still asleep. "Okay. Ready. Got it."

"Animal, vegetable, or mineral?" Sam asked.

"Animal."

"Mammal?"

"No."

"Reptile?"

"Yes."

He cocked his head and clucked his teeth as if running through likely reptiles, but then he asked, "What were you really afraid of? Why didn't you want to cross that bridge? Or go in that fountain?"

"That's not a yes or no question."

"What happens if you let me in, Ally? Is it really that bad? C'mon, tell me. I really want to know."

"You don't understand twenty questions at all, do you?"

"I don't understand you. I want to understand you."

He seemed sincere. What would happen if she let him in? Three police cars raced past them, their sirens wailing. Oh, hell, they were going to die anyway, she might as well spill. So she told him her grandmother's story that her parents were waiting for her.

"And why would seeing your parents be a problem?" he asked.

"You're not playing this right."

"I never play by the rules. You shouldn't either. Answer the question."

She took a deep breath and met his eyes. *What would happen if I let him in?* So she told him about how her parents had run off, leaving her. She left out the gambling part, not trusting him completely. By the time she finished, the streets had become cleaner, the houses kept up. Small lawns started to appear.

"Are you green?" he asked.

"Green?"

"Twenty questions. The reptile."

"Oh." She had forgotten their game. "Sometimes."

"Yes or no."

"Sometimes."

He looked her over. "Do you trust me even a little, Ally?"

She hesitated. "Yes."

"But you hate me, too?"

Not anymore.

"Yes or no. Or it won't count."

"No."

"C'mon. Yes. Say it. It's because of your parents. I remind you of them, don't I?"

"Yes."

"They were reckless and carefree, and they didn't stick around to take their responsibilities seriously."

"Yes."

"You think I'm them. That if you let me in, I'll abandon you just like they did."

"I'm done playing, Sam."

"Good. So am I."

He tapped his foot, watching her, considering. "Do I have any questions left?"

"One," she lied. She'd lost count.

"Can I kiss you?"

Granny Donny was asleep next to her. Mateo was listening to his iPod. The cry of "Gooooaaaal d'Argentina" escaped from his earphones, and he muttered something to himself.

Sam looked, as usual, like everything dangerous and irrational in this world. And she thought, *What if?* What if, for once, she was the irrational, crazy one? She could be the wild one. Wasn't that what this trip was all about? "I thought the next kiss was going to be from me," she reminded him.

"This doesn't count. It's just a thank-you kiss."

"Thank me? For what?" Ally asked.

"For you taking me seriously enough to tell me that story."

"Oh." She licked her lips.

"Thank you," he said.

"Well, er, thank you, Sam. For everything. Really. I know you think I don't notice—"

"You're just supposed to say, 'You're welcome.' "

"You're welcome."

"Excellent." Sam leaned toward her and her voice trailed off. She closed her eyes and he cupped her head in his hand and lifted her face to his. She opened her eyes to look at him as he lowered his lips. The world around her disappeared. It would be so easy to reduce her world to the chiseled planes of this man's beautiful face. So easy to fall into his bed and not care that he wouldn't be there the next day. Certainly not the next month. So easy to forget all her responsibilities and give in to being spontaneous just as her mother had. Would that be so bad? Was there something wrong with that? Who would she be leaving behind besides her childhood ghosts?

She was halfway to her own twenty questions when his lips touched hers. A shudder of pleasure arced through her. His lips were soft and searching. *Yes or no,* they seemed to ask. She let her hand fall to his thigh. *Yes.* He gathered her closer, and she let him. In fact, she opened her mouth for him—*yes*—and he responded by deepening his kiss—*yes.*

I'm making out next to my sleeping grandmother, and it's hot.

He separated his lips from hers. "How many questions left?"

"I have no idea." *Get those damn lips back here before I change my mind.*

He nipped at her lower lip but didn't return to the kiss. "Ally, are we friends now? Even just a little bit?"

"Sorry. You're out of questions." *Shut up and finish kissing me.*

He saw her need and flashed a grin. "Then I have to guess. Hmm . . . Let's see. Animal, reptile, occasionally green—you're thinking of me."

I'm thinking of wringing your neck if you don't get back here and kiss me again. She pulled him by his collar toward her. "Wrong. I was thinking of a chameleon. You lose. Game over. *Kiss me.*"

"Oh! Is that a request?"

She sat up, alarmed. Had she fallen that quickly? "No. Just a thank-you kiss."

"Thank me? For what?"

"For the previous thank-you kiss."

He gathered her to him and kissed her. "You've got two covers, Ally," he murmured into her neck.

"Two covers?"

But he refused to explain. He kissed down her neck, and she tried to remember why she had been resisting him. Right—responsibility, honor, sanity.

He felt her pull away and he leaned back to look at her. "Okay. My turn. Go on—ask me. I've got one."

"Animal, vegetable or mineral?" Her voice was breathless.

"Animal. Definitely animal."

And then he kissed her again.

* * *

Ally was confused. What was happening to her, kissing Sam like that? They had separated, and they rode silently, the carriage peacefully rocking. Paula moved smoothly through the streets, which were getting cleaner and less ominous. They drew some attention, but less than Ally had feared, mostly amused stares and delighted shout-outs.

"I'm going to pull over," Mateo called back to them. "Give Paula some water." He pulled to the side of the road in front of a small storefront restaurant called La Rosita. "And I'm going to run in and get a Cubano sandwich for me. Any other takers?"

"I'll go with you," Sam said.

"You watch the lady," Mateo said.

"We don't need to be watched—," Ally began.

"I meant Paula," Mateo said with the shyest slip of a smile.

Sam jumped down and took Paula's reins. The horse flashed him a disgusted eye roll. He fished in his pocket and handed Mateo two twenties. "Get four. To go."

The coachman disappeared into the restaurant.

"What's a Cubano sandwich?" Ally asked Sam.

"No clue."

"You know what to do if Paula bolts?" Ally asked, patting Paula's side.

"No clue." He smiled and she thought, *I've been kissing that,* and her insides flipped. *Have a fling with the duke? Why not?*

Granny Donny stretched. "Shall we go for a stroll, darling?"

"No." Ally looked down the quiet, abandoned street. It

looked safe enough, but she was anxious to get back on the road.

"Oh, nonsense." Granny Donny slid to the edge of the carriage seat. Sam had no choice but to help her down, as she looked as if she fully intended to climb down herself. She brushed off her dress and set off down the street, her parasol over her shoulder.

"I'll follow her," Sam said.

"You watch Paula. I'll watch her." Ally climbed down after her grandmother. She welcomed the chance to separate from Sam, think about what was happening to her, kissing him like that. *Worse, talking to him like that.* Telling him things that she'd never told anyone.

They strolled to the corner, then Ally managed to spin Granny Donny back toward the carriage. So, he was a great kisser. So, he had invited her to his room tonight. Why not an affair? This whole trip was a game, a fantasy. Why couldn't she have a little fantasy, too?

When they got back to the carriage, her mind was still whirling. Mateo gave Sam the sandwiches, and then he unhooked Paula's water bucket from under the carriage.

Sam positioned himself to help Granny Donny back into the carriage, but he put out his hand before they could climb in. "Stand back!" he cried.

"What's the matter?" Granny Donny asked.

Mateo looked up.

Ally's blood ran cold.

"There's a brigand in your coach, madam," Sam said. "Get back, all of you. I will deal with this."

Ally peered around Sam's shoulder, sick with worry. She was infinitely glad that Sam was there to protect them.

And then she saw it.

The smallest, dirtiest kitten she had ever seen was curled up in the middle of the plush red seat, fast asleep.

They made it to Mateo's friend's house by three o'clock. The kitten made the journey curled up in Sam's lap, purring like a broken air conditioner. Poor thing had eaten a good half of the meat from Sam's sandwich and then instantly passed out from the effort.

Ally looked up at the compact house with white aluminum siding and four concrete steps that led up to a solid white door. The house was under what seemed like the direct flight path of every plane in and out of JFK Airport. Ally ducked whenever one of them roared by overhead, about every five seconds.

The backyard was a postage stamp of grass dominated by a lovely weeping cherry. Mateo's friend had rigged up a rough shelter for Paula out of corrugated steel and wooden pallets. Paula didn't seem to mind the sloppy stall or the yard's small size. Nor did the local children, who had gathered around to pet her flank through the slats of the fence, begging for rides. Mateo let them feed her bits of carrot while he washed down her legs.

June and Will were there to meet them with the car Ally had rented and their own silver Prius. Ally's and Granny Donny's suitcases were stowed in the trunk of the rental, with more bags stuffed into the backseat. Her grandmother's dresses weren't compact.

Ally had never been so glad to see her friend. After her deeply confusing day with Sam, her head was swimming.

She pulled June aside the first chance she got. "He showed up on the bridge."

"I knew he would. I read the book. Remember? He doesn't let the princess go unattended into the dangerous countryside. So, did you get mugged? Was there a swordfight? Is he your hero, and do you owe him a booty call?"

"I don't think the princess in *The Dulcet Duke* did booty calls." Ally grabbed June's shoulder and pulled her closer. "June, he asked me to sleep with him."

June cocked her head. "Well, that didn't take long. So you said yes and game over, you're in love?"

"I would never give in so easily. I can totally resist Sam." Ally took her friend's arm and pulled her close, turning her back to the crowd so they could whisper. "But I wouldn't need to resist Sam, because it wouldn't be me and him."

"Okay. I'm lost."

"It would be the princess sleeping with the duke."

June's face was blank.

"Role play," Ally hissed. She stole a glance back to Sam. Her body fluttered like a twittering virgin's. Stupid body was role-playing already.

June squinted at her. "It wouldn't be you giving in to your obvious lust for Sam because it would be—?"

"Fantasy." She could feel the blush creep up her neck.

"Fantasy, sort of like the scene at the masquerade ball in *The Dulcet Duke* where the duke kisses the princess but he doesn't know who she is."

"Yeah, sort of that scene. Only instead of a kiss in the moonlight, it would be me screwing him in a crummy hotel room under the roar of jet engines while my grand-

mother had most likely escaped and was waltzing on the
runways at JFK with a homeless man, waving to the tourists in jet planes on their way to Florida."

June mussed Ally's hair. "You're role-playing! That is
so kinky. I am so jealous."

"You're jealous of me? You're the one with the perfect
fiancé."

"Yeah, but Ally, perfect gets boring. You—I mean, the
princess—and the duke, now that's fun. Do you have a
safeword?"

"What's that?"

"That's for role-playing. You have a ridiculous word,
like, maybe, *crocodile,* that one of you says when the
game is getting to be too much. That way, there's an out.
It's an S and M thing."

"And you know this, how?"

"Oh, Ally. I so don't know it from my own life, believe me. I think I read it in *New York* magazine, the May
'Kinky Sex Club' issue. Will is as boring as—" June
caught herself.

Ally leaned forward. "As me?"

"Sorry, hon. But it's kinda true," June said.

Ally changed the subject. "So this is new about Will."

"It's not new, actually. It's been bugging me for a while.
I thought maybe after you moved out, he'd loosen up."

"So you want a man who's more fun, and I want a man
who's stable and reliable. Maybe we could switch. I think
Sam would go for 'crocodile.' "

June shook her head. "I wouldn't do that to you, Ally.
He's yours."

"He is so not mine."

"That's just because you're being an idiot."

"It's not going to happen," Ally assured her friend. She studied June. "Wait, you look awful."

"They're making cuts Wednesday for Europe. I had an awful rehearsal today. But that is so boring. Let's get back to you having sex with not-Sam."

"Of course you'll go to Europe. Your life is perfect. You're a star."

"Forget me. Now, not-Sam. And not-you. Not-clothed. Knotted. In bed. You must. It's been too long since you had a boyfriend. How long has it been?"

"The math teacher. Charles."

"That was like a year ago, Ally."

"Fifteen months."

"Oh, Ally! Not-Sam is not-ugly. And not-dull. And definitely not-poor. Look at him. He even tempts me."

They both paused to look.

They both sighed.

Sam was horsing around, playing pickup basketball with the kids at the driveway net. He picked up the littlest boy and let him slam-dunk.

"Ally, promise me you won't back out like you backed out of San Francisco. The only thing standing between you and that man is fear."

"I didn't back out of San Francisco. I just delayed it."

"For another ten years? Sleep with him, Ally. Why deny yourself this?"

"You're supposed to be my friend, to warn me off bad men who will ruin my reputation and break my heart. Why would I ever get something started with a man like Sam?"

"Because he's sex on a stick, baby." June looked over her shoulder to where her fiancé was waiting, his attention alternatively on the basketball game and on his watch. He began testing his phone, pushing the buttons with annoyance. June frowned.

Ally was shocked by the look of regret on her friend's face. She filed it away as nerves. The tryouts must really be getting to her.

"What do you have to lose?" June asked.

"Time. Self-respect. My reputation." *My heart.*

"Listen, Ally, you don't have a reputation. No one has reputations anymore. In modern times, best friends are supposed to tell each other the truth. Like, for example, you need to get laid."

Ally looked at Will. Had she let down her best friend by never telling June what she thought of her boyfriend?

Now June was looking at her watch. "We have to be in New Jersey for Lula's rehearsal dinner by five. Have your way with that beautiful man, and then tell me every single disgusting detail." Her friend stopped and looked at her very seriously. "Ally, just because you want to have some fun with a beautiful man doesn't mean you're irresponsible. You're not your mother, and he's not anything like your father. No offense, but your father was a bit of a loser. Sam is a lot of things, but he's no loser."

Ally wanted to grab on to June and not let go. "I know. I know." And she did know that leaving her sleeping grandmother for an hour was nothing like her mother leaving Ally for a lifetime. But still, it was a slippery slope. It was too close to her parents' reality for comfort. *I will never be them.* I will be conscientious. Because if I act crazy— then what? What would happen? Why did it feel so dire?

"You and Will are still coming to stay with us next week, right? Did Will get off work?"

"Wouldn't miss it for the world. But I can't wait that long to hear what happens with not-Sam. Promise me you'll call me and tell me all about it before then."

They both looked at Sam. The game was still going, but Sam had left it to join the group petting Paula. He held one little girl up so that she could get closer. He told a tough-looking boy of about nine that Paula bites only boys who aren't nice to their little sisters. The boy pulled back his hand and the little girl beamed.

"There won't be anything to tell," Ally said, trying to put the image of Sam with the children out of her head. *I so don't want to marry him and have his brood like some overbreeding noblewoman.* But Sam held the little girl so carefully. Like a man who might be a good father . . .

"Then promise me you'll make something up. Ally, c'mon. You deserve a good time, too. That man may be a lot of awful things, but I'm pretty sure he's very, very good in bed."

Ally watched her friend go with a sinking heart. She wished she could go to a party with June's huge family, to drink and dance and then go off to Europe for the summer, to be famous and adored, then come back for a three-hundred-person, sit-down wedding with a kind, normal man.

Instead, tomorrow, Ally would drive the rental June had left for her to Lindenhurst to meet Eloisa Tyler, the housekeeper she was interviewing. If all went well, Eloisa would keep the car, give Ally a lift back to the carriage, then take the car on herself to Granny Donny's house. She'd air out the house and get it ready for them. Ally felt a pang of guilt for sending a scout ahead to see if the house was occupied, but she allowed herself this weakness because if her parents were there, she wanted to give them advance notice. She wanted them to know she was coming so they would be able to leave if they wanted. She wanted a family reunion to be a choice.

Ally hoped Eloisa was decent and trustworthy. Her references were excellent, and they had talked by phone several times, but you never knew. In a life spent avoiding chance, she was suddenly racking up an alarming number of risky bets.

"Ready to hit the Hilton?" Mateo asked, startling her.

"Is Paula rested?"

"She's doing great." Mateo was so relaxed, he seemed almost happy. Ally got the sense that Paula had relaxed, too. Maybe, from here on out, they could all relax.

"And Sam?"

"He's rested, too," Mateo said. "I'll drop your grandmother at the Hilton, get Paula settled, then me and Sammy are gonna stop for a drink."

"Of course." They probably couldn't wait to get away from the womenfolk.

Mateo drove Ally's grandmother the short hop to the hotel. Ally followed in the car.

It was time for dinner and bed.

And that was definitely all.

To resist was pointless. He was determined to ruin her.
But she had no intention of enjoying it.
—From *The Dulcet Duke*

Chapter 20

Ally woke up. Something was scratching at the door. She looked at the glowing red numbers on the clock: 1:37 in the morning.

Scratch, scratch, scratch.

Sam. Who else? Her heart pounded.

Granny Donny was snoring soundly.

Ally rolled over in her bed, wrapping her pillow around her ears. This was crazy.

The scratching continued.

Oh, hell. She threw back the covers and went to the door. She cracked it open with the safety chain still on.

"Princess, I need you. For alas, tomorrow, I go to war," Sam said.

Ally scowled. "Tomorrow, we go to Hempstead."

He cleared his throat, reset his feet, and raised his chest. "Nonetheless, I cannot go forth to Hempstead without at least one last kiss from your dewdropped lips."

"Dewdropped? Oh, please, Lancet is better than that." What was Sam wearing? She tried to look through the slit of the door, but her eyes were still sleep-logged and resisted the light. She unlatched the door and opened it wider.

Granny Donny stirred. Ally slipped out, leaving the door ajar behind her.

"You're wearing—er . . ."

"Admiring my fall-front knee breeches?" He turned around to show her the lacing at the back. "Easy access."

She *was* admiring his jaunty, tight pants. She could admire every detail, of course, because there was no shirt on over the pants. Sam in the pants was a breathtaking sight, despite the fact that he was obviously nuts.

"I shall resist the impulse to comment on your workmanlike and sensible sleepwear," he said.

She was as stirred by the effort that must have gone into finding old-fashioned pants as she was by the way he fit into their skintight fabric. Grippy thighs. Figured. Probably, it was no work at all to get the pants. Most likely that Charlie guy again. If he knew how to get a horse and carriage over the Brooklyn Bridge, surely it was child's play to get lace-up pants that fit Sam like a glove. She shook her attention from his crotch. "Sam. I don't think this is a good idea because—"

"Wait, look!"

She waited. She looked. "What?"

"My thigh muscles. They're rippling."

They were.

"I've been practicing all night."

Now that, she didn't doubt. "I'm sorry. Good night,

Sam." She turned to the door, but Sam got to the door-knob first.

He shut the door with a sickening click.

Ally's heart sank. "You cad."

"Rogue."

"I can go down to the front desk and get another key."

"Not if I don't let you." He stepped in front of her, blocking her path.

"Now see here, Sam. Just because we had a few little kisses—"

"Kisses? Marvelous idea." He grabbed her and stopped the flow of words with his lips, warm and insistent against hers. He smelled like leather, and she wondered if the pants were leather and so she touched them and—good God—the pants were baby-soft suede and under them was Sam and he pressed against her thigh and he was *hard.* She tried to pull away. "Sam!"

Only when he was thoroughly done kissing her did he mumble into her neck, "Why do you keep calling me Sam? I am the duke." He pulled her close and she let him because he wasn't wearing a shirt and it felt so impossibly good to touch his warm, smooth skin with so much muscle tensed just underneath the surface, ready to uncoil. Maybe just this once, he wasn't Sam, but the duke. What the hell? *Duke* Whatthehell. Her hands were trapped between their bodies and all she could manage was a feeble struggle, which felt so enormously sexy against his bare chest, she struggled again just to feel him deny her.

Then, all at once, he swept her off her feet and into his arms. She gasped with shock and indignation.

"You're coming with me, Princess, whether you like it

or not." His voice was gruff and dominating and not at all like the playful Sam she was getting to know.

He started down the hall with her in his arms. "I'm going to scream," she said, kicking at him.

He only tightened his grip. He was being a brute, and *it was fun*. She liked the way he carried her, as if she were a feather in his arms. She liked the way her shoulder wedged against his right pec. She especially liked the way he smelled, of leather and skin, warm and musky. And somehow, she told herself that it was okay to like all this because they were just playing—it was a game. A fantasy. Not real.

They had come to his door and he was struggling to hold her in his arms while extracting his key card from the waistband of his ridiculous pants. "No one would dare tangle with the Duke of Midfield, especially in matters of bedding a woman. So scream all you like. I'd enjoy it, actually."

She rolled her eyes. This was insane. It was silly. It was . . . fun. Also, sexy in a way that turned her inside out. She did owe him, after all, for helping them over the bridge. For being so sweet playing twenty questions. For protecting them all from the killer kitten. And, he had bought lunch . . .

He had gotten the card out of his waistband and was trying to insert it in the door slot. She took the card from him and managed the door. The small light blinked green.

He met her eyes. "Thank you, Princess," he said while he smiled such a devilish smile, she knew she was lost.

He pushed inside the room, knocking her leg on the doorjamb. "Ouch."

"Oomph." He hit his head on something.

"Bloody hell." Her robe was caught on the doorknob. Finally, they maneuvered into the small room.

"Tonight, Princess, you're mine."

"Oh, God, crocodile," she murmured.

"Excuse me?"

She explained June's idea of a safeword.

"So, crocodile?" he asked.

"Maybe alligator," she admitted.

"Really?" He didn't make another move.

"Okay. Well, gecko."

"Ha!" he cried, triumphant. "No tiny gecko would ever stop a woman like you."

He set her down and she stood before him and he began to circle her like she was a horse he was considering buying. "Sam—"

"Duke!" he corrected, continuing to circle. She felt absurd. And chastened. And controlled. She felt incredibly sexy. "Duke," she said, trying it out. The single word stirred her. She was in her cotton robe and under it were her men's striped vintage pajamas, and yet, she felt as sexy as if she had been wearing a negligee.

He removed her robe and laid it carefully on the bed.

She gulped. "I think—"

"Don't think. And for God's sake, don't speak. You are here for one reason, Princess. To become mine. I have been waiting years for this moment, since I first met you as a child of fifteen, in your first bud of youth."

"Okay, crocodile. That's gross."

"Yeah. You're right. Okay. Cut that." He cleared his throat, turned his back, and then turned again to her. She could feel the heat rise off his bare chest. "I have been waiting for this moment since the first time I laid eyes on you in your crummy apartment, hung over and dressed in these same despicable pajamas that I will now remove and burn." He unbuttoned her pajama top as if he had all the time in the world.

"Not so good either," she said.

He stopped. "Okay. You're right. Too much truth in all that to be a good fantasy. Wait. Let me think." He turned away again, loosened his shoulders like an athlete, dancing a little jig in place. He spun around to face her, his eyes blazing. "I am a man undone. I can't live without you, Princess. I must have you. Now. Or I will die of longing and regret." He dropped to one knee.

God, I'm easy. Ally's insides quaked with desire. "More of that." She knew he must be joking, but he seemed so sincere.

"Will you have me, Princess? Have me as I am, a scarred and despicable man?" He took her hand and kissed it. The kiss went all the way to her toes, then shot back up again.

"That's my favorite kind of man," she said.

"Are you sure?" He rose to take her in his arms. "Because once I begin, I can't be responsible for stopping." He kissed the base of her neck. "I am not a gentleman." He kissed her under her right ear. "I am a beast, beyond control. A scoundrel. A rogue." The line between playing and not playing had faded to nothing, and now she was Ally, talking to Sam, and he seemed to be telling her something important.

"Then I will control you, sir," she answered, bewildered. Where had that come from?

He smiled.

"Undress me," she said, not caring where the urge to talk this way came from, just caring that it felt so good.

"If you insist, madam. I am entirely at your service." Sam bowed his head and then got to work.

Ally shivered with desire, her body defenseless. She knew they had been joking around, but the look in his eyes now was no joke. That her body quivered was a dire matter in need of remedy. He wanted her as badly as she wanted him. *A terrible man is undressing me. A rake. A man with no regard for anything beyond his own pleasure.*

And I like it.

He pushed the fabric off her shoulders, revealing her flushed skin.

"Hmm . . . ," he murmured. "Lovely."

And then, he was upon her.

They were on the bed, somehow, a tangle of limbs and tongues. He wasn't kidding about being unstoppable. He loomed over her, a dark shadow pressing down. He was still wearing the ridiculous pants, and she felt cross at their impudent interference, pouty as befitted only a princess. "Remove the pants, Duke."

She could see a shade of his smile in the darkness. "As you wish." He raised his hips and shimmied out of the pants.

Oh my, oh my.

Her heart stopped beating as she took in the sight of him. She reached out to touch him, unable to resist. "Oh!" She hadn't meant to squeal like a virgin princess, but Sam was as endowed as Duke Blackmoore.

She felt his grin as he pressed his lips to hers and brought his body back to hover over hers, the tip of him tickling her stomach. "I await your command, Princess." But he didn't await her command. Instead, he reached down between her legs and felt her wetness. "That feels like a command to me."

And he's smart.

He slid two fingers inside her and she gasped with the pleasure of it. His thumb caressed her while his fingers moved inside. "Like this, Princess?"

"I didn't tell you to touch me," she managed, surprised she could sound so haughty when she felt so wobbly and weak.

He withdrew his hand, and she tried not to grab his wrist and command him not to listen to some dumb princess who obviously didn't have a clue what she wanted.

"Punish me for my transgression," he growled.

Her body went limp. She managed to squeak, "I think I will."

He waited, watching her. His flashing gray eyes took her breath away.

"Twenty minutes of hard labor for you, sir," she said when she had found her voice. She put her arms over her head, stretching out luxuriously. "Get to work, Duke. I don't want to hear another word until—" She hesitated. Talking dirty was turning her on, but the sensation of losing control was starting to make her queasy.

"Until you scream for mercy, Princess? Until you come so hard, I have to hold you down? Until I make you forget your own name and leave you quivering with exhaustion and desire?" Between each phrase, he kissed her. Carefully and thoroughly.

To hell with control. "Yes. All that."

"Very good, madam. I shall bend to your will."

God, she was beautiful.

He hadn't expected her to be so beautiful.

Small, creamy, white, *glowing.*

Okay, so it was a game to her still. He bit her neck and didn't give a damn. Kissed her lower lip and cared even less. Took her nipple into his mouth and remembered that she still thought he was useless except in her fantasy. But at that moment, her nipple growing hard and hot in his mouth as he rolled it on his tongue, he didn't give a damn. All he cared about was pleasing her.

"Sam. God. Now. Please."

She called me Sam.

She knew exactly what she was doing and who she was doing it to, even if she would deny it later. It hurt him to anticipate the denial that he knew would come.

But he couldn't rush. He would be a gentleman, no matter what she thought of him. "Protection?" he practically growled. "I have a Regency-era sheep-gut sheath—" She gasped and sat up, alarmed. Then relaxed when he flashed her the foil-covered Trojan.

He watched her face as he entered her, slowly, so exquisitely slowly, carefully, his princess. The exquisite sensation of opening her spread through every inch of his body. So, he had to dress up in laced pants and carry her off? Had to pretend he was someone else? None of it mattered. All that mattered was the way she desperately gripped his shoulder, the way she thrust her hips up to him, begging for more, now, faster, please . . .

Ally Giordano was the woman who would make him whole again.

He knew it as surely as he knew she was going to come, now, hard and strong, rocking in his arms, shuddering into the power of her release. *She is mine and I won't betray her, even when she betrays me.*

He knew she would as surely as he knew that he couldn't hold on in her wet, soft, smoothness another instant. She was playing, but his playing had ended. He pushed into her. Again. Again. Harder and faster as he came.

They lay limp, spent, in each other's arms.

"Duke?" she said.

He pushed a lock of hair off her face.

"I think someone is licking my toes."

Sam scooped up the tiny kitten. "It's just that dastardly troublemaker. Have no fear. I vanquished him once, I will subdue him again." He scratched the kitten under his chin and the little ball of fur instantly went limp with ecstasy. If only women were this easy.

Actually, for him most women were.

But not Ally. He had jumped through hoops to get her here. And this was only halfway at most. He stroked the cat, wondering what to say to Ally that would tell her how he felt about what they had just done. About how he didn't want to play games; he wanted to try to understand how he felt about her. He wanted to try to change the way she felt about him.

"Ally, that was amazing. I don't want you to think that this was no big deal to me. Because it was a big deal. I've slept with a lot of women, it's true. And I'm not sorry about it. But I think you and I could have something more than a game. I think I could . . . we could . . . Ally, tell me what you think." He stopped, breath held.

But she, like the kitten, was fast asleep.

Ally awoke in the duke's bed. She looked at the clock: 9:27 a.m.

Holy hell, what had she done? That scene last night was *not* in *The Dulcet Duke.*

And yet, she felt lovely. Positively tingly.

And decidedly quite *sore.*

I left my grandmother alone the whole night!

She jumped out of bed and pulled on her clothes. Sam slept soundly through her bustling, the cat asleep on his chest, which was a relief as she didn't want to face him. She slipped out of his room and tiptoed to her own, not remembering until she got there that she didn't have the key. She knocked. "Grandma? Are you up?"

No answer.

She knocked louder.

"Granny Donny? It's Ally. I locked myself out."

Nothing.

She looked around the empty hallway. Would she really have to go to the lobby and beg to be let in wearing her pajamas and sporting her bed-head hair like a blinking neon sign: I HAD AWESOME SEX LAST NIGHT!

From the silence all around her, that seemed likely.

Then the panic hit her like a sucker punch to the gut.

What if Granny Donny wasn't in there?

Ally raced to the lobby down six flights of fire stairs, unable to wait for the elevator. Her slippers flew off on the third floor, but she couldn't waste time to stop for them. She emerged into the lobby barefoot, the marble cold against her feet. What had she done, leaving her grand-mother alone like that? She pushed past the businessmen in black suits and families with small children, all of them either scowling or, worse, nodding knowingly at her disheveled pajamas and bare feet. "Excuse me. Emergency. Sorry."

At least she wasn't wearing lingerie.

"Hi. I have a problem," she began. But then she stopped. Out of the corner of her eye, she saw something—or rather, someone—waiting for a cab just outside the front doors. Her mouth went dry with fear.

Her mother? Here?

She left the counter in a daze, making her way through the bustling lobby full of stewardesses and bellhops pushing carts loaded with baggage. She bullied her way to the revolving doors just as her mother ducked into a cab.

"Mom?" This was impossible. How would she recognize her mother after ten years across a crowded lobby? How could her mother be here? Ally had so many awful memories of following strangers when she was younger, thinking they were her mother. The shock when they whipped around to face her was etched into her nerve endings.

The cab screeched away from the curb, the back of a woman's head next to that of a taller man (Her father? It was crazy to think it . . .) just barely visible through the glare hitting the back window.

"Mom?" she said again, more quietly, to no one. "Dad?" Her bare feet were cold on the recently washed wet concrete. The warm, early-morning wind whipped through her thin pajamas. Everyone was frozen around her, staring at her, and she couldn't have cared less.

"Cab?" the doorman asked politely, keeping his eyes on her bare toes.

"No. Thanks." It probably wasn't them. How could it have been them? She mumbled an apology to the crowd waiting for cabs, then went back inside the hotel to get her key, praying her grandmother was in her bed.

Granny Donny was in bed, peacefully asleep.

Ally tried to shake off the discomfort of her morning encounter. After all, it was most likely no encounter at all, but rather a case of mistaken identity. She had seen only the side of the woman's face, the back of her head.

Judging by Granny Donny's snoring, nothing had happened here. She dismissed her fantasy as residual weakness from her sex-ravaged night. A warning?

No. Pull it together. Ally had a lot to do today, and she was already desperately behind. She wasn't happy about leaving her grandmother with Mateo and Sam for the few hours it would take her to check out the housekeeper, Eloisa. Maybe they could change their plans. Wait together at the hotel and pay for a cab to bring Eloisa here to pick up the house key and car. After all, Ally ought to get used to having access to her grandmother's money.

Maybe she could send Sam.

Sam.

Oh. My. God. Sam.

What had she done? That delicious little interlude last night was a fluke. A one-timer.

The best sex she'd ever had?

Yes.

And more than sex. It had been wicked and playful and fun. Outwardly, they had kept in character the entire time, and she had felt as if she was his princess. He had accepted her whims like a true gentleman, and yet he still made love to her like a savage. How had he managed that? That a man was allowed to be that skilled in bed was not fair.

Although, she hadn't been half bad either, judging from his reaction to her touch. They had slept, then made love, then slept again. The night was a blur. She had shown him a thing or two about what a princess could do to a duke. She could still see his wicked smile flicker in the darkness as she pushed him back against the mattress, commanding him to be still while she tasted him. By the end, he'd been begging her to stop and not to stop and ohmygod yes . . .

She needed a shower.

By the time she got out of the shower, Granny Donny was sitting up in bed, her old-fashioned nightcap covering her thinning hair. The bed seemed enormous around her tiny frame.

"Did you sleep okay?" Ally asked her.

"The sleep of the just, my dear. Very well. And you?"

Was it Ally's imagination, or was her grandmother smirking? "Fine. Thanks."

"Delightful."

This wasn't the first time that Ally felt her grandmother wasn't the innocent she was making herself out to be. Had she really slept through the night?

Ally dressed quickly and began packing their things. "We have a big day. I have to meet Eloisa. She's going to help us with the house. Do you remember?" She continued telling her grandmother the plan as she moved around the room, helping the old woman out of bed and into the bathroom. She hovered outside the door, uncertain.

"Stop hovering. I'm fine. You're making my bladder shy," Granny Donny scolded from behind the shut door.

"Right." Nothing about her grandmother had ever been even the slightest bit shy, but Ally left her to lay out her grandmother's traveling dress, arranging yesterday's dress in the garment bag that was not made for a floor-length gown. Something fell from the dress, and Ally knelt to pick up what she thought were loose buttons, torn from the dress in her haste. She really had to slow down.

But they weren't loose buttons.

They were small white pills.

Ally stood, the pills in her hand. Blood rose in her chest.

Granny Donny came out of the bathroom and took small careful steps toward the dress, balancing herself by the tips of her fingers on the bed. "Lovely, dear. The purple will go so well with my pearls."

"What are these?" Ally held up the pills.

"I'm sure I don't know," Granny Donny said. She was fussing with the dress on the bed, smoothing its creases. "Help me get this on, dear. Oh, I can't wait to get to the country where my maid will be able to help me so you can tend to more important business. Like that lovely duke of yours."

"Granny Donny, are you not taking your pills? You need to take your pills if you want to get better!" Ally tried not to let her voice rise, but it wasn't easy.

Her grandmother straightened the lace around the collar. How did she manage to look a hundred years old and frail as a butterfly whenever Ally was upset with her?

Granny met Ally's eyes with her own. Her jaw was set defiantly. "Who says I want to get better?"

Ally was speechless. She fingered the unswallowed pills. How long had this been going on?

"Help me out of this contraption, dear," she said, indicating her nightgown.

Ally helped her grandmother out of the thin gown and into the purple dress. She tried not to look at her wrinkled, frail, blue-tinged body as she dressed her. Pools of dark bruises spotted her skin here and there, as if she were so delicate, every touch left a mark. "You need to get better, Granny. I can't be here forever." *I need you to be here forever* . . .

"So go." Her grandmother sat regally in front of the mirror, her hands folded in her lap, waiting to be groomed. "Lisa will take care of me as soon as we get to Carleton House."

Was her mother near? "What do you mean?" Ally's voice was thin.

"Your mother, dear. Surely you remember her. She'll take care of me, and you can run off with the duke. Isn't that why we're making this arduous journey?"

Ally felt dizzy. She dropped to a sitting position on the bed. "Did you see my mother? This morning?" If she had been here, she surely would have raced to Ally, embraced her, never let her go. She wouldn't be sneaking around, stealing visits, ducking into cabs. Granny Donny was delusional. Ally couldn't get caught up in the fantasy.

Granny Donny looked confused. "I'm so hungry, dear."

"Right. We'll get breakfast." Ally gathered her grandmother's toilette. "No one came into the room last night?

This morning?" She packed Granny Donny's things into her suitcase, looking longingly at the one black Dior silk suit she'd brought for her grandmother, just in case she came back to her senses.

"How should I know, dear? I've been asleep. I'm sure the maids have been in and out to keep the fire burning."

Her grandmother's face was so wrinkled, this close, she looked as if someone had dropped her and she had shattered. Ally started in on her thinning hair as gently as she could. The fragility of the old woman soothed her and angered her simultaneously.

Ally painted pink lipstick on her grandmother's puckered lips with a small brush. The woman's eyes were closed, her mouth offered up like a child's. She dotted her cheeks with blush, put up her hair as best she could.

Before they left the room, Ally watched carefully as her grandmother took each and every pill, followed by a big drink of water.

*One step off the path, and suddenly Alexandra was lost,
as if just outside her garden was a jungle. She realized for
the first time in her life how truly sheltered she was.
She had no experience with the outside world. She had
no idea how to get back to safety.*
—From *The Dulcet Duke*

Chapter 21

Mateo was waiting with Paula outside the lobby.

Sam was nowhere in sight.

"You have my cell?" Ally asked for the fourth time.

Mateo saluted. "We'll be fine. Don't worry about a thing. We're going to wait for the worst of the traffic to clear, and then we'll set out."

But Ally was worried. She drove the car as fast as she could to Lindenhurst to meet Eloisa. The housekeeper was younger than Ally had expected and much too pretty.

"As far as I can tell, the house hasn't been occupied for a while, and there might be a lot of work to do," she told Eloisa, who nodded and looked at her perfectly manicured nails. Ally hoped this woman was up for the work required of her. They had gone over all the plans for cooking and cleaning and stocking the house, including what to do if anyone was in it (*Get their names and call me!*). Ally slipped Eloisa a picture of her parents from ten years ago, so she'd know whom she was looking for. By the time they were done discussing everything, it was almost noon.

Ally called Mateo's cell phone. She hoped they had gone at least six or seven miles, although Mateo had warned her that it was another hot day and might be slow going.

Sam answered Mateo's phone.

"My girl!" Sam cried. "Come and join us. Where the devil have you been?"

Ally struggled to understand the sounds she was hearing through her cell phone. Cheers. Horns. *Sam.* "Why do you have Mateo's cell phone?" Thank God he couldn't see her blush. His voice alone set her nerve endings to tingling.

"Are you meeting us or not? We miss you! I miss you."

"Are you drunk? Where is my grandmother? Let me talk to her." It was impossible to smell a man through a phone, and yet she could: man, musk, sex, heat. The urge to press the cold, plastic phone to her nose and inhale as if it were Sam was irresistible.

She glanced at Eloisa, who was touching up her bright red lipstick in a tiny compact mirror.

She sniffed her cell phone.

Oh, help me, God . . . I want that man again so badly . . .

"Ally? Are you sniffing your phone?" Sam asked.

"No!"

Eloisa looked over, startled by the vehemence in her voice.

Ally put the phone back to her ear and heard shuffling, then her grandmother saying, "What is this contraption you're putting on my ear? You're messing my coiffure, young imp. Now shush and pass me my lorgnette. The race is starting." Sam came back on the phone. "Seems they didn't have cell phones in Regency England. Sorry, puss. You'll have to talk to me. Or, you know, *sniff* me."

Puss? Race? *He caught me sniffing him.* "Sam. Where are you?"

"I had an amazing time last night, too, Princess."

If she could smell him through the phone, could she smack him through the phone? "Where's Mateo? Why aren't you all on the road on your way to Hempstead? There's a schedule. A plan. We have to follow the plan." Ally was sweating. Sam and his leather pants were so not in the plan.

"We're at the racetrack."

"Racetrack?" Ally's blood ran cold. The family gambling disease! Had it struck Granny Donny?

"Belmont, baby. Your grandmother has made five K already. She's a natural. Brilliant on the bet-to-show."

"Horse racing?" Ally struggled to process the situation. She asked rapid-fire questions and learned that they had traveled just four miles to the racetrack; Paula was settled in the track's stable, happily munching oats while Mateo caught up on horse talk with his amigos; her grandmother was not just gambling vast sums of money but was an ace at it; and, worst of all, Sam's voice was melting her insides like nothing she had ever experienced, and he seemed to know it and was enjoying it immensely.

Ally flipped the phone shut in shock.

Please, not gambling. Of all the places they could

end up, the horse races seemed like an evil joke. Almost as if she was being punished for being with Sam. Last night . . . She sighed just thinking about it. Part of her felt guilty, another part of her wanted to smile, to place a bet, to join the fun. She was splitting in two.

She was getting carried away. She took a calming breath and, to her dismay, still smelled Sam.

Eloisa in tow, Ally rushed to the track. Of course, "rush" in Long Island midday traffic was painfully slow, and by the time they got there, it was early afternoon.

Someone here has to be responsible, or it'll all fall apart. Someone has to take care of things . . .

Having to face Sam again, she tried to remind her heated flesh, was the least of her problems.

Sam watched Ally march up the cement grandstand toward them, her mouth fixed in a tight line. Where was the woman who had screamed in his arms last night, begging him not to stop? The one who had—my God, she had done that, hadn't she? Twice. And he'd begged her to do it again. His body stirred with desire. This was the woman he couldn't wait to see again. The one who had just tried to inhale him through a telephone.

Hadn't she enjoyed herself? Had he been awful? No. He could still remember every blissful expression as he made love to her. The look on her face as she had come last night was brilliant, as if she were surprised all three times (Or was it four? He had lost count), as if she had no idea what her body could do.

But look at her now. She was just like that book, first cover. He mentally flipped from her outside cover to the racy cover underneath. He wanted to rip that outside cover off and mash it in the rubbish heap.

Granny Donny greeted Ally with a hearty wave and a lusty, "Join the party, Princess!"

Ally, for once, was speechless. Not a single fact or statistic escaped her lips. She was looking at him like he had unknowingly morphed into the devil.

Seeing the scene through Ally's horrified eyes, he had to admit their surroundings might look a wee bit seedy. The place reeked of stale beer and cigars. The sparsely populated grandstand was filled with clusters of obsessive-compulsive gamblers: the obese bloke shouting curses; the gang of open-shirted Italian lads; the greasy Russians who looked like they were packing heat; the chain-smoking, desperately thin man, alone, who was tearing his racing sheet to shreds. Ally and her grandmother were just about the only women there, at least, the only ones there with all their teeth.

Sam felt like a child getting caught playing hooky.

Sure, it had been Ally's grandmother's idea to come, but it felt bloody shabby to say so.

"Sam Carson! What are you doing here?" Ally demanded. She seemed to coil herself into a rage and then, to his astonishment, she smacked his shoulder. Hard.

He winced. Last night had been hard on his bruised ribs, and that smack didn't help. Why was she so upset about a little betting on the horses?

A woman came up the steps behind Ally. This was the housekeeper? The woman looked Italian, all black flowing hair and dancing eyes. She had a delicious tattoo of a rose on her shoulder. She was looking at him as if he were an ice-cream sundae with sprinkles, which felt considerably better than the way Ally was looking at him.

The contrast of the two women gave Sam pause. Was it worth pursuing Ally, when women like Eloisa were seemingly everywhere?

Yes. It was just that simple. *Yes.* After coming this far with her. *Yes.* After sleeping with her last night.

Definitely yes.

And then Ally shot him a look of pure disgust.

Or maybe, no. "C'mon, Ally. What's wrong with a little risk? A little excitement?"

Ally set her jaw. "Don't tell me about risk, Sam Carson. I know all about risk, and I want no part of it."

He grabbed Ally's arm and pulled her down into the seat next to him. He lowered his voice and spoke close to her ear. "What's the matter? Tell me."

"You are the matter. This is not okay. My grandmother is a fragile woman. There are dangers here you couldn't possibly understand." Ally was fuming. She looked anything but fragile. "This is just like you, Sam. Irresponsible."

He spoke softly but with the conviction of a man who knew he was right. "You're incapable of living life, Ally Giordano. You're scared of it. You're scared of me. You want me to be a wild man in bed and then a timid creature in life? I don't think so. I think you like all this the same way you liked last night, and you don't want to admit it."

Ally pulled away from him and crossed her arms over her chest.

Sam was exasperated. How could he get Ally to admit that she was the wild woman he had held last night and that it was okay?

The housekeeper adjusted the skinny strap on her tank top and winked at him.

Bingo.

He winked back.

Ally caught the exchange, and her mouth dropped open. For an instant, Ally's eyes faltered and he doubted himself. Was this plan too evil?

Or was it just what he needed to do to make Ally see her true feelings, her true nature, her true need? The need to live. To connect. With him. To go after what she wanted, damn the consequences. He had gotten the princess to sleep with the duke, but he hadn't gotten Ally to sleep with him.

But he was going to change that.

Even if it meant flirting with the hired help.

Ally was numb. *Gambling.* She could tear down the whole track, board by board, with her bare hands. And then Sam's wink at the housekeeper . . . She'd tear his head off . . .

Eloisa coughed, shaking Ally from her thoughts.

Right. Introductions. Life went on despite her twisting emotions. "Sam, Eloisa Tyler. Eloisa, Sam Carson."

"Don't forget me, darling," Granny Donny sang out.

"And my grandmother, Mrs. Giordano," Ally said.

Eloisa curtsied like a pro. "Lady Giordano! I'm so pleased to make your acquaintance."

Granny Donny beamed at Eloisa. "Give the young lady a cigar, Duke. The next race is about to begin, and I've got ten thousand pounds on it."

"Sam!" All the blood drained from Ally's body.

Granny Donny leaned back and touched Ally's knee

with a gloved hand. "The race is starting! My horse is Lady Sam! Isn't that delightful? We can't lose."

Ally had heard that before. "What are the odds?" Her stomach was a knot.

Sam said, "Seven to one." He looked at her, blinking, playing the innocent. "She really bet only a grand," he whispered.

Ally couldn't believe this was happening. Only a grand? How could Sam have let this go so far? And what was going on with him, going cold on her, then lighting up like a Christmas tree for the slutty housekeeper, whom she was ready to fire on the spot. Eloisa had sat down in the row behind them, and Ally felt as if she had a cougar at her back.

The horses for the race were being led onto the track by their trainers. They high-stepped with excitement and nerves.

Sam offered Ally a cigar.

What if . . . ?

She took the cigar and shoved it between her lips.

Sam's eye widened, but he didn't comment. He lit the end.

Ally puffed.

"Gah!" A wave of coughing overcame her. She was going to die. Vile smoke filled her lungs, coated her tongue, and was most likely coming out her ears.

Sam pounded on her back.

When she could breathe again, she mumbled, "Lovely."

"Indeed?" But Sam wasn't watching her anymore.

He was watching Eloisa puff her cigar effortlessly, her red lips practically caressing it. Ally wouldn't have been the slightest bit surprised if the white smoke emerging from her mouth had formed the letters *S-E-X*.

Ally felt as restless as the horses, ready to bolt.

Sam turned his attention back to Ally. "You okay?"

"Fine." *Humiliated, but fine.*

"It's just for fun," Sam said. Then he lowered his voice. "Like last night, right? Just for fun."

She felt a rush of lust as she thought of last night, but one look around made it dissolve like the smoke.

His lips were so close to her ear, she could feel his breath on her cheek, smell his scent over the stink of the cigar. "Remember me? We made love?"

The horses bucked in their starting stalls.

"That wasn't you," she whispered fiercely. Embarrassment for not being able to puff the cigar mixed with jealousy at Eloisa for being so capable. "I made love to a noble duke."

He flinched, then leaned in even closer. "My mistake. You're absolutely right. I mistook you for someone else. I made love to a willing, sensuous princess, full of passion and heat and fun. Certainly not you."

She felt as if she were teetering on the edge of a cliff. "Guess we're both suffering from a case of mistaken identity."

"Bloody shame." He leaned back, spread his arms over the backs of the seats to either side of him.

Then he turned and looked at Eloisa again.

Ally couldn't help it; she had to look back.

Eloisa shot him a flirty smile and puffed away, happy as a cat in the sun.

To get Alexandra, the duke would have to pursue another.
—From *The Dulcet Duke*

Chapter 22

The gun sounded and the horses broke out of the starting gate. Lady Sam fell behind in an instant. Ally sank back into the seat next to Sam and hid her face.

But then she had to watch. She felt the sickness that was gambling creep into her veins: hope. *What if? Just this once?* She peeked out from between her fingers. What if Sam was really a good, trustworthy man? What if Eloisa wasn't the slut she was turning out to be? What if the horse won? Lady Sam was in fourth as they rounded the first bend. Granny Donny's face was alight with excitement, her eyes blazing as she cheered her horse on with a breathless, "Go, go, go! Like the wind! Fly!" Ally could see her mother's face in her grandmother's. The hope, the excitement, the forgetting about the future as she became lost in the moment. This was how mothers forgot about daughters. How men forgot about their lovers as they turned to loose housekeepers: the hope of something more, something better. Gamblers could never stop with what they had. Sam was just like the rest of them.

But maybe she was, too. Waiting for her parents was the long shot of a lifetime. And she had lost half her life to it. If she was really a gambler, she'd go after Sam right now. Risk it all. But she couldn't. She couldn't risk anything more. There was so little left. She could hear her father's voice in her head: *When you have nothing left to lose, that's when you really start to play.* She could turn to Sam and tell him that, yes, she wanted him, all of him, again and again, forever.

But what a risk. Look at him.

The horses came out of the second turn with Lady Sam in second place, a head and neck behind the lead horse. She held her place as they rounded the third bend.

Eloisa's hand clenched Sam's shoulder as Lady Sam inched up on the leader. They came to the straight run toward the finish, and Ally found herself more focused on the hand than on the horses. Around them, the sparse, spotty crowd cheered, as if cheering for Eloisa. *Go, go! Touch his pec! Lean in close and kiss him!*

Ally tore her eyes away and watched her grandmother instead. She was sitting upright, one hand holding her parasol, her chin in the air, an image of gentility and poise, except for the curses she shouted to egg on her "goddamn hunk of dogmeat!" Ally loved those glimmers of the old Granny Donny. Was she coming back? Maybe the pills were taking hold? The doctor had said there was a chance, however slim, that her condition was treatable. Ally tried not to dwell on the weeks lost while her grandmother had resisted the drugs.

Lady Sam pulled up neck and neck with the lead horse.

Eloisa's mouth nestled just behind Sam's left ear and she bit her lower lip. Ally thought she heard growling.

And then, at the last instant, the lead horse pulled ahead, crossing the finish line a nose before Lady Sam.

Ally let the defeat wash over her. She would not look at Sam and Eloisa. "I'm going to kill you, Sam."

"But why? Your grandmother bet to show."

"I have no clue what you're talking about," she lied. She had been around racetracks enough that she could already calculate her grandmother's winnings in her head, before and after taxes. Not bad.

What if . . . ?

Sam explained. "Show means the horse can come in second and she still wins. Your granny just made another bundle. What have you done today for her, Princess?"

*Alexandra knew what the duke was up to, and she
wouldn't fall for his tricks. His eyes, on the other hand,
were harder to resist. There wasn't a woman in London
who wouldn't fall for them.*
—From *The Dulcet Duke*

Chapter 23

Eloisa suggested the celebration dinner, and Sam and
Granny Donny merrily agreed. Ally refused to be the
party pooper. She didn't want Sam to think she was jealous. What did she care whom he winked at? She had slept
with the duke—once!—and that was all. Mistake. Done.
Over. Sam could do what he liked. She had no claim on
him.

So why not have a blowout dinner with some of Granny
Donny's winnings? Her grandmother was, Ally had to
admit, having fun. More fun than she'd had in years. So
what if she thought it was 1812? So what if she had no
idea who or where she was? So what if they'd gotten almost nowhere today? So what if Sam was flirting with the
hired help?

The last one hurt most of all, but Ally refused to acknowledge the ache. Or the anger.

They went down to the stables to find Mateo sitting in

a circle of folding chairs with a group of horsemen, drinking out of a silver flask they passed from man to man.

After some good-natured banter and bowing and explanations of their odd party, they said their good-byes and got ready to get back on the road. Mateo led Paula from her stall and back to the carriage.

As Mateo adjusted Paula's tack, a man joined him. He motioned to Paula's yellow, green, and blue plumes. "Hey, amigo, you should take these folks to the Settle Inn. It's run by a Brazilian *mulher* just a few miles down the road. It's got a stable in the back for your horse, and the avo cooks a *rango com quiabo* not to be believed."

"Maybe, *obrigado*," Mateo replied, but he didn't look at the man. In fact, he seemed to be trying to hide his face from him.

"Should we?" Ally asked, trying to interpret Mateo's reluctance. She had no idea what rango com quiabo was, but she hadn't eaten all day, and rango com anything sounded pretty good.

Mateo hesitated. Then he touched Paula's flank as if for luck. "Sure. No problem. I'll make the call."

"Mateo, one more thing," Ally said, catching him before he rejoined the others. "We have to get my grandmother to the house and get her settled. We can't keep making these stops."

"It was your grandmother who wanted to stop here," Mateo said. "She insisted."

Ally was surprised. Why hadn't Sam told her the track had been Granny Donny's idea?

"And I wanted to give Paula a break," Mateo went on. "These new streets are hard on her. She's been shuttling like she's on tracks between Central Park and her stables.

Now I take her out to all these new places. She's feeling it. She's under stress. A day of rest did her good."

Ally looked at Paula. She had no idea how to tell if a horse was stressed out. Paula wasn't smoking or biting her nails or splurging on pints of Ben & Jerry's. "I'm sorry. I didn't think of her."

Mateo petted Paula's warm side. "Also I was hoping maybe one of these guys would want her. Or would know someone who would. After. You know."

Ally let the horse's mane slip through her fingers. "After what?" She'd been so lost in her own head these past few days, had she missed something he'd said?

Mateo patted Paula. "After we finish this trip. I'm not taking her back to Manhattan, Ally. No working horses in Manhattan after they're twenty-five. Rules are strict."

Ally tried to follow. "You mean, sell her?"

"I can't afford to keep her if she's not working, and I can't keep her working in the city. Out here, I was hoping, maybe someone would see her and want her."

Ally looked into the mare's huge black, liquid eyes. "Oh, Mateo. I wasn't thinking. Of course. I'm sorry." Compared to the racehorses surrounding her, Paula seemed small and frail, almost like another species. "Who buys old horses?"

"You mean besides the glue factory?"

Ally gasped again. "Don't say that!"

"She doesn't speak English," he joked, but his voice was wistful. He adjusted her tack a final time. "It's the way of the world. A time to live, and a time to die. That's life, right? You gotta get as much as you can out of it before your time comes. In a way, Ally, you and I are making the same journey, no? Hoping to bring the old ladies to a kind of peace."

Sam watched Ally talk to Mateo and his skin grew hot. The way she looked at him. The way she deferred to him. It wasn't that Sam thought she was interested in the coachman. Not in *that* way. What he was watching between Mateo and Ally was worse than a sexual attraction. She was *talking* to Mateo. Having a real conversation about something—who knew what—that touched them both.

Sure, Sam was fine in her bed for a night, or to turn to when she needed diversion in the carriage. But otherwise, he was *still* nothing to her.

Except that he wasn't. He knew they'd had something more than role-playing sex last night. There had been a connection. Ally was just too pigheaded to realize it. Competitive spirit stirred his resolve. A duke had to do what a duke had to do.

Even if it broke her.

Or him.

"You're going with Eloisa in the car?" Ally asked Sam. Her heart was beating wildly with anger and jealousy, but she'd be damned if she was going to let it show.

"See you at dinner." Sam waved happily.

Ally gave Eloisa the car keys and watched her and her long, lean, bare legs and her perfect little body climb into the car with Sam. Ally, her grandmother, and Mateo followed in the carriage. After they passed the third strip mall, the town began to thin out, getting greener and sparser. Granny Donny took Ally's hand. "Thank you, dear," she said. "I had a lovely day."

Paula clopped along the quiet streets.

Ally tried not to think about Sam. "Grandma, please don't gamble anymore. It doesn't become a lady." She couldn't believe those words had come out of her mouth. She *was* the good woman and she was so darn—no, so *damned*!—tired of it.

"I expected to see your dear mother at the track," Granny Donny said. "I was so disappointed."

"Why did you expect that?" Ally held her breath.

Granny Donny sighed and ignored the question. "Oh, it doesn't signify, dear. I'm so excited for the ball, when you and the duke can be together and dance and be young and let the sparks fly! I do think that he'll propose there. Don't you, darling? And your father and mother will give you away. It will be like old times!"

Ally couldn't look at her grandmother. Granny Donny had let her live her life with the fantasy that her parents would be back "any day now." It would be cruel for her to deny her grandmother the same hope. Her grandmother had let her pretend for so long. But the irony that Ally had finally left the fantasy behind just as her grandmother picked it up tore her heart apart.

Even if she couldn't destroy the fantasy of her parents' return, though, Ally could nip the fantasy of Sam in the bud. "Sam is not going to propose to me at a ball or anywhere."

"Well, of course not."

Ally was stunned by her grandmother's abrupt about-face.

"Not unless you do something about it. I can feel the

love you two share. The way you ran to him when he was injured in that duel!"

It took Ally a moment to realize her grandmother was talking about the soccer game.

"Or the way he kisses you."

Yeah, well, you should see how he makes love to me. She felt the urge to bolt from the carriage, catch the car by sheer will, and yank Sam out by his messy hair. *Mine.*

But she didn't make a move. "First, I don't even know him. Second, he isn't interested in me. Third, even if he was, he isn't my type." *Fourth, that's animal lust you're picking up, and lust does not equal love.*

"How can you know he isn't your type if you don't know him? Darling, that makes no sense at all. You must get to know him. To discover the pain beneath his flawless surface. To find out why he cannot love."

Ally glanced at her grandmother. "You've got to be kidding."

"Of course not. He suffers the pain only true love can heal."

"Sam? Suffering? I don't think so."

"That's because you're too closed off to see."

Ally watched her grandmother closely. Despite her risky behavior today, she was starting to sound more aware of the real world. Was it because she had finally taken her pills? If Ally kept supervising her carefully, would this whole episode end? Would she be able to go to San Francisco after all at the end of the summer? Was that still what she wanted?

Or did she want Sam? All of him? Forever?

*   *   *

The houses were getting bigger, settled in the center of green lawns. They had crossed out of the city and entered a place that seemed quaint and old-fashioned, frozen in time. This was the way Ally had imagined their journey. She and her grandmother, a beautiful dusk, the clip-clop of the horse's hooves. It was peaceful. Lovely, even. Granny Donny was stroking the kitten, which they'd named Bandit. Bandit looked as if his tiny bones had gone to liquid as he sprawled on Granny's lap.

Ally wished she felt so peaceful. Instead, her mind and body felt as if they were separating. On the one hand, Sam meant great sex with a beautiful man. On the other, he meant great sex with a beautiful man who personified her parents' lifestyle—carefree, risk-taking, irresponsible, *disloyal*. She felt a black hole open in her gut and resisted spiraling into it. Admitting she wanted Sam, all of him, would be admitting that her mother had done the right thing in following her father. That a rogue could be okay. *Better than okay.* That a rogue could be worth following. *To the ends of the earth.* Worth loving. *And then loving again.* How could that be? How could she risk that?

"Granny Donny, do you think my mother did the right thing when she left with my father?"

"Oh, yes, of course, dear," Granny Donny said with not a moment of hesitation.

"Why?"

"She followed her heart, dear. She had no choice."

"But what about her leaving me?" Ally heard the childishness of her words, but the pain was still there; she couldn't help it.

"You had me, dear. You were better off with me. We all agreed."

So they had come to a logical decision?

Was there a logical decision to be made about Sam? Could a man who treated Veronica and apparently all the women who came before her badly treat Ally any better? It wasn't logical. Case in point: him running off with Eloisa.

They passed under a towering maple and Ally looked up at the majestic, soaring trunk, the sedate green leaves.

Logical? She was in the back of a carriage pretending to be a princess.

She looked at her grandmother, swaying happily, stroking the kitten.

Logical?

This trip was lovely, the best thing Ally had ever done for her grandmother, and it was completely nuts. Maybe it was time to forget logical and lay her cards on the table.

To make the bet of a lifetime.

The sign for the Settle Inn pointed up a long driveway that meandered around a copse of trees. They slowly made their way around the curve, where a charming 1920s, multicolored, gingerbread-style cottage welcomed them.

Sam and Eloisa were already on the porch swing out front, sipping wine.

Mateo stopped the carriage in front of the inn and leaped down. Ally realized she was waiting for him to take her hand as if she had spent her entire life riding around in carriages with attentive coachmen.

Eloisa had kicked off her shoes and was blissfully settled on the swing, as if she had spent her entire life with Sam.

Ally approached the porch of the cottage, her grand-

mother clinging to her arm. Sam and Eloisa were swing-
ing, singing, and drinking red wine, without a care in the
world.

"We've ordered up dinner!" Sam called. "We're the
only ones here tonight, so Mrs. Maltez, the proprietor, is
making us a special Brazilian meal!"

"Delightful!" Granny Donny said, but her voice was
tired, and Ally wondered if she'd make it to dinner without falling asleep. Maybe it was the pills that were wearing her out. Ally hoped she wasn't being too strict with
her grandmother.

Sam jumped up to open the door for them.

"Opening doors for ladies doesn't make you a gentleman," she said.

"Oh, Ally, you're no lady," he whispered. And then he
shut the door behind them.

Mateo was in the inn's stable, counting bills. He had
rubbed down Paula and now she was happily munching
hay. He was glad she'd had an easy day today. This trip
was taking it out of her, and he had to be careful not to
push her. He had to keep her healthy if his plan to find
her a new home was to work. No one but the glue factory
wanted a sick old horse.

Mateo overturned a pail and sat on it while he watched
her. He folded the money he had won today and pushed it
into his pocket. He had dabbled in gambling before, but
never like that. Donatella Giordano was an idiot savant
at the track. She picked horses by sense of smell or messages from God or maybe a complex and intricate study
of the wrinkles of her palm. Who knew? Who cared? The
eight hundred dollars he'd walked away with today was

more than he made in a month carting tourists around Manhattan.

The feel of the money reminded him of better days. He had been rich once. This would have been pocket money. Enough for a night on the town. But he didn't want to think about everything he had left behind.

What he had to think about was Paula getting old. He couldn't take her back to Manhattan. Mateo believed, more than anything else, in loyalty. He was going to save this horse, even if it cost him everything. The eight hundred bucks would help, but it wasn't enough. It cost a lot more than that to board a horse for any length of time. And although he had once been a rich man, he had given everything he had to the local church before leaving his country. It had been an apology as well as a way of starting over. But now he wished he'd kept a little of his riches; he hadn't anticipated Paula. And he had no way to make that kind of money here without going back to his old life.

Which he wasn't going to do.

The small stable sat across the mud parking lot from the main house, and as the summer sun set, the lights in the house went on one by one. Mateo could see Sam flirting with Eloisa at the large round table. Stupid man had no idea what he had in Ally.

Mateo should go in, shower, join them. But what if the mulher recognized him? A real Brazilian would know he wasn't Brazilian. It was amazing that the two Argentineans in the crowd of Mexican stablehands hadn't recognized him at the track. Those boys at the fountain, however, had known exactly who he was. He didn't have to worry about Ally or Granny Donny or Eloisa knowing the difference between an Argentinean and a Brazilian. He did have to worry about Sam. The man might not know Spanish from Portuguese, but he would know in an instant who Mateo was if he wasn't thrown by the Brazil nonsense.

When would Ally kick that gringo out? He liked Sam, but he was dangerous. Good thing it looked like Sam was blowing it with Ally big-time. He'd be gone soon at this rate.

Fool.

Mateo's stomach growled.

He turned to watch Paula, who was nodding off to sleep. Poor girl, working so hard to drag them all through these filthy streets. She was a good horse. She deserved a rest, deserved to get out of that stinking city, and deserved not to be sold for her parts.

"Some of us, Paula, we were just born unlucky." He patted Paula, who neighed softly. Then he went inside for a shower and dinner. After all, he wasn't about to miss Mrs. Maltez's cooking. He might not be Brazilian, but he still loved the food.

He'd just be sure to keep his head down and his mouth shut.

Ally awoke in the narrow single bed. "Ouch!" Bandit was pouncing on her feet.

Her grandmother snored softly beside her, then stirred, and then sneezed.

Ally could just make out the black hands of the antique clock in the darkness: two a.m.

The cat attacked again. His tiny claws dug into her leg. "Stop." She gathered him up. He purred and bit her hand

and she wondered whom Sam was biting—or worse, who was biting him.

Granny Donny sneezed again.

Ally tried to go back to sleep, but it was hopeless. Between wondering about Sam and Eloisa, being attacked by Bandit, and Granny Donny's restless sleeping and sneezing, she gave up.

She put on her bathrobe, gathered up Bandit, and crept down the hall. She knocked on Sam's door.

He answered the door, but sleepily—which was good as it meant he'd been sleeping. But he opened the door only a crack, as if trying to keep something inside hidden.

Ally held out the kitten. "I think my grandmother is allergic. Can you keep Bandit for the night?" She tried to peer around him into the room without seeming to peer around him into the room.

He took the kitten. "Sure."

She hesitated. "But maybe Eloisa is allergic, too," she suggested.

He smiled the faintest of smiles. "Maybe. Guess we'll find out." And then he shut the door.

Ally stood in the dark hallway, alone, fuming. .

She stomped back to her room, then returned to Sam's door a moment later.

She knocked, perhaps louder than was necessary. "Sam, one more thing," Ally said through the door.

Sam opened the door. Ally held out Bandit's tiny litter box and a scoop.

"Ah!" He took them but then returned the door to its narrow slit of an opening. "Anything else?"

She hesitated. "Yes."

"What?"

She took a deep breath. "Tell me about yourself," she said.

"Excuse me?" He rubbed the sleep out of his eyes.

"You. Who are you, Sam?"

"Ally, it's two a.m."

"So you're saying you're busy?" she asked. The need to figure Sam out was humiliating. But her grandmother was right: She hardly knew him and she had been judging him and it was wrong and she couldn't sleep and they were almost in Lewiston and she was coming undone.

"I'll be right back." He shut the door and her heart shut, too, and then he emerged a few moments later, with Bandit and a piece of string, and her heart fluttered open again. He shut the door behind him, then sat down on the floor outside the door, his back against the wall. He played with the delighted kitty. His long legs stretched in front of him, crossed at the ankles. He was wearing what looked like a very expensive pair of Henley pajamas, solid navy on top with blue-and-gray plaid flannel pants. She tried not to look at his exquisite toes. "What do you want to know?"

She sat down, too, leaving a good foot between them. Not that the distance stopped her from feeling the heat of him. "In *The Dulcet Duke*, Duke Blackmoore is a rogue, but it's not his fault."

"Ah. Right. I remember. That prologue about his father despising him because of his lisp. Ridiculous."

"It's not ridiculous. It's lovely. Sam, I need to know your prologue."

Bandit leaped over his legs, then skidded to a clumsy stop against her legs and crouched down for his next attack on the string. His tiny, furry head bobbed back and forth, following his prey.

"I think it's bullshit for a grown man to blame his parents for making him an ass. My past doesn't matter. At some point, you need to be responsible for yourself."

"It does, Sam. It matters to me."

"Why?"

"So I can forgive you and—"

Bandit pounced.

Sam scooped him up and let him bite his thumb. He looked sideways at Ally. "And what?"

"And—are you sleeping with Eloisa? Is she in there?"

"Does it matter?"

"Yes."

"Why?"

He was going to make her say it. She closed her eyes. "Because I don't want her to be." Bandit climbed onto her lap and settled down for another pounce.

"Why?" he asked again. His voice had gone husky, and Bandit reconsidered his attack, backing away with his tail down.

"Because I thought we had something more important."

His eyes fixed on hers. "Do we?"

"Did you have a stutter as a kid?" she asked. "Have an abusive mother? Were you stolen by pirates at twelve or raised by wolves?"

"Bears. But we hung with the wolves on Friday nights. Ally, listen, because this is important. I don't want to be forgiven. I do what I do because it's what I want to do. I'm here because I want to be here. I am who I am, and I don't make excuses for it. And if I want to change, I'll change because I want to. Digging into my past is useless. Take me for who I am and trust me."

"Tell me one story. Just one. Make it up," she practically begged.

"Why? So that you can feel sorry for me? I don't think so. I will not be pitied." She must have looked at him like he was a lost puppy dog, because his voice grew more serious. "What if I was married and then widowed within a year? What if my parents disowned me for marrying down? So what? I'm a grown man. I am responsible for my actions."

Ally shook her head. "I'm a grown woman, and I'm terrified that my mother is waiting for me in Lewiston."

"Well, yes, but you're a *woman*."

She was starting to get it. To get him. "Ah, so if you were a woman you could feel emotion and admit that you've been hurt?" *Married? Widowed? Disowned? Sam?* Was that true, or had he made it up as an example of a romance-novel tortured hero?

"I'm not hurt!" he insisted. "Ouch!" He pulled his thumb away from Bandit and a drop of blood appeared where he had bit him. "Are you two teaming up on me?"

"You're not going to tell me anything?"

"Ally, my past is past. What matters is that you came to me in the middle of the night because you were jealous of another woman and now you should kiss me; you should be overcome with passion; you should forget the past. What matters is what we feel and do here, now."

She wanted to feel and do it here, now. But something held her back. His midnight stubble, dark on his chin and cheeks, seemed to grow even darker as she watched him.

"Don't say it," he warned.

"What?"

"What you were going to say."

"I have to get back," she began.

He hit the wall with his fist, startling the cat. "You said it. Damn it. You've gotten nowhere, Ally. It's like day one. You feel me, you want me, and yet you don't trust me."

"I left my grandmother alone. I have to go back." She stood.

"Ally, don't come to me in the middle of the night again unless you intend to follow through."

And with that, he scooped up Bandit in one hand, went inside, and shut the door behind him.

Granny Donny awoke and sat bolt upright. Where was she? Some kind of hotel. The bed next to her was empty but used, as if someone had gotten up in the middle of the night.

She felt uncomfortable. Something was on her head. Granny Donny pulled it off.

She had been sleeping in a hat? Who wore hats to bed? Especially little, white frilly ones?

Her head hurt and she felt immensely tired, so she sank back into her covers. As she drifted off to sleep, she felt peaceful, as if things were going well.

Except that she smelled faintly of horse, which was odd.

She was so sleepy.

She'd figure it out in the morning.

In the end, a woman has only herself to count on.
—From *The Dulcet Duke*

Chapter 24

Sam slept with Eloisa.

Sam didn't sleep with Eloisa.

Of course he didn't. Wouldn't Eloisa have come out into the hallway if she had been in Sam's room? But then, maybe she had already left by the time Ally came with Bandit. Or maybe she was sound asleep, exhausted and naked in his bed.

Ally harrumphed as she finished her breakfast in the inn's small dining room. She was the first one up, and she was glad to eat alone. Not that Ally had much of an appetite. The inn was so small, there was no way for Granny Donny to leave her room without Ally seeing her.

Ally had woken up that morning furious with herself for not going through with what she had intended with Sam. But what had she intended? That he'd break down and admit he had a wounded soul and that was what made him behave the way he did?

But then, didn't he sort of admit he was wounded by denying it? Wasn't that classic rogue behavior right there? *Married. Disowned. Widowed.* That was intense if it was true. She picked at her oatmeal in despair. *The past doesn't matter.* Was it that easy to forget the past? Then why couldn't she?

No, he was full of it. He had no idea how to face the fact that life had scarred him and left him a man who had no idea how to love.

She wasn't the only one blowing this big-time.

She had to get more details. Find out more. And now that she saw how reluctant he was to play along, she had no idea how she'd do that. Especially now that she'd made him mad.

Granny Donny got dressed and left her room at the same moment Sam closed his own door. He turned and faced her and his jaw dropped. "Lady Giordano!" She was wearing a black Dior suit—totally modern. She wasn't even wearing gloves.

"Lady?" She harrumphed. "Who are you?" she asked.

"Who am I? Duke Whatthehell."

"What the hell?"

"Exactly. Oh my God. You're back." He was amazed.

"What is going on here, young man?"

Sam took her arm. "It is so nice to meet you. Come into my room. We have to talk."

She glanced at him. "You think I'd go into a strange man's room?" Then she lowered her eyes and batted her eyelashes. "Although, you are a rather attractive strange man."

"Why, thank you. But we better just talk, for Ally's sake."

"Oh, delightful!" That seemed to convince her. She marched to his room, giving him a sideways stare when he bowed her inside. "So, how are you involved with my granddaughter? Carnally, I hope!"

He told her the whole story and she listened, astonished. When he told her the part about Ally's parents waiting at the house, she gasped. "But they can't be at the house!"

"Ally thinks they might be."

"Why?"

"You told her they were."

"But you just said yourself I was mad as a hatter."

He shrugged. "Ally believes what she wants to believe. She's a little hard to sway."

Granny Donny shook her head. "Oh, the poor dear."

"So who is at the house?" Sam asked.

"How should I know? I have a company handle it. I only pay attention to the checks. Although, come to think of it, I don't pay much attention to them either."

He explained to her about the lack of records.

"Oh. My. Well, it's a great mystery for all of us."

They looked at each other for a moment, unsure what to do next.

"So, do you love her?" Donatella asked.

Sam was startled. "I do." Oh. Now he was even more startled. Had he really said that? *I love her.*

He did.

"So it's settled."

"Nothing is settled." He felt another wave of anger like the anger he felt last night. "She won't have me. She thinks I'm a rogue, like her father. And she doesn't want to be like her mother."

"More than she knows," Donatella murmured. Then she said, "Wait, did you say rogue?"

He smiled. "*The Dulcet Duke.* Like I said, we've been sort of caught up in the early nineteenth century."

She eyed him. "So you haven't been sleeping together?" Granny Donny seemed aghast at his deficiency.

He felt the absurd need to defend himself. "We, um, we have, Ally and I—slept together. But not exactly."

"And I'm the one who was supposed to be nuts?" Donatella mumbled. "I suppose you'll explain that nonsense?"

So he did.

"I see. Well, then we have to keep on with the book."

"We do?" he asked.

"Well, of course we do. If Ally is too stupid to sleep with you as herself"—she gave him a once-over worthy of a true connoisseur—"then we have to keep pushing her along. I better change back into my costume. And you better run off ahead with the housemaid."

"Oh, I don't know. Ally did come to my room last night."

"To talk! Young man, you go off with the housemaid and let me worry about the princess."

Someone was coming down the stairs to the kitchen. Ally hoped for Sam. But it was Eloisa. Alone. She looked awfully happy as she joined Ally at her table. "Good morning!" she sang, tucking herself demurely into the seat.

Ally sniffed, wondering if she'd be able to pick up the scent of Sam. All she could smell was bacon cooking in the kitchen. Which was good, because sniffing the hired help was decidedly nuts. "Morning."

Eloisa scanned the menu as Ally scanned her for bite marks. She didn't see any. She glanced under the table to see if she could spot tiny claw marks on Eloisa's ankle.

"Sleep well?" Ally couldn't help but ask.

"Lovely!" Eloisa cooed. "This is turning out to be a much more fun job than I expected." She signaled Mrs. Maltez to the table and ordered a full, post-awesome-sex-worthy breakfast of rice, beans, eggs, sausage, and coffee. Extra hot sauce.

Ally looked down at her lumpy oatmeal. She gulped her coffee, trying not to want to pour the hot liquid on Eloisa's head. She badly wanted to fire her, but she just as badly wanted Eloisa to go ahead to the house so she could report back on what she found there. "So," Ally said finally, trying to appear cordial. "Did Bandit bother you last night?"

"Oh, Bandit wasn't with me last night," she said, accepting her coffee. "I can't abide cats. Terribly allergic."

"Good."

Eloisa gave her a strange look.

"I mean, I'm glad you slept well. Good." Or was it bad? Ally had no idea.

Mateo drove Paula slowly out of Hempstead while Ally repeated to herself: *What do I care if Sam went on ahead with Eloisa in the car?* Who could blame him? She hadn't exactly given him a reason to stay with her.

But as the carriage glided behind Paula's slow gait, Ally wished she hadn't let Sam go. She should have stopped him. The trip wasn't the same without him. She wanted to play twenty questions with him. She wanted to jump in fountains with him. She wanted to tell him facts about the history of Long Island so that he could tell her to can it with the lectures and then kiss her.

She missed him.

"Ally, dear, you're a million miles away," Granny Donny said. "Are you thinking of the duke?"

"No. Yes. I don't know." She turned her attention to her grandmother. She looked different somehow, more jaunty and full of life. "You look good. I'm so glad you started taking those pills again."

"Oh, fiddle-dee-dee," Granny Donny said. Then her tone changed and Ally could swear she was her old self again. She looked positively sneaky. "You have to get that man back."

"Shouldn't a gentlewoman wait for the man to make the moves?" Ally asked.

Granny Donny snorted. "*Gentlewoman*. Ally, don't be a prude. There is nothing wrong with a rogue that a real woman can't fix."

"Granny!"

Paula turned a corner, and Ally could see Mateo trying to hide a smile.

"It's not true," Ally insisted. "Mom couldn't tame Dad. She threw her life away."

Granny Donny flinched. She watched Ally for a long moment, then said, "You mean she threw you away."

"No. She threw everything away."

"How can you know that? She gave her life for love. That's not throwing everything away," Granny Donny said, her voice heavy with emotion.

Before Ally could respond, her cell phone rang.

She held her breath and answered. "Sam?"

"Ally. We got to the house."

Ally's stomach clenched. "And?"

"I'm sorry, Ally. Your parents aren't here," he said.

She waited for her world to go black, but it didn't. In fact, she wanted more of Sam's voice, no matter what he said. This shocked her. How could she care more about a man she'd known a few weeks than about her own parents?

"The house isn't in such great shape," he said.

"How bad is it?"

"You won't be here tonight, will you?"

"No. We were going to stop in Lindenhurst for the night. There's a stable there for Paula."

"Good. Take your time."

Ally felt a chill of foreboding.

"Ally, I'm sorry about your parents," Sam said.

"It's okay. It's best, really. Bye, Sam." She closed the phone and looked at her grandmother.

"They're not there."

"Who, dear?"

"Mom and Dad. Lisa and Ross. There's no one at the house."

"The house?" Whatever sanity Granny Donny had found seemed to have faded away.

"The beach house? Remember? We're going there?"

Granny Donny asked, incredulous, "Why would they be there?"

"Because you told me they would be," Ally reminded Granny Donny.

"Yes, about that. I—" She stopped, searching for words.

Ally hadn't ever seen her grandmother look so defeated. "Is something wrong?"

"Wrong? No. Of course not. Everything is fine. Let's enjoy the rest of the ride. Let's speak of balls and picnics and dukes with black hair and gray eyes!"

They stopped at a local park to rest Paula and eat a picnic lunch they had picked up along the way. After lunch, the dark pond beckoned, and Ally excused herself to walk to it.

It felt odd to suddenly be alone after so many days of being surrounded by people. She scooped a handful of pebbles and tossed them one by one into the water.

It was time for her to decide what to do next. Her grandmother had been showing small signs of becoming her old self all day, and it struck Ally as oddly sad.

My parents aren't waiting for me.

The fantasy was over.

She grabbed another handful of pebbles.

It was time for her to let go of all her fantasies and get on with real life. That was what going to San Francisco was all about, and she had to turn her attention back to getting there.

She tossed a stone—her mother. It made a small splash, then sank.

Another—her father. Splash. Gone.

She held the last stone, turning it in her fingers. She felt numb. *People don't really change.* It was ridiculous to think her parents would be there, waiting, living conventional lives. As absurd as thinking a lifelong rogue would settle down and love her just because he said he would.

She threw the last stone—Sam—just to see how it felt.
It didn't even make a splash before it disappeared.
It felt lousy.
She turned quickly and hurried back to the carriage,
wondering, *Are my fantasies all I have? All I ever had?*

A man sometimes had to choose between looking good and doing good. The duke held his breath and chose doing good, despite the unfixable problem that made him look like less of a man.
—From *The Dulcet Duke*

Chapter 25

The carriage crossed the bridge to Fire Island five minutes after four o'clock the next day. Luckily, this bridge was small and untended, with no rules against horses, or, if there were rules, there wasn't anyone for miles who cared about enforcing them.

As they got closer to the ocean, the smell of the sea and the beauty of the one-lane sandy road that led to Granny Donny's house made Ally feel hopeful. This was real. This was facing her past. This was moving on with her life.

Granny Donny and I will have a lovely vacation, she promised herself. *A beautiful summer.* This was how she had wanted it, after all. Sam and Eloisa would leave. She'd find another housekeeper. Then Ally would take Granny Donny on long beach walks. They'd sit together on the porch, drinking lemonade and watching the waves. Here would be good. Granny Donny could live in the world she'd created, safe and well cared for in a beautiful place full of happy memories. How bad could the house be? Whatever was wrong with it could be fixed.

There was only one loose end to tie up.

"Mateo. Can we stop? Can I talk to you for a minute?"

Mateo pulled the coach to the side of the small road. He unhooked Paula's water bucket from underneath and gave it to her.

"I'll be right back, Granny Donny."

Her grandmother waved her off. She looked preoccupied, but Ally wrote it off as nerves. It had been a long trip.

They stood by Paula's head, and Ally stroked the mare's silky nose. "Mateo. What would you think of staying out here with my grandmother? Let her buy Paula. Then you stick around to take care of her and be my grandmother's private driver?"

"She'd buy Paula?" His interest was aroused.

"Sure. Why not? My grandmother has plenty of money. We'll have to check the zoning. Probably keeping her at the house isn't okay. But we could find somewhere nearby to board her." Ally wrung her hands. It was too much to hope for a happy ending for everyone, but she could at least give one to the horse and Mateo. "I think my grandmother is getting better, Mateo. She's showing signs of her old self. Just little ones. But I think taking the pills is making a difference. The doctors said it was possible." She explained about the pills, and how she'd been making sure that Granny Donny was taking them. "So I've decided that if I can get everything set up here, I'm going to leave as soon as the summer is over." Mateo looked surprised so she explained. "I had planned to move to San Francisco before all this happened, and now I realize I need to go."

Mateo looked surprised. "San Francisco? What about Sam?"

"Sam?" A jolt of desire ran through her, but she repressed it. "I planned this move a long time ago. I have a job and an apartment set up in California. I had always planned on going. This has been a kind of good-bye trip."

He nodded, taking in this new information. After a while, Mateo said, "We'd be honored to stay with your grandmother, Ally. Thank you. From both of us."

They pulled into the driveway of the beachfront house. Sam came down the front porch steps to greet the carriage. His lips were set in a grim line. He looked so oddly serious, Ally almost didn't recognize him. She tried to ignore the way her body sparked when he appeared, tried to hold down the urge to smile just because he was there.

Sam helped Granny Donny down from the carriage. There was paint on his shirt and sawdust in his hair. How odd. Ally looked around for Eloisa and wondered just what kind of hard work the two of them had been up to. At least Sam had all his clothes on. Eloisa, nowhere in sight, most likely didn't.

"Ally, we need to talk," Sam said.

Ally swung down from the carriage. His sternness puzzled her. Maybe Eloisa had been more than he could handle. Ally pulled her small travel bag from the carriage and took Granny Donny's arm to help her navigate the rocky, crushed-shell-covered driveway to the house. Ally fought off the waves of nostalgia that were competing with her yearning for Sam. The smell of the sea was overwhelming in its power to take her back to her childhood. She felt a little shaky, and she wanted to fall into Sam's arms for comfort. Instead, she squeezed her grandmother's frail hand. Her grandmother squeezed back, with alarming strength.

"I know, dear. I know," she whispered.

Sam took their bags, throwing them over one shoulder. He took Granny Donny's other arm. Sam hadn't smiled once.

Something didn't look right about Sam.

Or Granny Donny, who kept stopping and looking at Ally as if she were trying to come to some kind of decision. Ally realized what it was about her grandmother that made her seem almost back to normal: She was noticing Ally in a way she hadn't in weeks. She seemed tuned in—really tuned in—to what was happening around her.

And what was happening wasn't good.

One shutter hung from a second-floor window. What looked like a faded, printed sheet hung in one of the windows downstairs. Her grandmother, a meticulous housekeeper in her day, had imported all the draperies from France and had them washed every year at the end of the season. "What's that smell?" Ally asked. A twinge of foreboding crept up Ally's spine. Undercutting the sweet, salty smell of the sea was something sharp and piercing. It drifted in and out of range with the breeze.

Granny Donny didn't seem to notice. "The smell of the

sea," she muttered. "It's so strong. It's—" She trailed off. Were there tears in her eyes?

"Well, it's the smell of my youth, that's for sure," Sam said, still grim.

Mateo, who had been tending to Paula, caught up with them. He mumbled something and whistled softly.

Granny Donny straightened as she approached the two-story, blue-shingled square house.

Behind the house, the dunes rose up, and beyond them, Ally could hear the promise of the waves. In the front, two huge weeping willows and a few scraggly holly trees screened the porch, creating delicious shade. To either side, there were more trees and dunes, blocking out the neighbors' houses almost completely. Ally had forgotten how much she had loved summers here before her parents left. She felt weak, undone by memories.

"Ally." Sam's urgent, commanding tone stopped her racing thoughts. "I think your grandmother might enjoy an iced tea on the porch with Mateo before she goes in." He pointed to a tray set up on the porch with a pitcher and two tall glasses. A vase holding a bouquet of wildflowers sat in the middle of the tray.

"Where's Eloisa?" Ally asked, trying to take it all in.

"No worries. Come, sit." Sam put his hand on Mateo's shoulder and whispered something in his ear.

Mateo whistled softly again and shook his head. "*Si*, Lady Donatella. Let's sit and enjoy the shade."

Had Sam scared off Eloisa? Of all the irresponsible—

The breeze blew her way again, and this time Ally knew what the smell was—marijuana. Of course she knew it from teaching school, but it had been so incongruous in this paradise, it hadn't clicked. Then she noticed a pile of at least six huge black garbage bags just outside the front door and her stomach sank. "Granny, why don't you sit and enjoy the breeze on the porch with Mateo? I'll be right back."

Granny Donny stared at the house, her mouth a determined line. "What happened to my house?"

They all stopped. Something was different about Granny Donny's voice. It had lost its slight British inflection.

"Granny Donny?" Ally could barely hear her own voice.

"Oh, forget this blasted ruse! Who ruined my house?"

Was the old Granny Donny back? Or had she just slipped further away? "Granny Donny, do you feel okay?" Ally asked.

"No. I don't feel okay. Last thing I knew, I was in Manhattan, in normal clothes, and now I'm standing in front of my house in a ridiculous dress, wondering what the hell is going on here."

Ally tried to control her elation. "Do you know where you are?" she asked her grandmother.

"Well, I seem to be in Lewiston," she said. "With two very beautiful men and very silly gloves." She ripped off the elbow-length white gloves.

"What year is it?"

"Ally, what is the matter with you? I need a drink, and I'm not talking about iced tea." She threw her bonnet on the ground and cursed it in a most unladylike fashion.

They all looked at one another, unsure how to proceed. Ally felt as if she had been caught playing an embarrassing game.

"Welcome back," Mateo said.

"The house looks like shit." Granny Donny scowled, marching to the porch. She climbed the steps and looked down at them, still mute on the driveway. "Well, c'mon, let's you and me have some iced tea, young man. I feel a little woozy and could use the rest. Then we'll drive that contraption of yours out to the liquor store for more appropriate supplies."

They all still stared.

"C'mon, don't be daft," she said to Mateo. "Obviously these two want to ditch us to be alone."

"Granny! Certainly not!" Ally bolted up the steps and hugged her grandmother. "It's so good to have you back! How could I leave your side? There's so much to talk about. I have so much to tell you."

"Oh, please. I'm just an old bag of bones. Run off with that man. And don't you dare come back until you're good and ready."

Ally's mind was reeling. She felt like dancing, and at the same time, she felt inexplicably sad. Sam was watching her. As much as she wanted to stay glued to her grandmother's side, she also wanted to talk to Sam and make things right. Mateo and Granny Donny sat down at the porch table, leaving Ally and Sam alone at the base of the steps.

"I think the house shocked her back into herself," Ally said.

He shrugged. "Maybe."

"Sam, I'm really sorry I was an idiot last night. If you want to be with Eloisa, I totally get that. Because I've been very confused and—"

"Pigheaded?" Sam suggested.

"Right." She glanced up at him. He still hadn't smiled, but at least he didn't look as mad. "Where is Eloisa?"

"She split," Sam said.

"Sam. You didn't scare her away! We need her!"

"Come inside. I think you'll understand."

Chapter 26

Ally dropped her bag. Mateo's and her grandmother's voices from where they sat on the porch were oddly normal; they chatted away as if they were meeting each other for the first time.

Nothing else about the place was normal. Ally was speechless at the destruction around her.

"This actually looks pretty good. It was shagging well awful when we first got here," Sam said.

The house was still pretty shagging well awful. It looked as if a punk band had trashed it. Ally fought back a mixture of anger and hopelessness.

"The bloke at Bart's"—Sam named the local grocery and lottery ticket store—"told me what he knew, which wasn't much. The real-estate management company that was meant to run the place, Grouse and Grouse, went out of business two years ago when Mr. and Mrs. Grouse retired and moved to Florida. I guess your grandmother didn't read her mail or no one rang her or some unfortunate bollocks. The tenants who had been here moved on, and, from what I can read of the graffiti, Zed, Monica, and George—a bunch of effin' pissheads—broke in and made themselves at home."

"Zed, Monica, and George?" Ally could hardly find her voice. The house stank of pot and beer. Not only were her parents not here, but the house was wrecked.

"The three geniuses behind the punk band Blue Fish Rule."

Punk rockers *had* wrecked the house.

Ally thought she might throw up. Her grandmother's beautiful house was so ruined that the housekeeper fled in terror, despite Sam and his abs.

Well, at least now Ally wouldn't have to fire her.

Ally moved through the rooms as if through a dream, touching the graffiti on the walls. *Rock on!* the wall up the beautiful old stairway read. *Blue Fish Rule!* shouted the wall in the dining room. *F#%@ the power!* screamed the ceiling.

They had to be kidding.

Everything of value—from the candlesticks on the mantel to the antique china—was either gone or smashed to bits.

Ally couldn't get out any words. How was she going to show this to her grandmother? It wasn't the house that upset her as much as what it represented: her past. Empty, destroyed, unlivable.

"I threw the blockheads and their groupies out when we got here. Scared the piss out of them. They backed down pretty quick. They won't be back." He paused, and when he started talking again, his voice had softened. "Of course, Eloisa won't be back either. She said she didn't sign on for hard labor. She called her brother and he was here to pick her up within an hour. She left a bill for two days."

"Thank you, Sam, for getting rid of the squatters." *Thank you, God, for getting rid of Eloisa.*

"It was easy." He shrugged. "Saw it on an episode of *Crime Unit L.A.* But I wish I had at least kept a few of the lads around. Ally, I've been trying all day to hire someone to come in here. The whole island is booked. High season, they all say. Can't even get a Dumpster."

Ally sank against the wall, then thought better of it. Too late. She separated herself from the sticky surface.

She had brought her grandmother to a dump.

How was she going to replace Eloisa if the whole island was booked? The fantasy paradise she had promised her grandmother was like the rest of her fantasies—over.

They could be back in Manhattan in two hours. But then they'd be right back where they'd started.

She looked at Sam. *No.* Eloisa had left, and he was still here.

Her heart was racing. "We need to find another house to stay in. Or a hotel." She dreaded the thought of another hotel. She had thought they had arrived at something like home, but instead it was just another disappointment.

"About the hotels. It's like trying to find workers. I tried like mad, Ally, but again, it's high season. Everything is booked solid except for the places that are even scarier than this. You'd have to go back inland."

"And then we might as well just go back to Manhattan."

"If you want to be on the beach, this is it."

"Then this is it." The smell alone was enough to curl her hair. The molecules of Ally's body were starting to come undone, shaking apart in a whirlwind of emotion. *I can't go back. I can't stay here.* She was going to spin into a million pieces. In front of Sam.

Sam's hand tightened on her shoulder. "Ally, listen to me." He turned her toward him. "Oh. You're crying." He dropped her shoulder and took a step back.

Was she?

She was.

She blinked back the tears and put on what she hoped was a solid, useful, can-do face. "I am not. I have sand in my eye. Stupid beach." Her voice wasn't as steady as she would have liked.

"Both eyes?" he asked.

"Yes."

"Ally, come with me to the bedroom," he said firmly.

She threw up her hands in disbelief. "For the love of Pete, Sam! Sex isn't the answer to everything!"

"Well, that's not true. But it's beside the point. C'mon. I want to show you something." He made his way toward the back of the house, threading through the graffiti-covered kitchen and onto the back porch. At least the porches were okay. She didn't want to know what was in the huge black garbage bags pushed into the corners. It touched her that he had filled all those bags himself. Through her panic, a thought caught her attention like a small blinking light of hope in the distance: *Sam stayed, and he helped.*

A flight of wooden stairs led from the lower deck to the upper deck. He took the lead, and she reluctantly followed him, as if on autopilot. She hoped that Mateo and her grandmother were still on the porch. She didn't want Granny Donny to have to see the house.

They reached the top deck, and Sam slid open the glass door to the bedroom. He pulled her inside.

"Sam, I am so not in the mood for nonsense."

"Oh, I think you'll be in the mood for this."

At first, all she could see was darkness through her sun-bleached eyes. But she could smell the rich, cloying odor of lilacs.

She blinked away her blindness. As her eyes became adjusted to the dimness, she saw—a canopy bed? She touched the fabric.

"My plan was to bring your grandmother around the back of the house and straight up here. We'd try to keep her from the rest of the house until everything is cleaned up. Now, of course, I guess it doesn't matter. But at least she'll have a place to sleep. And you, too. I did the next room also. Your bedroom."

Ally could see colors now. The room was done in pinks and greens. The canopy bed was opulent, luxurious, with layers of pillows of all shapes and sizes covered in beautiful fabric and lace. "How did you do this?" Confused emotions zigzagging through her made it hard to form the thought: *Sam had done this. For her and Granny Donny.*

"I raced back to Manhattan for supplies after Eloisa left. I only wish I could have found someone to come out to put it all together. I did the best I could on such short notice."

He did this. For us. "It looks exactly like a nineteenth-century bedroom."

"Correction. It looks *exactly* like the grand dowager's bedroom in *The Dulcet Duke*. I tried to match the book as best I could. Lancet never went in much for describing window treatments and bed linens, so I had to wing the details."

"Did you—?" She could barely get the word out, it was so incongruous with Sam. "Sew?"

"You got a problem with a man who can sew?"

"No."

"Good. That would have been very disappointing. But, sadly, no. I can't thread a needle. Bought it all."

If someone had asked Ally the color of the grandmother's bedroom in *The Dulcet Duke*, she would have been stumped. But now that she was in it, she remembered reading about lilacs and four-poster beds. Sam had remembered every detail.

His gray eyes were serious. His hair was still a raucous mess, but it seemed like it was trying to control itself. The pair of faded blue jeans he had worn in his apartment on the day he had kissed her—she never would forget those jeans—were now covered with paint and grease stains.

A wave of gratitude overtook her, but she tried to temper it with reality. "Oh, Sam. You shouldn't have. I can never repay you."

"You can repay me by stopping crying." He stared at her with an intensity that made her skin tingle. "You're not stopping."

She snuffled. "I am." *I could repay you in other ways . . .*

He watched her. "Complete stop. Or the canopy goes. I built it with all the wrong tools and much too fast, so it won't be hard to dismantle."

"Working on it." She wiped her cheek. Snuffled some more. "There."

He wiped her other cheek with his thumb. "And there. Okay. Now we're good. Right?"

Heat lingered where he had touched her. "I'm not feeling so good." She could hear her own voice as if it belonged to someone else.

He took her into his arms and she melted into him. *Stay, Sam. This is the nicest thing a man's ever done for me.* He kissed her cheek. Then again. Then he took her face in his hands and kissed her lips. Softly. She let her eyes flutter closed. It wasn't bad being cared for.

"How are you feeling now?"

"Better. A little."

He kissed her again, fully, the warmth of his lips spreading through her. "Now?"

"Almost . . ." It was hard to reconcile the Sam part of him and the duke part of him, but at this moment, they came together. "This room is amazing, Sam. Imagine if we had shown up without you here first. You saved us."

"I redecorated. It wasn't very heroic."

"It was. You're a man who can do what needs to be done. Even if it involves toil."

He didn't take his eyes off her.

"What are we doing, Sam?"

"Getting ready for makeup sex, I hope."

Sam had wanted to bolt the moment he laid eyes on this sorry house. He was mad at Ally for being, well, Ally.

But when he and Eloisa had pulled into the sandy driveway to find the Blue Fish on the front porch, smoking dope and downing whiskey shots at eleven a.m., he knew his plan of making Ally jealous had to take a back-seat to making sure she didn't catch a nasty communicable disease from the scum squatting in her grandmother's house.

Eloisa had accepted a joint at first offer and settled onto the porch with the Fish, which made Sam realize that the kind of woman who'd flirt with her employer's lover was maybe the kind of woman he needed to start avoiding if he wanted Ally to take him seriously.

After her joint, Eloisa took one look at all the work that had to be done, and then she was on her cell phone and soon gone.

So Sam had thrown himself full force into the bed-room remodel. He had to drive to Manhattan to find suitable bedspreads, curtains, and supplies, calling in favors from some of his most reliable sources. He had worked all night. But it was worth it to see Ally's face.

And now, her hand resting on his as she took in her bedroom, she seemed warm and impossibly vulnerable.

Had he convinced her to trust him?

She very carefully let his hand go, leaving behind a million tiny pinpricks of desire that floated from his hand through his body directly to his crotch.

"I don't know how you did this so fast," she said.

"Money, honey. Money and a lot of elbow grease. Do you like it?"

"I love it, Sam. Let's get Granny Donny up here before she goes in through the front door and has a heart attack that sends her right back to 1812," Ally said.

Let's throw your granny in the closet and make love. He shook off his lust and tried to concentrate. This was him, proving that he could be more than a sex machine to her. He had one more surprise. "First, dinner. It's almost ready."

Her eyes opened wide.

"I threw a little something together. After all, what's more manly after redecorating than cooking?" It felt like Christmas to see her regard for him rise another notch. *So talk to me,* he thought. *Let me in.* Was she finally coming around?

She was clearly shocked. "You fixed up the house *and* made us dinner? Who are you?"

He shrugged. "Well, I sort of ordered dinner in. But if I could cook, I would have." His face grew serious. "I want us to try to be together."

"I want us to try, too," Ally said.

"You're not just saying that? 'Cause, Ally, I haven't done this in a long time. If we're going to try this, you have to trust me. Have faith in me. You have to let me in. Tell me what you're thinking, feeling. It can't just be a game anymore. Can't just be the duke and the princess."

"I'll sort of miss them," Ally admitted.

"They did get us together." He kissed her lightly. "Ally, I'm serious."

"Sam, you have to let me in, too. Not just be Mr. Tough Guy."

"Hey, I cooked and sewed."

"Sort of."

"Well, it's a start."

The princess had deceived him. The duke, having never played the role of the hoodwinked innocent before, was stripped of all his bluster, and what was left was laid bare and exposed.
—From *The Dulcet Duke*

Chapter 27

Sam served Mateo, Ally, and Granny Donny dinner on the beach while Paula stood by, watching and sniffing at the sea air. They ate and ate as if they hadn't eaten in days. Aside from their odd little party, the beach was almost deserted.

Ally watched the flames of the bonfire that illuminated their circle in the fading light. For the first time in a long time, she felt hope. They had made it. It wasn't what she expected, but at least they were here, safe, eating, her grandmother back to her senses, although still wearing her long dress, proclaiming it "slimming." The clams, potatoes, and corn Sam had ordered from the local seafood shack had been excellent, especially when washed down with white wine that slid down Ally's throat so easily, she knew it must be something unpronounceable and expensive imported from Manhattan along with the bedroom decor.

She looked out over the blackness that was the ocean, then at her grandmother's beautiful face, flickering in and out of shadows of the flames. Sam and Mateo had started another game of soccer, kicking the ball around on the edge of the circle of light. Sam intercepted a ball with his chest. It fell to his feet like a dead bird, and he juggled it with his feet before putting the moves on Mateo. Mateo snuffed him like he was a pesky insect, stole the ball, and scored. Ally felt kind of sorry for Sam.

They stopped for a while, having a conversation Ally couldn't hear. She leaned back and closed her eyes.

Granny Donny, next to her, patted her hand. "It's lovely here, dear. Thank you for bringing me."

"Thank you for bringing me," Ally said. "It's been an adventure. I think I needed it more than you did. Do you think it was the scent of the sea air that brought you back to reality?"

Granny Donny said, "Or maybe the scent of the marijuana."

Granny Donny was totally back, in all her glory. "Proust's madeleines, but in reverse," Ally said.

Granny Donny shrugged. She was never much for literature. "So they thought I had a stroke, huh?"

"They didn't know. They never found physical evidence of it. Just the symptoms. They said it could have been that or it could have been something else, something that could be fixed with the drugs you were taking. Well, supposed to be taking." She told Granny Donny about finding the pills in the hotel.

Granny Donny shrugged. "I never was a very good patient. How long has this been going on? When did it start?"

Ally thought back. "Sometime between when I last saw you and June twenty-fourth. In those two weeks. I'm sorry that I didn't visit for so long. I was busy getting ready for San Francisco. And before then, I was probably too distracted even when I did visit."

Her grandmother stared into space. "June thirteenth," she said. "It happened June thirteenth. I remember not being able to get out of bed. Deciding to just order in and read. Oh, I am getting old if I slip so easily into madness! Never get old, Ally."

Ally watched her grandmother struggle with an emotion that seemed alarmingly close to grief.

Granny Donny turned to Ally with tears in her eyes. "Oh, I'm so sorry, dear. I should have told you right away. I shouldn't have kept it from you. I'll tell you now!" Tears began to stream down Granny Donny's face.

Ally was paralyzed with fear. She took her grandmother's hands. "What's wrong?"

"It's time I told you, dear. If something happens to me, then, well, oh dear. Now is the time. Yes. Too late, really. If I slip again, you'll never know."

Ally was afraid her grandmother was slipping again now.

But Granny Donny shook her head as if to clear her mind and went on. "A year after your parents left, June thirteenth. They, they—" She cleared her throat. "They died in a car crash, Ally. I just couldn't bring myself to tell you. Then, after a while, it seemed too late to tell you. I am so sorry, dear. You just clung so hard to the idea they'd come back. I couldn't bear to take that away from you. It was all you had. Then the years passed, and it seemed better to leave it as it was. But every year on June thirteenth, I'd have fits of indecision. What to do, what to say. Maybe, somehow, I knew this was the time you had to know and I couldn't tell you and that's why I slipped into the past. Maybe it had nothing to do with strokes or drugs. Just the tired mind of an old lady."

Ally stared at the dark sea, unable to think or speak or even feel. *Dead?* All these years, her parents were—

She couldn't even think the word.

Granny Donny wiped the tears from her eyes and pulled herself together. "Yes. I don't think I had a stroke, Ally. Or whatever you called it with the pills. I think I had a breakdown. Every year, I'd want so badly to tell you. It ripped me apart. I'd imagine telling you. I wonder if somehow, all that holding back caught up with me."

Ally didn't know what to say, so she said nothing.

She didn't know what to feel, so she felt nothing.

And she thought only one thing: *Sam.*

"So, you scared off the housekeeper, eh, hombre?" Mateo asked Sam. He juggled the ball easily from foot to foot.

"Would you stick around if you had to clean this dump?" Sam asked. He was pretending not to watch Mateo's style closely. If he could pick up a weakness in his technique, maybe he could score on the show-off. But then, Mateo wasn't exactly showing off. Didn't have that Brazilian flair at all. More of a stealth player. Seventeen, eighteen, nineteen—the man juggled the ball with his feet, his knees, his chest, his head. No one could do that unless—

Unless . . .

"Who are you, really?" Sam asked, hoping to catch Mateo off guard.

Mateo missed the ball. It hit the ground with a thud. "The coachman. Or at least I was. Now that Lady Giordano is back in the present, maybe I'll be the chauffeur." He picked the ball back up with his right foot. He began juggling it again. "I don't blame Eloisa for running out on you. I wouldn't stick around if I had to deal with you," Mateo said. He winked at Sam. The ball was still going, and there wasn't a single weakness Sam could pick out. He could barely tell if the guy was right- or left-footed, he was so agile.

"You played professionally, didn't you?" Sam asked.

"A little." He juggled the ball easily. Right foot. Left. Head. Shoulder. Chest. Knee.

"For Brazil?" Sam held his breath. What a brilliant stroke that would be. He'd seen this wanker somewhere. If not Central Park, then on the telly. His mind flicked through the Brazilian players, but none matched Mateo.

Mateo only smiled slyly. "Your princess had better find a replacement for Eloisa quick. 'Cause I like the old *mejore* just fine, but I can't care for two old ladies, sane or not. Paula is enough for me."

Sam would go along with the change in subject until he figured Mateo out. The guy would drop a clue eventually. "Ally will get things in hand."

"Yup. Now that Lady Giordano is back, she'll hire new help and Ally will be able to leave."

"Leave? Back to Manhattan?"

"No. Didn't you know? She's moving to San Francisco to live just as soon as she can. She's got a job and an apartment and everything. She's just biding her time here until Lady Donatella is settled."

Sam felt like he had been sucker punched in the gut. He tried not to let his surprise show. "Why didn't she tell me?"

"Didn't you know, man? And here I thought you were sleeping with her." He still hadn't let the ball touch the ground.

Sam was glad for the dark, hoping it hid his hurt. Why hadn't she told him? If he meant anything at all to her, she'd have confided in him at least before her coachman. She had said that she'd try to be with him, but she hadn't meant it. Or, maybe she meant it in the bedroom. Was she still just using him, only this time it wasn't for sex, it was for interior decorating *and* sex? An ugly green hulking hand seemed to grab him around the chest and begin to squeeze the breath out of him.

I love her, and she's treating me like I'm below the hired help. Not worthy of her confidence.

He tried to breathe evenly.

I love her.

She's still not letting me in. After everything.

Why, after all these years of not loving anyone, had he fallen for the one woman who wasn't capable of fully loving him back? That was the kind of love he had lived and never wanted to experience again, the incomplete, conditional love of his family. Who was he to think he could get more?

The hand tightened its grip.

He made a lame move on Mateo, but the other man evaded him easily and kept on dribbling and kept on talking. Sam watched Mateo's feet, but the fun was long

gone. *I am an asshole.* He had thought she was starting
to take him seriously, but she had no intention of including him in her real life. She hadn't even told him about
her real life. He was pure fantasy to her still, after everything he'd done for her. She was incapable of believing
he could change.

I don't need her. I don't need anyone.

The hand released him and he almost collapsed with
relief. "Don't ever try to be a hero, Mateo," he said. He sat
down in the sand, catching his breath. *I don't need her. I
don't need anyone.*

The ball plunked down beside him, followed by the
Brazilian coachman. Mateo put his arms on his knees
and stared out at the sea. "You don't have to tell me
that."

" 'Cause who'd want to be a hero, anyway? It's damn
hard work and for what? You just get dissed."

"Despised," Mateo corrected.

"Exactly. It's not like she owed it to me to tell me she
was moving across the country. But to treat me—" Sam
stopped. "Wait. What are we talking about?" He looked
at the other man, squinting in the dark at the shadow
beside him.

Mateo broke out of his reverie as if he'd forgotten Sam
was there. "I'm talking about you. I didn't know you didn't
know she wasn't sticking around. They're never loyal. No
one is loyal. They'll turn on you. That's why I hang with
Paula now. That old girl is loyal till the end." His voice
was cold.

Sam watched Mateo's profile. He wasn't talking about
Ally. But what was he talking about? Sam had seen this

guy before. Who was he? *They'll turn on you. Don't be a hero* . . .

Sam caught a glimpse of despair on Mateo's face, and all at once, he knew who he was. "Bloody hell. You're not Brazilian."

Mateo had him by the collar and down in the sand on his back in an instant. "Enough. Not another word."

"You're—" Sam couldn't believe he had missed it. The fake Brazilian accent had thrown him. The blue, yellow, and green on Paula's rigging. No Argentine would show those colors. Like a Brit sporting German yellow, red, and black. The world's best camouflage because any true Argentine would rather scoop out his guts with a rusty rake than show Brazil's colors. "But how—?"

Mateo slammed him harder into the sand, straddling him. "I'm not."

Ally called, "Are you okay? What's going on over there?"

"Grand. Just grand." Sam didn't fight back. He let the smaller man hold him down while his mind raced. He glanced at the fire, but he was pretty sure Ally and her grandmother couldn't see them in the dark, outside the small circle of light. But he could see Mateo's face, all right. Well, not Mateo, Sacco. Bloody, bloody hell. Who knew? The man was wild with anger. "Okay, okay, you're not who I think you are." *Sacco fucking Poblano is sitting on me, wanting to kill me.*

What an honor.

"Don't you forget it," Mateo hissed.

"Were there really death threats?" Sam asked. Mateo—Sacco—had played right midfield on the Argentine National team. Two years ago, his team had made it to the finals in the World Cup, the biggest prize in soccer. It was the Super Bowl and World Series and NBA Finals all rolled into one. *Real* worldwide competition. Nothing compared.

"Death threats?" Mateo said. "You think I'm that big a coward to run from threats? There were death attempts."

Sam thought back to the fury of that game. After ninety minutes of some of the best soccer ever played, the game had ended in a tie. Nil-nil. It came down to penalty kicks. An almost unheard-of event in World Cup finals history.

A player had to be brave to take a penalty kick. The advantage went to the kicker; they were expected to make the goal. There was little a goalie could do unless he got lucky. Or if the kicker missed . . .

But missing was unacceptable.

The penalty kicks came down to Sacco. If he scored, Argentina would win the biggest prize in soccer. If he missed, Italy would take it all.

That fact that "Mateo" was on this beach, working as a coachman and pretending to be from Brazil, said it all.

He had missed the net.

Sam cringed as he remembered. It was an unforgivable sin to miss the net. If his shot had been blocked, well, that was bad, but forgivable. But to miss? In the World Cup final? The game on the line? Players had been shot on the street in South America for lesser sins.

"You thought you'd be like Escobar," Sam said. Andres Escobar was a Colombian player who mistakenly put the ball in his own net. He was shot dead outside a bar in Medellín. His girlfriend claimed the shooter had yelled,

"Gooooooooaal," as he fired the bullets, mimicking the famous call of the Latin sports announcers.

But Sacco hadn't just missed his shot. He hadn't even been close. He had shot like a child. *Skied it.* The Argentines went as far as to say, *like an Englishman.*

All of Argentina would never forget that shot.

Italy had won the cup.

"My name was dirt," Mateo/Sacco said. "My countrymen shunned me. People spit on me in the streets. Then the death threats started. People said my kick was so bad, I had thrown the game. Schoolchildren started to mimic the Colombian shooter, using their fingers as guns, pointing at me and shooting while they yelled 'Goooooaal!' It got so I couldn't go into the streets anymore. And then, well, I got shot at in the grocery store. Hit my leg. I ducked behind the canned goods, then ran like hell and never looked back."

Mateo's story made Sam think of Ally. "The trouble with trying to be a hero in the real world is that sometimes, you fail," Sam said.

"You know it," Sacco said.

"Sam? Mateo?"

All Sam could see of Ally from his position in the sand was her ankles. It was a flashback to a million fights he had gotten into in school: a teacher's ankles. The toe tapping irritably. But no teacher had ever been barefoot with ankles as thin and tempting as Ally's. Of course, there was no little rose tattoo or sexy ankle bracelet or even painted toes. And yet, he still wanted those plain, knobby ankles like a starving man wanted food. *I don't need her. I don't need anyone . . . Don't try to be a hero . . . In the real world . . .*

"You got it?" Mateo whispered into Sam's ear. "Not a word to anyone."

"Got it." No way was he fighting Sacco Poblano. He'd just as soon fight Jesus. If Jesus had played soccer, he'd have been bloody Sacco, taking the fall for the team.

Mateo let him up and Sam shook the sand from his shirt.

"What is going on here?" Ally asked.

"Just a little friendly competition," Mateo/Sacco said.

"He's just mad because I finally scored on him," Sam said. He brushed sand off his shirt and out of his hair. *Sacco Poblano, the up-and-coming Argentine soccer whiz kid.*

"Liar. I've seen you play, Sam," Ally pointed out. "You couldn't score on him to save your life."

"Hey! That's not fair! I'm a damn good player. It's just that he's—"

Mateo's body coiled. "Watch yourself."

"It's just that he's rather good," Sam said. "For a *Brazilian.*"

Sam sank next to Ally into the cooling sand. Ally could feel his dark mood as if it were something she could touch. The news of her parents hung over her like a fog that disconnected her from the world. Sam felt like her link back. She wanted to throw herself into his arms. But his mood stopped her.

Granny Donny had gone back inside, and Mateo was a shadow, talking softly to Paula as he got ready to lead her back to her makeshift stable in the garage.

"You and Mateo okay?" Ally asked Sam.

"Fine."

"Thanks for dinner. I'm so tired, I feel like I'm fading faster than the fire."

"No problem."

He sure was terse tonight. "Thanks for staying to help with the house. I really—"

"No biggie," he interrupted.

They sat in silence for a while. Men. Maybe she should jump him and pin him to the ground as Mateo had, wrestle his feelings out of him.

Mateo called his good-byes to Ally, then disappeared as he led Paula into the darkness.

Ally had been planning what to say all night, but now, her breath caught. Everything had shifted after talking to her grandmother, and her footing felt unsure. Now her bet on Sam felt more dire. All her cards on the table. She resisted the familiar urge to retreat and cleared her throat, trying to sound casual. "Will you sleep with me tonight, Sam?" She held her breath. She didn't want to be alone tonight. She wanted him to hold her. She wanted him to make love to her, and then she'd tell him about her parents and he'd tell her it would be okay, she wasn't alone; she never had to be alone again. Her heart pounded as she waited.

But Sam didn't answer. Instead, he stood, grabbed the bucket, and walked to the ocean, becoming a shadow along the shore. He returned and doused the fire with water. They both watched as the embers sizzled and smoked to a dull gray. He began tossing sand over the soggy remains. A year or so later, he said, "So, do you want to fuck me or the duke tonight?"

Ally's heart sizzled out like the fire. His voice was so cold, the night around them turned frigid as his words floated in the air between them. "I don't want to *fuck* anyone," she said.

"No? What about the princess? I think she likes that."

"Sam? Are you okay?" *'Cause you're acting like a real jerk.* Why had she taken this risk? What made her think she could risk this? The pain of his rejection spread through her.

"Is there anything you want to tell me, Ally?"

"No." She didn't want to talk about her parents now. All she wanted now was to hold Sam. To have him hold her. But he was pushing her away.

"Ally, you never told me you were moving to San Francisco."

"That's what you're upset about? Me moving?" She had forgotten San Francisco. It seemed unimportant, trivial.

He sat down next to her. "Not important? This isn't a game, Ally. But it seems to be one for you. Still. After everything."

Her already scattered thoughts were blown into further confusion by his attack. She needed to process everything that had happened tonight. It was running together. Sam, her parents. Sam asking her to run off with him. Not run off, that was her parents who ran off. Who were dead. Her head was spinning. "We've only known each other a few weeks."

Sam scowled. "Ally, hell, I've known you since 1812. It's been almost three hundred years. We have something, Ally. Or I thought we did. Except then I find out that you were planning on leaving for California. You told Sacco—" He paused. "You told Mateo, and not me. Were you going to tell me?"

She blinked away the black spots that were dancing in front of her eyes so she could focus on Sam.

"You think I take falling in love lightly?" His voice was heavy and rough.

Love? Her heart hammered as if it might be trying to tear itself out to find life in a more worthy chest. "What do I know about love?" Except that everyone she loved most left her.

"You know everything, in your heart." His eyes were dark and growing darker. "But you don't really feel your heart, do you, Ally? You ignore it. You ignore everything around you. Your grandmother saw something deeper in me that made me a better man. But you can't see it. You won't ever see it, no matter what I do. I'm fed up, Ally. I did my best. Life is too short to keep chasing something that isn't there. So tell me now that you trust me. That you think I'm worthy. Tell me now that you might be able to love me. Tell me, Ally, or, frankly, that's it. I'm done trying to convince you that we should be together."

Guilt, anger, and pain rose inside her. It wasn't his fault her parents were dead, but he represented everything her parents had stood for—had died for. Fun. Passion. It all rushed together, converged and melded and boiled over. They say they love you but then they leave you. The pain seared her insides.

Her hesitation sent Sam over the edge. His eyes narrowed and he stood up and took a step back.

The black heaviness of her parents' deaths consumed her. *Love isn't possible. It's a fantasy, like everything else.* "You should go, Sam."

"Ally."

"I'm sorry." It felt good to push him away. To feel her pain and loneliness as deeply as she could. To be the one who did the leaving, not the one who was left. She knew she was hurting him. She even knew she was hurting herself. But at that moment, she didn't care. Her heart felt black and she needed to be alone, to feel that pain as deeply as possible.

*There was something raw about the duke, in his eyes,
his touch, and in his voice. Alexandra couldn't have said
what it was, but she knew instinctively, the way all
women do, what to do about it.*
—From *The Dulcet Duke*

Chapter 28

Princess?"

Ally stirred on the guest room bed in her Regency-palace bedroom. Earlier that night, Sam had stalked off down the beach. Ally had gotten into bed, expecting to cry. But instead, she fell into a deep sleep almost instantly.

She had been dreaming of the duke.

And now here was the duke. Well, no. It was Sam by the side of her bed.

"Hmm?" She tried to sit up, but before she could, Sam was kissing her.

She struggled to wake up fully, but instead, she fell even deeper, not into sleep but into his lips, his warmth, the intoxicating smell of his musky skin. She opened her lips, tasting him. She remembered that taste like a dream. *My secret lover, the duke, coming to me in the night . . .*

"Sam—"

"No. This is the duke." He covered her body with his and she melted into him. "Sam is pissed."

She was starting to wake up, but a part of her didn't want to wake up. She wanted to stay in the hazy fantasy of her dream and not think about what she was doing and where she was going with this dangerous man. *He wants from you what you want from him . . .*

"Don't ever use me, Princess." His hand snaked under her pajama top and he grasped her breast roughly, almost clumsily.

It felt divine. *Human contact.*

He pulled up her shirt and bit her nipple just exactly right. Warmth spread through her.

"I wasn't using—"

"You were. You are."

She moaned. "That's. Not. True." He knew exactly how to touch her. She could barely stand the ecstasy of it. He kissed her, working his way down to her stomach, past her stomach, holding her hips firm so she couldn't struggle away.

She surrendered to his touch, the roughness of his face against the inside of her thighs, the pull of his mouth. She came, spiraling even further out of reality, exactly where she wanted to be.

He said, "Let me make love to you."

She pulled him up to her as she tried to find her breath. Her whole body was humming with desire and need. She pulled him tightly to her, his body long against hers. She felt some of the tension he was holding ease out of him as he entered her.

"I thought I was losing you," he said as he pushed his body against hers, pushed into hers, as though if he pushed hard enough, their bodies would fuse. "But I never had you."

What was he talking about? She didn't care. Her body rose up to meet his. His hand was between her legs, and she fell back into the sensation of him inside her and his hand against her, not caring that she wasn't sure what was happening, why he was upset at her, whom she was even making love to, the duke or Sam.

No. This was Sam. No one else could make her feel this way. But he was different tonight, rougher and more demanding. It wasn't like the love they'd made at the hotel, which had been tender and even lighthearted. This was the love of a gentleman injured and a gentlewoman in pain, each easing the other in the most ancient way of the world. *Whatever is wrong in the world, there is still this; there is still us. We can attack each other until we've reached the core, and there, no matter how violent the approach, is peace.*

"Come for me," he murmured, his voice rough with need as his hand moved against her. She felt him shudder inside her and she held him to her as closely as she could as her own body trembled.

It felt ridiculously, amazingly, perfectly delicious.

It felt like a healing.

Sam woke up early. The first rays of the sun were piercing through the blinds. Ally's head was on his chest and her perfect mouth was just slightly open. She was curled up against him, her legs around his.

Bloody bollocks, he hadn't been able to keep his hands off her last night. Worse, he wanted his hands right back on her now. He didn't understand the pull she exerted over him. She had, after all, told him to leave. She had spoken everything he had feared. Everything he knew all along but hadn't wanted to admit. He'd been her dupe. *I don't need her. I don't need . . .*

The way the morning sun lit up the side of her face. The way they were both alone in the world. The way she made him be a better man . . .

Bloody hell.

Something had clicked deep inside him. But to her it was always a game. She had shut him out completely. A woman who couldn't love. Couldn't feel love. Couldn't recognize it. He was a fool to have ever thought she'd feel otherwise. He had broken his own rules by getting serious about a woman again.

He gently slid from under her. She stirred, then curled back up with a contented sigh. Well, he'd played the duke for the last time. He was back to being Sam. Back to his old life. Who the hell needed this?

I do.

He wanted to talk to her so badly that it hurt, but he hadn't done much talking in his life, and it was impossible to know where to start. She had accepted him last night, without words, had even been tender with him in a way he didn't entirely understand. Which, of course, made every-thing worse. Her soft moans. Her begging him for more. Her brown eyes fixed on his like he was her hero.

Don't try to be a hero. He would never forget Mateo's words. In the real world, heroes were punished. Exiled. In the real world, heroes failed and were not forgiven.

In real life, out of her bed, he was nothing to her. She still didn't trust him. Still didn't believe in him. It was the story of his life, fighting for conditional love. The worst damn feeling in the world. He'd had enough.

Sam was gone.

What had she done?

She had woken up that morning, thinking he'd be there. But he wasn't. She had searched the house, feeling like a fool. Even searched the beach. He was gone.

Ally tried to keep busy and not think about last night. She spent the morning buying supplies and doing drywall patchwork, and now she was draping the furniture with the sheet-curtains the Fish had left behind. Her grandmother had tried to help, but Ally had chased her out to take a ride with Paula and Mateo. A few neighbors had come around, and Ally knew they would have to find Paula a permanent place to stay before people started to complain. Granny Donny was pleased with the task of saving the horse. Mateo had told her Paula's story the day they got to the house, and Granny Donny had risen to the occasion with gusto before she even finished her iced tea.

Ally was relieved Granny Donny was gone. She wanted to be alone with her thoughts so she could untangle them. She poured paint into a small can and started cutting in the corners of the room.

It felt good to get the first coat of primer on the graffiti-covered walls, as if she could paint over her entire past. As she painted, she thought about Sam. She knew she had been cruel to him by telling him to leave.

Do I love him?

She finished the edges and started in with the roller. Big, broad strokes, covering the graffiti with the clean, white paint. Thoughts of Sam faded into thoughts of her parents. She was angry at Granny Donny for not telling her the truth about them sooner, and just as angry at her for telling her so soon, with no time to prepare.

It seemed unreal to have waited for them all her life for nothing.

She finished the first pass at the room and fell onto the sheeted couch, exhausted. What was she going to do now?

At least she had decided one thing.

She pulled out her cell phone. "June, it's Ally. Can you come out here? I think I've done a terrible thing." And that's when she started to cry.

Step Three:

Every rogue has a heart. Break it.

A man driven by passion was by definition untrustworthy.
How could she give her heart to such a man?
More urgently, how could she not?
—From *The Dulcet Duke*

Chapter 29

June arrived the next day.

Ally told her everything, and June listened and cried and said all the right things, including, "I have next week off. Let's get this house fixed up together."

The work helped to focus Ally's mind. After a day of cleaning and painting, Granny Donny finally chased them out of the house to get some air. They set two low chairs in the shallow surf, facing out to sea. The beach was deserted, except for two couples walking in opposite directions and a jogger with a German shepherd. The sun was just starting to dip under the horizon.

"So? What are you going to do about Sam?" June buried her feet in the wet sand, the waves lapping at her ankles.

"Let's forget Sam and talk about you. We've been talking about me all day." Ally had no idea what to do about Sam. She needed more time.

"You don't want to hear about me not making the European touring troupe."

Ally's heart ached for her friend. She had been afraid June hadn't made the tour the instant she'd seen June's stoic face in the driveway. No wonder she said she could spend the entire next week at the shore. "I'm so sorry."

"And I left Will."

Ally gasped. "June? When? Why?"

"I left him because of you."

"Me?"

"Well, you and Sam." June let her hand dangle in the gentle surf, drawing a triangle in the sand. "I realized watching the two of you that I wanted more than I had. I wanted a man who wasn't safe, a man who loved me despite everything."

"But Will loved you."

"Not despite everything. Ally, you should have seen him when I didn't make the European tour. He was so disappointed. More than I was. That was when I realized that something was wrong. My whole life, I've done what other people wanted me to do."

"But you've always loved dancing."

"Not as much as I'd have to if I wanted to truly succeed. It was more about pleasing my family. Pleasing Will, too." A wave splashed into their laps, and they moved back a few yards to drier ground.

Ally stole a glance at her friend. "They were idiots to cut you."

"I don't know if they were idiots. I'm getting old, Ally."

"You're twenty-eight."

"For a dancer still in the corps, that's getting old. If

I'm not a star by now, I'll never be one. And after I got cut, I knew I needed to reassess. It doesn't get better for a dancer. Just harder. And while I reassessed, I saw you and Sam and thought, *That's how to live life—just go for what you want; forget what you think other people want.*"

They watched the sand plovers peck at the outgoing waves, the tiny birds undulating along the sand like waves themselves. The sun was half hidden behind the ocean now.

"I was really awful to Sam," Ally said.

"He'll forgive you."

"Looking at him was like looking at the embodiment of everything my parents were. I just went nuts on him. Like it was all his fault."

"So tell him that. Tell him you were an idiot and confused by grief. Don't tell me." She offered Ally a small smile. "And Ally, don't wait ten years to do it either."

The only thing worse than a broken heart was being surrounded by lovers, their hearts sickeningly intact.
—From *The Dulcet Duke*

Chapter 30

By the end of the week, the house was almost back to its original state. Ally and June had finished painting over all the graffiti, replaced all the curtains, and ripped out the beer-stained carpet to expose the hardwood underneath. They had even spent an afternoon knickknack shopping at the local tourist traps. Shell sculptures and pictures of lighthouses made the house look beachworthy and normal. Granny Donny had joined them at the end. She and Mateo had finally found a stable not far from the house to board Paula. To celebrate, she bought some not-so-beach-like knickknacks: fuzzy dice, a Zen entry fountain, and way too many cat toys for Bandit, including a battery-powered mouse that Bandit tore to ribbons in less than an hour.

Looking at the mouse wreckage, Granny Donny said, "With Bandit around to destroy any intruders, all I need is a housekeeper, and I think I could get used to staying out here."

Ally was shocked. She climbed down off the chair she was standing on to hang a shell mobile in an empty corner. "Stay out here? In Lewiston? What about Manhattan?"

"I was wondering if you wanted my place," Granny Donny said absently, not looking at Ally. "I'm getting tired of the hustle of the city. I like being surrounded by the sea and by good memories. I think I'd like to stay."

What she didn't say, but what Ally understood, was that in Manhattan, she was surrounded by bad memories. Ally pushed Bandit aside and sat down on the couch next to her grandmother—her grandmother who had just offered her a beautiful apartment in one of Manhattan's most beautiful buildings. But Ally didn't even have to think about her decision. "I don't want to go back to Manhattan either," she said.

Granny Donny nodded, and Ally knew that they understood each other well enough not to have to dwell on what New York meant to them: the past. "If we got you a housekeeper out here, a cook, a driver—"

"Mateo said he'd stay and be my driver until I found someone permanent." Granny Donny said.

Ally nodded and took her grandmother's hand. "Then I could go to San Francisco."

"Then you could go to San Francisco," Granny Donny repeated. "And I think you should go. Except for one little thing you're forgetting." She paused. "Sam."

Ally hadn't forgotten Sam. In fact, she thought of him all the time. She just didn't know what to do about him.
So she worked.

Her body ached all over. She had lost at least five pounds from the unaccustomed physical labor.

June, on the other hand, had actually gained weight in the week she'd been there. To Ally's amazement, she had begun eating food instead of her customary picking at it. Maybe it was the sea air, but Ally had a suspicion it was something else. June was spending an awful lot of time with Mateo. What they had in common was a mystery to Ally, but they had long, hushed discussions that stretched into the early evenings. So far, June had returned to sleep in the extra bed in Ally's bedroom every night. But she seemed to be coming back later and later.

Ally was jealous. Seeing June and Mateo together made her miss Sam even more.

Then, the next night, June didn't come back to her single bed.

"It's not what you think," she told Ally the next morning as they ate on the porch with Granny Donny. Mateo had gone first thing to the stable to check on Paula, and Granny Donny had whipped up a batch of her famous blueberry pancakes. "Did you know that Mateo used to be a professional athlete? He was a soccer player. A really famous one."

"So you're trying to tell me you spent the night talking about soccer?" Ally asked. There was something sweetly romantic about June and Mateo together, something inevitable. Something eerily familiar.

"Yes. We were *talking*. About a lot of things."

Granny Donny harrumphed. "Then you're a bigger fool than I thought."

Ally said, "I've seen that man without a shirt." She realized that a part of her wanted June and Mateo's relationship to be base and silly, even though she knew it wasn't. Why was she so insistent? She searched her emotions, trying to uncover her motives. Was this not about June and Mateo but about her and Sam?

"We're not all sluts for men without shirts," June said. But she blushed as she poured the syrup.

"Silly girl," Granny Donny muttered.

June ignored her. "I think you're jealous, Ally, because I'm brave enough to go for it with a risky man, when you wimped out with your Prince Charming."

Ally reached for a fourth pancake and smothered it in butter and syrup. Maybe June was right, but there was a bigger truth that Ally was just starting to understand: June and Mateo were perfect together. They had to be together and they both knew it.

They are like my parents.

And it was lovely.

"What if he wants to go back to Brazil?" Ally asked.

"He's not Brazilian, he's Argentine," June explained.

"I'm a schoolteacher," Ally reminded her friend. "I know my flags. Brazil is blue, yellow, and green, just like Paula's plumes." Ally was beginning to feel lighthearted as the truth of her emotions hit her: She wanted June and Mateo to run off. Granny Donny could hire someone to look after Paula and be her driver. She'd be fine just like Ally was fine when her parents left. Ally watched her friend carefully and imagined her own mother, making this decision to follow her heart, no matter what.

"I'm telling you, he's from Argentina," June said. "He used to be an athlete, and—well—something didn't work out." June hesitated. "Anyway, that's not important. What's important is that he understands what it means to give your heart and soul to something and then fall flat. He gets me. I know we've only been together a week and it sounds nuts, but Ally, it's not."

"Do you even know where Argentina is?" Ally poured herself another cup of coffee. *My mother was happy when she died. She was following her heart.* A huge weight lifted from Ally's chest as she watched June not care about her silly objections.

"Sort of. Not really. I don't care."

"It's in South America, June. We're talking crocodiles and pumas."

"Mmm . . . crocodiles." June wagged her eyebrows.

"They eat beef for breakfast in Argentina."

"The crocodiles?"

"No. The people. Really big, fat, bloody steaks. You don't even eat red meat."

"Don't! Ally, I don't want the facts. I don't care if Argentina is in Antarctica with the penguins."

"Which are in the North Pole," Ally said quietly. She was proud of June. She was proud of her own parents. She was the only coward in the bunch.

Granny Donny rolled her eyes. She started to clear the table, and June and Ally jumped up to stop her.

June cleared the plates. "I want to go after my fantasy, to go after fun, wherever it takes me. I want to not care what the right thing to do is. I was a good woman even more than you were, and I didn't even realize it. I've never met a man like him, Ally. The way he makes me feel. It's—I can't even explain. I'll follow him anywhere—" She stopped, suddenly aware of what she was saying. "I'm sorry, hon. But that's how I feel."

"Don't be sorry. I think it's great. Your skin is glowing.

You can't keep a smile off your face. You're even eating the pancakes, carb bombs you never would have allowed yourself days ago. I'm happy for you, June."

June swiped a whole pancake off the platter that Ally carried back into the kitchen and ate it with her fingers in three huge bites. "Anyway, don't worry about Argentina. We're going to start with the exotic island of Manhattan. As soon as Paula's set at the stable and he finds a driver for your grandmother, Mateo and I are going back. Just for a few days. Just to, you know, be alone. See what happens. Will you be okay here by yourself?"

Ally hugged her friend. "I'll be fine. I've always been fine. I've just been too dumb to know it."

Ally went on long walks and played cards with Granny Donny, who cheated like a sailor. She cooked food and sat on the balcony and reread *The Dulcet Duke*. Then *The Duke Who Loved Women*. Then, *The Marquis and I*.

After her seventh Regency-era novel, she knew exactly what she had to do.

She borrowed Granny Donny's fountain pen and India ink and a few sheets of her heavy vellum-like paper and she began: *Dear Sam* . . .

By the time she had finished the letter, her hands were shaking. Her signature came out wobbly and uncertain, but she couldn't bear to rewrite the whole letter. She was terrified that he'd return it unread. Hadn't he said that was what his mother had done with his letters? What if he had written Ally off? What if she poured her heart out on the page, and he didn't care? What if he laughed?

For a moment, she considered tearing up the letter. This was what Send buttons were for. Impulsive missives

sent off on a whim. But to fold the paper, address the envelope, find the stamp, put it on, and walk half a mile to
the blue mailbox was hard. Every step gave her a chance
to wimp out and forget the whole thing.

She stood in front of the blue mailbox. She was trembling. Her heart pounded in her chest, and the part of her
that had controlled her actions for the last ten years practically shouted, *No!*

But she was done with that part.

She was going to put on the ball of the season: an orchestra, caterers, hundreds of guests, and only one that
would matter: Sam.

If he would come.

Sam ate his sushi, then washed it down with hot sake.
It was ten o'clock at night and he was back in Manhattan,
back to his old life. He and the rest of the creative team
at Donnel/Woody/Smith had just paused for dinner in the
main conference room. After leaving the beach house, he
had gone back to work with a vengeance to keep his mind
off Ally. This was the second agency this week that he'd
been called in to bail out.

They were preparing for the introduction of a diet
pomegranate-grapefruit juice. They'd have it sewn up by
three a.m. at the latest. Three of Sam's concepts had made
the final cut, which was pretty good, considering that he
had come in to pinch-hit for these jokers at the bottom of
the ninth.

"So, what's new?" Ray asked, stuffing a wasabi-coated
tuna roll into his mouth. "What's-her-name good?"

Ray was his old buddy. They had worked together
when Sam was just starting out, bouncing from agency to

agency, eager to learn everything he could from everyone he could. He and Ray used to go out every night to the local bars, looking for women and alcohol, not necessarily in that order. "Veronica. She's out of the picture."

"Has it been more than a month since we've worked together?"

"Christ, am I that predictable?" Sam speared a tuna roll.

"Yup. As long as I've known you. Got a new one yet?"

"Yes. Ever get involved with a woman who hates you?" Sam asked.

"This could be a long month, huh?"

"I didn't read this one the one-month act; she read it to me."

Ray's eyebrows went up. "Really? Does your lawyer know?"

"We have this sex-only relationship." He struggled to explain.

"Sounds like just your thing."

"It is. Only, usually, the woman wants more from me. This one—" He paused.

"You're *her* boy toy?" Ray thumped him on the back and Sam flashed back to the old days, when he and Ray would go out. Had Sam gotten nowhere in his life*?*

"She thinks I'm a creep."

"But you are a creep," Ray pointed out. "Which is exactly why I was hoping you'd come out with me tonight when we're done here. Old times' sake. I have someone I want you to meet."

*   *   *

The woman pressing against Sam's side in the red crushed-velvet half-moon booth of the Idyll Club was gorgeous. She was young. And she was giggling.

And yet, Sam couldn't keep his eyes off Ray, who sat across from him, a similar girl pressing up against him, his arm tossed casually around her bare shoulders.

When had Ray gotten so old? He looked like the woman's father.

Sam could see his reflection in the mirrors over Ray's shoulder.

He looked old, too. Maybe not father material, but big brother for sure.

He scanned the crowd, which was pulsating with energy and alcohol. He was definitely on the upper-age end, and Sam didn't like the looks of the other men who were about his age. They were trying too hard. You couldn't help but imagine the families who were waiting for them at home.

Sam didn't even have a family at home to ignore.

A group of hipsters moved aside, and Sam's whole body lurched as if he'd fallen into a bottomless pit.

Because staring back at him was an old man. He must have been sixty at least, shaky on his barstool, holding a martini identical to the martini Sam held. The man was wearing the exact same tie as Sam. The stranger caught Sam looking at him and raised his martini in greeting. He nodded and drank.

Sam's throat tightened, and he felt short of breath. He needed a drink, but he wouldn't drink. Not to that image of himself staring back at him. He wanted to rip off his tie. As soon as he got home, he'd burn it. He stood. "I gotta go."

"But we just got here, buddy," Ray protested.

"Actually, we got here fifteen years ago," Sam said.

He threw two fifties on the table and left Ray, who already had his spare arm around Sam's discarded girl.

He couldn't go back to his old life.

He'd be damned if he was going back to Ally.

Which left him—where?

He walked back to his apartment, fuming. He nodded at Misha, who called his name. Damn, the last thing he needed was to have to talk to that creep.

But Misha was waving an envelope.

"Delivery for Sam Carson," the Russian sneered. "Maybe it's soccer talent."

There comes a time in every man's life when he knows he's lost,
and only a woman can bring him back to life.
Preferably, an elderly, spinster aunt.
—From *The Dulcet Duke*

Chapter 31

*I*nside the envelope was a letter from Ally. It was written with a fountain pen on thick, rich paper: *Dear Sam, I'm writing to invite you to a ball* . . .

Then another letter came the day after, starting with, *Dear Sam, The weather is lovely here* . . . It ended with, . . . *and that is why I am very sorry. I hope you can forgive me.*

Another letter came the day after that.

At first, they were dotted with ink splatters. By the third one, Ally had managed to get the pen under control and the page was clean, beautiful, even.

After the third letter, Sam did the only thing that seemed right. He went out and bought himself a fountain pen and some beautiful paper. In his first letter to Ally, he told her about what he was doing in Manhattan. How he had gone on a carriage ride last week, alone, for old times' sake.

In the second letter, he began telling her about work, but somehow—who knew how?—he ended with a story of when he was ten. He had managed to get himself kicked out of school just to see if anyone would notice. After being sent home late on a Friday with the family chauffeur, he had shown up at the breakfast table and his mother had jumped up in shock, not having any idea he was back in London. She had him shipped off again the next day to a new school before he'd even had a chance to see his father.

Ally lived for Sam's letters. Sometimes, her tears streaked the ink on the pages as she read. Sometimes, she laughed so hard, she had to stop to catch her breath.

She poured her heart onto the pages of the letters she wrote, surprising herself with how easily the words came. She wrote about what it was like spending her whole life waiting and hoping. *I took two-minute showers for ten years, certain that my parents would call for me as soon as I stepped under the steamy water . . .*

Writing about her memories sparked darker thoughts, not about herself, but about her parents. How irresponsible and unreliable they had been when they were around. How she had mothered them. How she had sometimes wished she could live with her wealthy grandmother, not with them.

As she wrote page after page, she would sometimes look down and find her hand shaking with anger. All the years she had wasted, waiting for her parents to come back and rescue her, when it had been her job to rescue herself. That was what writing to Sam meant to her now—her rescue. She needed to make it right between them.

She admitted to him, in a letter written by candlelight with an unsteady hand, that she was terrified to become her mother, chasing after a man who wasn't trustworthy but was charming and fun to be with.

> *A man like you, Sam. A man I could lose my heart to. But I'm starting to see now that maybe my mother did the right thing by following her passion. Maybe my father needed my mother more than I did. Maybe my mother knew she was a terrible parent, and that Granny Donny was there to take better care of me. Maybe following my father was the right thing for her to do. Following her heart. Maybe it's about time I followed my heart.*

Something about writing the letters, the scratching of the pen across the page, made Ally feel better. Seeing her words in black and white, then sealing them into an envelope and sending them away to a person who might still love her was like sending the problems she wrote about away, too. She felt lighter, more at ease. It was as if he received her words, then put them carefully away someplace safe, where they couldn't cause her any more problems.

They wrote nearly every day for three straight weeks, and she still hadn't told him that her parents were dead. Those were the only words she couldn't bring herself to write.

And Sam still hadn't said if he'd come to her ball.

Sam's heart wasn't in his Saturday morning games anymore. They seemed like everything else in his old life—pointless. He warmed up listlessly, taking shots on goal and missing.

A commotion on the Latin side caught his attention.

Mateo.

The goofball was wearing dark glasses and had a baseball hat pulled low over his eyes, but Sam recognized that easy gait anywhere. Sam jogged over to the enemy sideline.

"New player?" he asked. "Got ID?"

Mateo/Sacco kept his head down. "I got all the ID I need right here," he said, making an obscene gesture that sent his team into happy catcalls.

Sam put his hand on Mateo's back and whispered in his ear, "A Russian shows up. About so high. Blond hair. Do me a favor: If he plays, humiliate him."

"You got it, Sammy," Mateo/Sacco said.

"Good to see you here," Sam said.

"I don't know if it's a good idea, but I promised June."

Sam looked around, and, sure enough, on the sidelines stood June. "Nice work," Sam said. "How long has this been going on?"

"Long enough. Anyway, I'm not a pussy like you. You should see Ally, man; she's miserable."

"Really?" Sam perked up. "Tell me." They'd been writing letters for weeks, but they hadn't spoken. And as much as he wanted to jump into his Porsche and go out there, he didn't. It didn't seem the gentlemanly thing to do. Plus, something was happening with the letters that he wasn't sure he could handle in person: He was writing the truth, writing stories and words and thoughts he might never be able to voice face-to-face.

But the game was about to start. "Later, buddy. I got more important things to do first. Like kick your butt."

Mateo scored in the first thirty seconds, leaving both teams stunned. Then, he scored again in the next minute, easily working around the awestruck defense.

"Cool it, man," Sam whispered. "You want to get found out?"

"I don't know," Mateo said. "It feels good. It's been a long time."

"What'd you say your name was, hombre?" The questions were starting.

"Don't I know you from somewhere?"

"Take off that hat, hombre."

Sam whispered, "When you get murdered, I'll try to hold them off. But we're a bit outnumbered."

"I'll play defense," Mateo said. But he couldn't stay back, and before five minutes had passed, he scored again.

Misha, who had come late and was still on the sidelines, came into the game, took one look at Mateo/Sacco, and said, "What the hell is Sacco Poblano doing here?" loud enough for everyone to hear.

By the second half, a crowd had formed along the sidelines. It was as if the quarterback of the New York Giants had shown up, or the center for the New York Knicks. Cell phones were buzzing, people texting and taking pictures. When schoolchildren started to appear, Sam began to get worried. "Don't you think this might get out of hand?"

But Mateo was in heaven. "What, someone will shoot me here? In Manhattan?" He had taken off the hat and the dark glasses. People were calling his name from the sidelines.

"Well, yeah. Right? They might. Wasn't that the point of lying low?" Sam asked. He was nervous for his friend.

They went back out on the field, Mateo matched against Misha. "You're a coward," Misha sneered before the ball was in play.

Mateo ignored him.

"You let your country down," he said louder. A few shouts of agreement reached them from the sidelines. *Traitor. Traidor!*

"Put the ball in play," Sam insisted.

"With this weasel?" Misha said. "I refuse." He shoved Mateo.

More cries from the sidelines reached them, including, "Gooooaaaal," the cry of the Colombian shooter that had become a stand-in for a cry to kill.

"He threw the game!" Misha said, raising his arms. "The World Fucking Cup. He handed it to Italy." He shoved Mateo again.

"We earned it," one of the Italian players said, enraging the crowd further as they took up the heated disagreement.

"Play," Sam said.

But as soon as the ball was kicked, Misha rushed Mateo and it seemed as if half the crowd followed, shouting for another goooooaaaaallll . . .

Sam didn't hesitate. He dived at Misha, pulling off the bigger man with the force of his anger. Someone punched Sam in the gut, and he staggered back, losing Mateo in the melee. Bodies seemed to be everywhere. June watched, horrified, from the sideline. Sam finally located Mateo at the bottom of three Argentines, getting pummeled and kicked. Sam tried to drag one of them off and was rewarded with a kick in the groin.

As he stumbled backward, he saw his salvation.

He had to get Mateo out of there before they killed him.

He ran for the nearest carriage, jumped onto the box, and informed the surprised driver that this was a hijacking. The terrified tourists in the back squealed.

"It's to save one of your own," Sam told the driver. "Mateo. Drove an old gray-and-white mare. White carriage with chrome?"

"Hey, yeah. He drove for Torredo Stables. Nice guy," the driver said. "Where's he at?"

"At the bottom of that pile. They're trying to kill him."

"Not on my watch," the driver said. "Hold on!" he called to the tourists. He hawed to his horse and drove the carriage to the field, bumping hard over the curb. "C'mon, girl, you can do it," he urged his beautiful black horse.

The driver rode the horse and carriage to where Sam pointed. The confused fighters looked up just long enough for Mateo to bolt. Sam yanked Mateo into the carriage as June jumped in the other side. The driver flicked the reins, and the horse picked up speed. The carriage creaked and listed over the rough grass while the fight continued on the field.

The last thing Sam saw was Misha going down under the Polish goalie, who'd hated him for years.

Mateo wiped the blood from his mouth. "How was that for a comeback?"

"Well done," Sam said. "But enough about you. About Ally. I want to hear everything, fast, before they catch up and finish you off."

"You know, Sammy, how I told you it sucks to be a hero?"

"Yeah?" Sam looked at the bloody man. A dark circle was blackening around one eye, and his shirt was torn almost in two.

"Well, it's not true. It's actually a lot of fun."

The letter came the next day telling Sam what Mateo and June had already told him: Ally's parents had died nine years ago, and she hadn't known until that night on the beach.

So Sam took out his fountain pen and began to write. But instead of starting with *Dear Ally*, he wrote something else, instead:

Prologue:

Sam Carson defied his family and friends when he married Hana Smith, daughter of a plumber and his Irish wife. Sam was twenty-one and instantly disowned by his titled family. He and his beautiful wife set off for America with nothing and no one. But they didn't care. They were in love.

Hana died two days after they arrived, a victim of a virulent strep infection that they had neither the experience nor the money to treat.

Sam was alone in America. He wrote his family, but they refused to respond. He was dead to them.

He vowed to make himself never need another

human. He grew rich and self-sufficient. But what he didn't realize was that Hana's death had killed something inside him. It was impossible for him to love anything or anyone. Until one day on Central Park West, when everything changed . . .

When all else fails, have a ball.
—From *The Dulcet Duke*

Chapter 32

*T*he day of the ball, the tent crew arrived at dawn. Ally and her grandmother watched from the upper porch in awe as twelve men struggled against the wind to set up the most enormous white tent Ally had ever seen. Maybe she had gotten a *little* carried away. But her grandmother had told her to spare no expense, and for the first time in her life, Ally obliged her.

More trucks began to arrive as the sun rose: Zimmerman Event Lighting, Bogart's Generators, Portfeld's Tables and Chairs. Freddy, the event planner from Freddy's Festive Fetes, arrived to boss everyone around. He shook Ally's hand and paused only long enough to ask if any of the guests were allergic to nuts, to roses, to wheat, to elephants?

Elephants?

Ally didn't remember the elephants. She hoped he was joking as he kissed both her cheeks and ran off to direct the small army. He had a stack of invitations in a see-through purple plastic envelope under his arm, which he passed out to everyone he met. What would the college kids next door wear to a nineteenth-century gala? Salvatore the tailor had come twice in the last two weeks to make sure Ally and Granny Donny were suitably attired, and he'd return today with the final dresses.

Ally kept a lookout for Sam, but he was nowhere. He had never RSVP'd, and Ally hoped against hope that he would come. This was, after all, for him. She felt like an anxious schoolgirl.

Groups of curious people came out to watch, and a frenzied energy buzzed in the air. Everyone Freddy could catch received an invitation. Even the seagulls screamed and swooped, as if they were after their own invites.

But where was Sam?

To Ally's dismay, she was sick with fevered anticipation. She retired to her room and lay on her bed, fanning herself and trying not to swoon like a maiden.

And it wasn't even noon.

Watching the proceedings but not being a part of them made Ally edgy. She played a round of gin rummy with Granny Donny until June and Mateo showed up. He still looked awful, both his eyes blackened and an angry slash over his lip. June told Ally what had happened, and Ally's anticipation to see Sam ratcheted up a notch. June and Mateo left for a walk on the beach, and Ally paced the house. Finally, after organizing all the seashells in the huge decanter on the mantel by color and size, Ally caught sight of the vintage wedding dress that Sal the tailor had delivered an hour ago along with the other dresses for the ball.

Ally fingered the fabric of the antique wedding gown. She really shouldn't.

But then, why not? What else did a princess do when she was waiting for the ball to begin? She had, after all, already retired to her bed once with nervous agitation.

She took off her sundress and put on the delicate gown. Sal had done a masterful job, and it fit her perfectly.

Oh, what the heck? She put up her hair and then sneaked into Granny Donny's room and borrowed a string of pearls. The finishing touch was her mother's pearl drop earrings, which Granny Donny had given her as a birthday present.

She slipped back into her own room, breathless as a schoolgirl, and looked in the mirror. *I look pretty good.* The weeks of sun and hard labor had made her tanned and thin. *What if he doesn't show?*

She took the fragile lace veil out of its box and tried that on, too. She pulled the veil over her face and walked down the center of her room, pretending it was an aisle. *Who would give her away if she ever got married?* The thought made her stumble in her bare feet. But she recovered. She was getting carried away. Marriage? She didn't even know if Sam would dance with her.

She went out on the balcony and watched the activity.

She longed for Sam. She wanted to tell him that she'd been a fool. That she had finally felt in her own bones how unhappy her mother would have been without her father. How she finally understood that her mother had left her *because* she loved her and she knew that Granny Donny could give her a stable life. She didn't blame her mother anymore for leaving. In fact, now, through loving Sam, she understood that her mother following her father was an act of love, not stupidity. She forgave her parents. And it felt sublime.

When Ally appeared on the deck in a wedding dress, Sam dropped his binoculars. He'd been watching the proceedings from behind the dunes; he wanted to make an entrance befitting a grand duke.

Seeing Ally in that dress, he thought he would want to bolt like a wild animal. But instead, he felt an entirely different emotion: *love*.

She is the one.

And tonight, they would finally waltz.

By eight o'clock, the makeup people and hairstylists were gone, and Ally, Granny Donny, and June had updos worthy of a period movie. Their faces were glowing and powdered. Their gowns were impeccable. The caterer had the grills going and the tables set. The twelve-piece orchestra had set up their instruments, and Ally could hear them tuning in the distance. The sun was just starting to set as someone threw on the lights in the tent.

It was time for the ball to begin.

But she still hadn't seen Sam.

Sam stood at the water's edge, his heart pounding. He could throw himself into the waves and swim for England. He could bail out and go back to his old stupid life.

Or he could do this.

His palms were sweating.

He picked up a shell and threw it into the ocean. "Good-bye, Hana. Wish me well."

And then he walked slowly toward the music.

"Where's Sam?" June asked Ally.

Ally couldn't take her eyes off her beautiful friend. Long curls dangled past her shoulders and smaller curls framed her beautiful face. She wore a baby-blue dress that made her look radiant. "I have no idea. Maybe he's making out with a cute waitress."

"No way. I read his letters."

"June!"

"Sorry. But you left them out."

Mateo approached them.

"Looks like your prince has come," Ally said. "My God, Juney, are you blushing?"

Mateo let out a long slow whistle. "You look amazing," he said to June. He held out his hand and she took it.

"Your duke will come," June said over her shoulder. She walked with Mateo to the dance floor, and they started to waltz.

Ally watched Granny Donny, who had formed a one-woman receiving line. She was in heaven, enjoying herself immensely. Ally had finally given her a fun, fantasy-filled night worthy of her uniqueness. She felt proud.

Ally was getting restless.

The tent was filling with locals that she vaguely recognized from the house next door and her long walks on the beach. The clerk from the grocery store down the street waltzed with the woman who walked a small poodle every morning at dawn.

But where was Sam?

Ally went to the appetizer table and picked up a chicken sate. She ate it without tasting it.

"Is it good?"

It was Sam.

He had come. And he looked amazing.

Not the title. Not the riches. Not the bravery. Not the glory.
Just the man. The simple man, standing before her,
looking into her eyes as if he saw just the woman.
For the first time in their lives, they were truly alone.
—From *The Dulcet Duke*

Chapter 33

Madam, may I have this dance?"

Sam, in his old-fashioned pants and tails, looked as if he'd just stepped out of *The Dulcet Duke*. The orchestra had begun a waltz behind them, and—except for Ally being barefoot, surrounded by tourists and locals in brightly colored neon beach wear, and the hem of her gown growing heavy with accumulated sand—she could have been in a London ballroom, waiting breathlessly for her duke.

"Of course."

He led her onto the dance floor, an expanse of sand in the middle of the tent. Christmas lights were strung all around, and it seemed half the town had come out to experience the spectacle. Everyone but Ally, Sam, and Granny Donny wore modern clothes; a few were even in bathing suits and skimpy cover-ups. And yet, under the twinkling lights, the moonlight shining in through the open flaps, and the music, everything looked perfect because Sam had come.

Naturally, Sam was a divine dancer. He waltzed Ally across the sand. "Still haven't really learned to waltz?" he asked.

"Still haven't learned what to say to your dance partner to keep her from stamping on your toes," she said.

"I missed you," he murmured into her ear.

"I loved your letters," Ally said. He had his hand on the small of her back and his barely there touch electrified her. "I'm sorry about Hana. I wish I could have met her."

"Ally, this is magical. Thank you."

"This is nothing. Wait until the dancing elephants show up."

He spun her and pulled her closer. His face grew serious. "Ally, I meant everything I wrote to you." He twirled Ally across the floor as he spoke, and the world spun around her. In Sam's arms, it seemed as if anything might be possible. She was finding it hard to speak. So she decided not to. Instead, she took his hand and pulled him through the tent flaps and into the darkened night.

Their lips met and their bodies met and Sam pulled her down into the sand. They could hear the orchestra in the distance, but they were out of the light, which was good as Ally was yanking his ruffled white shirt out of his lace-up pants and he was undoing the endless stays on her dress.

"Who invented these ridiculous clothes?" he asked.

"I thought of everything tonight but scissors."

"Good thing I brought my teeth."

As they struggled with their layers, Sam stole bites and kisses and they fell into the sand.

They made love so softly and slowly, as if they were discovering each other for the first time. The only words were each other's names, whispered breathlessly. With not a mention of the duke or the princess.

It was the first time they had made love as themselves.

And then the second time.

And then the third.

The music slowed. Then the guests started to file out. But still, they lay together, just the two of them, unable to separate.

"I don't even miss the duke and the princess," Ally admitted.

"Told you we'd write our own book," Sam said.

"Chapter one, page one," Ally said.

"Chapter one, page one, the rogue corners the maiden in the dark and vows she will be his," Sam said.

"I'm not sure I like that book," Ally said. "How about, chapter one, page one, the good woman sees the rogue, and decides that the two of them together could conquer all of London, with her brains and his stunning looks."

"His brains, and her stunning looks."

"And all of polite society watched in wonder—"

"Scandalized as she ran off to San Francisco without him," Sam said.

"Nonsense, they run off to San Francisco together," Ally said. It was as much a question as she dared. "My place is kind of small."

"We'll get a bigger place," Sam said.

She turned to him. "Really? You'll come with me?"

"Sure. Why not? It's not like I have any commitments here."

They watched the last of the guests leave the tent. They could hear the caterer cleaning up inside. The musicians left in pairs and threes, carrying their black cases. Ally hoped her grandmother was inside to tip everyone.

"Of course, it wouldn't be very proper for a gentle-woman to run off with a man unless they married," Sam said.

The night seemed very still.

"No. That wouldn't be proper at all," Ally said.

"So what happens next in our book?" Sam asked.

"I suppose they marry," Ally said. Sand was on his nose. She kissed it away, so what could he do then but kiss her? Deeply.

"Are you sure, Ally? Would you marry me?"

"I'm absolutely sure," she said.

"And they lived happily ever after," Sam added when he had thoroughly kissed her again.

"Well, of course happily ever after," Ally said. "That's the way they all have to end, or they aren't any good."

Acknowledgments

I'd like to thank everyone at Grand Central Publishing, especially Michele, for making this the best book it could be. Also, I'd like to thank Carolyn Pouncy, for her insane knowledge of historical romance and for turning me on to Georgette Heyer. And, of course, my unending gratitude to Ellen Hartman, for reading this manuscript way more times than it's right to ask a friend to do.

The One True Love Series:
Make Me a Match,
Sexiest Man Alive, and
Hungry for More

Readers who like books in a series, are in for a treat with Diana Holquist's "One True Love Series". But where to start? Should you read the books in order? Do you have to read them all to get to the happily ever after? Well, just like with love, there are no rules. Each book in this series about three part-Gypsy sisters stars three very different heroes, so why not start with the one you like best?

Finn Concord
from MAKE ME A MATCH: Book One

Occupation: Carpenter

Eyes: Green, Smoky

Favorite clothes: Jeans and a faded T-shirt

Interesting facts: Single father; ex-minor league baseball player

What draws him to a woman: Honesty, humor, and has to be good with kids

Favorite line: Likes it best when he doesn't have to speak; more the strong, silent type.

Favorite Review: "Finn was delicious, broody, and so sweet, you wanted to keep him for yourself . . ." (coffetimeromance.com)

Josh Toby
from SEXIEST MAN ALIVE: Book Two

Occupation: Movie Star

Eyes: Violet, often behind sunglasses

Favorite clothes: Armani tux from last year's Oscar night

Interesting facts: Has terrible stage fright; loves dogs and pastrami sandwiches

What draws him to a woman: She doesn't care about fame or fortune

Favorite line: Anything that's not from one of his *Mitch Tank: Tank Command* movies

Favorite review: "Fans will be drooling over the cover but remember, that is just the beginning of something amazing." (Strictlyromancereviews.com)

James LaChance
from HUNGRY FOR MORE: Book Three

Occupation: Chef

Eyes: Brown

Favorite clothes: Chef whites

Interesting facts: Dyslexic, can barely read a menu

What draws him to a woman: Who has time for women? He's got a restaurant to run.

Favorite line: "Cooking, like sex, is best done right or not at all."

Favorite Review: "James LaChance . . . can cook both in and out of the kitchen . . ." (Cheryl's Book Nook)

THE DISH

Where authors give you the inside scoop!

♥ ♥ ♥ ♥ ♥ ♥ ♥ ♥ ♥ ♥ ♥ ♥ ♥ ♥ ♥ ♥

From the desk of Rita Herron

Dear Reader,

I have to admit that I'm a TV junkie. I love comedies, dramas, crime shows, and paranormal series, especially those with a romance in them. Of course, I always find myself drawn to the strong heroes.

Two of my favorites are Jack Bauer from *24* and Cole Turner from *Charmed*. Both are charismatic, tough, sexy, dark tortured guys with tons of emotional baggage. In fact, my husband, who is also a huge *24* fan, named our cat Jack Bauer.

When I first decided to write about demons, I wanted my heroes to have the same qualities as Jack and Cole, to be larger-than-life men who risked their lives to save the world—and of course, the women they love.

In DARK HUNGER, the second book in my paranormal romantic suspense trilogy *The Demonborn*, (out now!), I combined Jack and Cole and created Quinton Valtrez, Vincent's long lost brother.

Quinton is a loner, a government assassin, and a man determined to keep his job and supernatural powers secret. Like Jack, he fights terrorists. Like Cole, he battles demons—as well as the pull of evil inside him.

Pit him against a sassy, tenacious, struggling reporter named Annabelle Armstrong who is determined to unravel his secrets, and the sparks immediately fly. Quinton doesn't know whether to kill her or love her.

Quinton also faces a new kind of terrorist—a demon who has the ability to exert mind control over innocents and turn them into killers. Soon he and Annabelle realize they must work together in a race against time to stop this demon. But Annabelle isn't quite prepared to be thrust into this terrifying demonic world, or to face Quinton's father Zion, the leader of the underworld, who will use her to get to Quinton.

For any paranormal story, setting and worldbuilding is important. Blending the real world with paranormal elements makes the stories more frightening. In DARK HUNGER, I also take you to three of my favorite southern cities: Savannah, Charleston, and New Orleans. All three are steeped with folklore, ghost legends, history, and a spooky ambience that adds flavor to the world of *The Demonborn*. If you haven't visited those cities, put them on your TO DO list. And don't forget to take one of the ghost tours and be on the lookout for demons!

Enjoy!

Rita Herron

♥   ♥   ♥ ♥

From the desk of Robyn DeHart

Dear Reader,

I've always been a huge movie buff and my very favorite genre is romantic action adventure; think Indiana Jones and *The Mummy*. Toss together some archeology, a dash of history, and a nasty curse, add in two protagonists with lots of sizzle and I'm one happy woman. I suppose it's this love that brought me to my Legend Hunters and the first book in that series, SEDUCE ME (on sale now).

I admit I'm a geek at heart, but there's something so compelling about old things: ancient texts, antiques, dusty old tombs. I mean, who hasn't dreamt of going on a dig and unearthing something so amazing it changes your life? Well, this is precisely what happens to our heroine Esme Worthington. She ends up getting herself kidnapped, but in doing so she comes face-to-face with the object of her life-long obsession, Pandora's box.

Enter our hero, Fielding Grey, a treasure finder-for-hire who is none too happy that his latest assignment comes with a damsel in distress. But he can't walk away from her while she's literally chained to a wall. So he snags Esme and the fabled box and thus begins an adventure neither could have imagined. Not only does the box come with a unique curse that has Esme acting the wanton, but a nefarious villain is hot on their trail and will stop at nothing until he possesses Pandora's treasure.

This new series is about Solomon's, a luxurious gentleman's club equipped with all the accoutrements one would expect from such a fine establishment. Membership is by invitation only, because in this club there's a hidden room where secret meetings occur. In these secret meetings some of London's finest gentlemen gather to discuss their passions; their obsessions. Some are scholars, some collectors, some treasure-hunters, but each of them is after the find of the century. I can't wait for you to meet the Legend Hunters . . .

Visit my Web site, www.RobynDeHart.com for contests, excerpts, and more.

Robyn DeHart

♥ ♥ ♥ ♥ ♥ ♥ ♥ ♥ ♥ ♥ ♥ ♥ ♥ ♥ ♥

From the desk of Diana Holquist

Dear Readers,

When my family moved from the big city to a tiny rural town for my husband's work, there were no jobs for me. I wept for about a week. Okay, maybe two weeks. Then I realized that this was the perfect time to start something new. Because I was incredibly naive, I opened a file on my computer and typed, "Chapter One."

Uh-oh. Now what? I needed a story. But what? What did I care about enough to pour my heart and soul into? Later, I learned that what a book is about—what it's *really* about—is called a premise, and every good book has one. What was my premise?

I started lurking on the Web site of a woman who was looking for her soul mate. She wanted him to be a certain height and make a specified income and on and on. But no matter how hard she looked, she couldn't find her "one true love."

What if there was a soul mate put here on this earth just for this woman, but he wasn't tall and rich? This woman needed a guide to the world of love.

Thus, Amy Burns was born, the psychic gypsy who can tell you the name of your One True Love. She starred in my first three books, creating chaos, love, and a premise I could believe in: only when we face our true desires can we find happiness.

In my first book, MAKE ME A MATCH, Cecelia Burns is a doctor about to marry the "perfect" man: a rich, successful, handsome, charming lawyer. Along comes her psychic sister Amy, to announce that Cecelia's one true love as destined by fate is not only an underemployed single father, but that he might be dying. If she wants her one shot at experiencing true love, she's got to act fast.

In SEXIEST MAN ALIVE, Jasmine Burns, the shyest woman alive, learns that her one true love as destined by fate is Josh Toby, *People* magazine's Sexiest Man Alive. Uh-oh. She can't talk to a regular man; how will she ever get near this one?

HUNGRY FOR MORE is Amy's book. She has to choose between learning the name of her own one true love or keeping her psychic powers. When she meets a sexy French chef, she realizes that accepting true love is harder than she thought it would be.

The One True Love series got great reviews, a RITA nomination, and won awards like the New York Book Festival romance award. But more important, this series introduced me to so many wonderful readers, some of whom I now count among my friends. When I look back on those first days of moving away from the city, I laugh when I think about how what I thought was the end was actually a new beginning. I didn't realize then that I was living my own premise: be careful what you wish for. Because when you try something new, open your mind to the possibilities that life offers, and focus on your true desires, good things happen.

Happy reading!

Diana Holquist